STRIVE AND PROTECT

Other Books
by Sharon S Darrow

Bottlekatz,
A Complete Care Guide for Orphan Kittens

Faces of Rescue:
Cats, Kittens & Great Danes

From Hindsight to Insight,
A Traditional to Metaphysical Memoir

Tom Flynn, Medium & Healer

Navigating the Publishing Maze,
Self-Publishing 101

She Survives, Laura's Dash Book 1

Coming soon:
Desperate Choices, Laura's Dash Book 3
Her Triumph, Laura's Dash Book 4

Strive and Protect

Sharon S Darrow

Samati Press

Samati Press,
Sacramento, California
Copyright @ 2021

by SharonSDarrow.com

First Edition, 2019
Second Edition, 2021
ISBN-13 — 978-1-949125-18-4 (Print Version)
ISBN-10 — 978-1-949125-19-1 (Digital versions)
ISBN-13 — 978-1-949125-04-7 (Audio version)

Library of Congress Control Number: 2019905224

Edited by Sue J. Clark
Cover Design by Leslie Clark

Publisher: Samati Press
Sacramento, California

Manufactured in the United States of America

Dedication

This book is dedicated to my daughter, Sheryl Wilson, an amazing woman of courage, character, and integrity. She has overcome fearsome challenges that would have broken other women, but faces each new day with hope and faith.

Sheryl wanted children more than any woman I've ever known, and her twin sons, Nicholas and Christopher, have grown into fine young men. She has always been their staunchest supporter and strongest advocate.

Thank you, Sheryl, for being a daughter your father and I will always love and treasure .

Contents

CHAPTER ONE
Betrayal
November, 1923

Laura was excited throughout dinner, eager to see the highest rated movie of the year. She skipped rather than strolled at Bruce's side when they finished eating and headed toward the Argosy. Bruce had parked the car, a shiny black Buick Touring Car convertible, and his most prized possession, a block away from the cafe.

The theater's large marque announced The Covered Wagon, in huge letters. The names J. Warren Kerrigan and Lois Wilson, stars of the film, appeared right below the title in smaller letters. Bruce gave their tickets to the usher at the door, then led Laura into the opulent interior.

Laura's low-heeled shoes sank into thick maroon carpeting. Heavy tapestries hung on the walls between glass cases containing posters for upcoming feature films, and muffled the whispered conversations around her. Soon they settled in plush seats, waiting for the heavy curtains to rise.

She was glad the interior was dim after being surrounded by pretty women that made her feel almost dowdy by comparison. They wore shimmering silk and satin, accented by fur wraps and feather bedecked hats. Her forest green wool frock with pale gold at the cuffs, collar, and narrow band accenting the dropped waist above narrow pleats seemed ordinary by comparison. Her patterned black stockings and cloche hat sporting a pale gold bow couldn't compare to sleek, silken hosiery and high fashion hats.

Laura took a shallow breath -- all she could manage with the tight brassiere that compressed her chest -- and gazed at the heavy velvet curtains. She resolved to think only of the movie and the handsome man next to her.

Laura's attention never wavered from the film, entranced from the movie title to the closing credits. She loved movies and the magnificent music and sound effects produced by the magnificent Wurlitzer theater organ. Her fingers danced over imaginary keys along with the organist seated at the gold and black console in the orchestra pit.

"That was the bees knees. No wonder it's the most popular movie around." Laura and Bruce maneuvered through the dense crowd. "Thank you so much for bringing me. Tonight has been the best evening ever."

"You're welcome." Bruce placed his arm around Laura's slim waist, holding her close even though she stiffened at his touch.   At last, they got out of the theater and headed for the car.

"Let's find a quiet place to talk. I've got something important to ask you."

Laura's mood changed from excitement to worry in an instant. She cared about Bruce very much -- in fact, sometimes she thought she might be in love with him -- but his tone sounded serious. She stayed quiet until they got back into the car, listening for any clues to what was on his mind.

Bruce chattered about the movie, paying no attention to Laura's distracted responses. He parked the car near St. Thomas Catholic Church, then led Laura to a secluded bench under the trees on the park-like grounds.

"It's so peaceful here," Laura said, settling on a bench. She shivered a little, wondering what was coming.

"Yes, and perfect for us," Bruce said. "Hey, don't look so serious. I've got an exciting idea."

Laura tried to control her rapid breathing, waiting to hear what he had to say.

"What are you doing for Thanksgiving?" Bruce said.

"Uh, just having dinner in the dining hall, I guess," she said, a little surprised by the question. "Nothing special. The YWCA has a lot of rules, but we're not required to eat there. I could skip the Thanksgiving dinner if you want me to."

"Well, my family celebration should be over by three."

The family celebration? Is he inviting me to join them?

Bruce continued talking. "What would you say about us going to Oklahoma City for the weekend? If we left at three thirty, we could get there Thursday night, and then come back Sunday evening. I'll get us a room in the best hotel in town. We can do whatever you want for two whole, wonderful days." Bruce pulled her to him.

Laura shoved him away, not sure she understood what he'd said. "What? Are you asking me to join you for Thanksgiving dinner and then take a trip?"

"Wish I could, but my parents are old-fashioned. I've told them how much I care about you, but Mother is hung up on her society rules. She'd never be able to see past you being half Indian."

"How can you say you care about me? It sounds like your mother isn't the only one hung up on stupid society rules."

Bruce reached for her hand but Laura stayed out of range. "It's not just that. My father's most important goal is having me take over the bank when he's ready to retire, but he insists that I have to find a wife with the perfect pedigree or he won't pass it on to me."

Laura stood and stepped away from the bench, shaking her head in shocked disbelief.

"Don't be like that, doll. I'm in no hurry to settle down with some boring society debutante. I'd rather keep seeing you, and a weekend together would be so great, just the two of us." Bruce leaned forward and his voice thickened. "Say yes, baby, please. You know you want to."

Laura's emotions cycled from confusion and shame, to pain, then blinding anger. "You and your parents don't think I'm good enough to sit at your table, but you want to take me to a hotel in Oklahoma City? You can't even consider me for a wife, but I'd be okay as a girlfriend on the side?"

"Don't look like that," Bruce implored. "We've had fun together, and I just want to keep having fun. I never said anything about us being more than that."

Laura fought hard to keep from crying. "Going to a movie or having dinner is different from sharing a hotel room for the weekend. I can't imagine what I've done to make you think that would be okay."

She trembled from head to toe, throat burning. "Take me home, right now."

"Oh, come on. Stop acting like some kind of innocent little school girl. You told me your history. What's the problem? It's not like you're a virgin ... and with your own father yet."

Laura slapped Bruce as hard as she could, almost knocking him off the bench. "He raped me," she screamed. Her hand stung like fire, but the flaming red mark on Bruce's face was worth it.

Without saying a word, Laura ran away, back the way they'd come.

Bruce yelled. "Come back here, you little bitch. No girl hits me and gets away with it. Where the hell do you think you're going?"

"Leave me alone. I never want to see you again." Laura spit the words back over her shoulder.

"You know you don't mean that. Come here and I'll take you home." Bruce's words were softer, but his tone couldn't make up for what he'd said.

Laura ran even faster, staring straight ahead as she passed the ivy-covered stone walls of the church. She angled toward the road, sliding on the damp grass as she passed dark trees, lit only by the moonlight.

No more words pursued her, but Laura heard Bruce's car starting. When he drew even with her, Bruce leaned out the window and said, "It's a long way to the YWCA. Get in the car. You know I'm right."

Laura didn't turn her head or acknowledge him at all. Bruce drove alongside her and kept talking. Then he gave up and sped away. Only then did she slow down to a snail's pace, struggling to see through the tears that coursed down her face.

How could she have been so stupid? A handsome, rich guy like Bruce with his college education and a Father who owned a bank? Why, oh why had she trusted him?

Hot tears still fell as Laura reached the YWCA front door. She was late and had to listen to a lecture before being allowed to go to her room. Once there, Laura paced back and forth, from wall to wall, raging inside.

She pressed her hands into her temples, unable to keep the words inside. "What's the matter with you? Miss Emma warned you and warned you not to tell anyone about your past. They will use whatever you tell them to hurt and manipulate you."

Over and over the same phrases reverberated inside Laura's mind, even after she stopped speaking them aloud. At long last she stopped circling the room and sat down. She had only one choice, and that was to get as far away as possible. Tulsa was a big city with plenty of room to start over. She'd be smart this time. She'd gotten along just fine without a boyfriend before.

Decision made, Laura pulled her suitcase from under the bed and started to pack her things. She left fresh clothes for the morning on the dresser, together with her comb and toothbrush, set the clock for an hour before dawn, then climbed into bed.

CHAPTER TWO,
Start Over

The next morning Laura woke up before the alarm went off, gasping for breath, covered in sweat, and tangled in twisted bedclothes. She blinked and shook her head, trying to free herself of the nightmares. The awful images still haunted her, vivid and real. Her pa's red, sweaty face looming over her as he held her down and thrust himself into her. Her brother Ben's ugly laugh and clutching hands pulling at her clothes. And the ranch hands, Daniel and Frank, who had attacked her at Miss Emma's.

She never thought her nightmares would come back. Last time they bothered her was at Emma's after she'd pulled a knife to get away from two hired hands. She shivered, remembering the agony of the horrific dreams

20

that lasted almost a year. Laura stood and picked her way through the dark room to the window where the faintest hint of the coming day softened the darkness on the other side of the glass. She knew she had to find a new job and a new place to live.

She shuddered, "I need to get away, no telling what Bruce might do since I hit him." Speaking the words aloud helped strengthen her resolve. Looking at the moon outside reminded her of when she ran away from the family farm so long ago. She'd started over then and could do it again, but she sure felt lonely with no one to help her.

Laura slipped into her green flannel bathrobe and tightened the belt while thrusting her feet into her slippers. Then she wrapped a threadbare towel around her shoulders, grabbed her toothbrush and headed for the bathroom. She made as little noise as possible taking her bath. She slipped back into her room without waking anyone.

After getting dressed and packing away her alarm clock and personal items, Laura sat on the bed. She pulled a pencil and pad out of her purse. "I'd better make a list, or I'll forget something," she said under her breath, then dampened the pencil point on her tongue and wrote.

    1. Quit my job

    2. Find a new job across town

Putting things on paper made them look easy. Her supervisor, Mrs. Ellsworth, would be mad if she didn't get a proper two week notice, but Laura didn't dare explain. She thought a moment, tapping the pencil on her pad. "I could tell her I have to leave because of a bad personal problem. At least that would be the truth." Nodding at the sound of the words, Laura went back to the list.

She added the next two items, then crossed out the first and changed the number on the next one. She'd better find a new place before she gave this one up. If the job search didn't go well, she could end up in a real mess.

    ~~3. Give up my room~~

    4̶. 3. Find a new place to live

Doubts pushed their way into Laura's mind. If she couldn't move away and find a new job, would Bruce come after her? Maybe even call the police on her? Stop it. She couldn't think like that.

    4. Give up my room.

    That was a hard one, even if she didn't have a choice. Laura'd been happy there and didn't want to leave. For the first time in her life she'd made friends with other women and would miss them. She didn't dare tell them she was leaving or they might tell someone. Laura started tapping the pencil again, trying to think of another way out of her predicament, but came up with nothing. She straightened her back, took a deep breath and continued writing.

    5. Close my bank account

    6. Find a new bank and transfer my money

    She didn't want one penny in Bruce's family's bank. Leaving the bank business for last was best since she wanted her money close to her new place.

    Laura stood and tossed the pencil and pad in her open suitcase. She dropped her robe on the bed and got dressed for work.

CHAPTER THREE
I'll Take It

Laura stopped by the kitchen to pick up her dinner, a thick wax-paper wrapped meatloaf sandwich, an apple, and two cookies packed in a brown-paper bag. When the front door closed behind her, Laura headed to the right. The Centurion Insurance Company where she worked was six blocks away. Most mornings she loved the energy from the busy pedestrians on the sidewalk and the noisy street traffic, but this morning the ugly scene with Bruce kept playing over and over in her mind.

She resented leaving the comfortable life she'd enjoyed for the last two years. Tulsa had felt like an alien world after living in the country her whole life. When Laura walked to work the first time she'd stared at the people around her. The ladies' dresses and some men's shirts and pocket handkerchiefs were bright and colorful as flowers, nothing like the dull colors she'd grown up with. And the city people wore store-bought clothing, with shiny shoes and boots, instead of the home-made hand-me-downs and bare feet she was used to.

When Laura arrived at Centurion, her heart was pounding and her hands were wet and shaky. She went straight to her supervisor's desk. "Good morning, Mrs. Ellsworth," she said. "I, uh, I have a problem."

Mrs. Ellsworth sighed, then slipped off the glasses that rested on the end of her nose. She dangled them by the silver chain attached to the temples. "What's the problem?"

"Well, it's personal. I hate to do it, but I've got to quit today."

"No notice?" Mrs. Ellsworth shook her head, but not a single gray hair dared to move out of place. "All the work we have and you'll leave me without a chance to hire someone before you go? After two years here I thought you were different."

Laura started to speak, but Mrs. Ellsworth put her hand up. "I don't need to hear any excuses. Go see to Mr. Ames in payroll."

In less than an hour, Laura found herself outside on the sidewalk, unemployed, but with a week and two day's salary, $31.80. She had $1.80 in her purse, and the rest tucked into her brassiere. It felt funny carrying this much cash around. Good thing her brassiere bound her chest so tight, since it was lots safer than keeping all the money in her purse.

Laura swallowed the fear that threatened to close her throat. Thank goodness she'd crept down the stairs and talked with the YWCA night receptionist, Miss Adam, before anyone else was awake. Nobody else would have taken the time to help her. Laura double-checked the hand-drawn map Miss Adam had made for her, then marched three blocks to the nearest trolley stop to catch a ride to Tulsa Central Memorial Hospital.

Laura hoped Miss Adam was right about the hospital hiring people since they'd added a new wing. She'd told Laura there were cheap hotels nearby, too.

Laura joined a group of people waiting for the trolley minutes before the clanging bell announced the car's arrival. The double doors hissed open, revealing the three steps leading up into the interior of the shiny green and red car. Running with the crowd, Laura dodged between cars into the middle of the street. A mass of people clambered down the steps headed for the safety of the sidewalk while Laura and those with her waited for their turn to climb in. As Laura handed the conductor her dime, she told herself she had to find a place to live within walking distance of the new job. A dime a day for a trolley was way too expensive.

The trolley ride seemed to last for hours, what with stops every few intersections, but was only about thirty minutes. Laura stepped down from the trolley right across the street from the hospital. She saw a sign advertising the new wing. She could also see that construction was still underway on the grounds. The main building, set back from the street, had manicured grounds dotted with trees and flowerbeds on both sides of the walkway leading up to the entrance.

Laura entered through the front door, surprised by the number of people waiting around and the cacophony of noise. She straightened her back, lifted her head high, and threaded her way through the crowd to a long counter that divided the lobby, determined to make a good impression. When she reached the receptionist, Laura told her she was looking for a job. She received a map of the hospital and detailed instructions to the staffing office in the basement. The directions led her down a wide flight of stairs only somewhat less crowded than the lobby. She took another look at the map, then wound her way through a maze of hallways to a room with the number B18 on the door.

Laura knocked, then stepped inside and stood in front of the largest man she'd ever seen. He was tall and wide, body spilling over the sides of his chair. He was massive rather than fat, the tight muscles of his neck and torso straining the fabric of his dress shirt over his chest and arms. His huge hands lay flat on the desk in front of him, one almost covering a letter-sized piece of paper.

"Hello, miss, I'm Mr. Armstrong, and I'm guessing you need a job." His voice was surprising -- soft and high pitched for a man -- didn't seem to match his huge body. "Sit down and tell me about yourself." He waved her to a chair in front of the desk and leaned back, his chair creaking in protest as he readjusted his position.

"Yes, sir." She balanced on the edge of the chair and took a deep breath. "I'm willing to do whatever you need, sir. I've done filing and office work, and almost every kind of chore there is on a ranch. I don't have any formal training, but I learn fast and I'm a hard worker. All I need is a chance."

"You have a good attitude, but without hospital experience, I'd have to start you in housekeeping on the wards. You'd be at the beck and call of the medical staff for whatever they need, including cleaning many body fluid messes. Patients will also ask you for help when they need something or if there's some kind of spill in their rooms. Both of those examples are in addition to the regular housekeeping tasks, such as scrubbing floors, cleaning bathrooms, making beds, dumping trash, and a whole list of other duties." Mr. Armstrong paused and stared at Laura, his face an impassive mask.

Laura waited a moment, not sure if he was expecting a response. "I can do all those things, sir. If you'll just give me a chance, I won't let you down."

After their conversation, Mr. Armstrong hired Laura, reminding her once again that the work was difficult. He also told her that if she proved herself, there was always a chance to advance. Laura was thrilled and determined to prove her value. She completed a stack of paperwork and left with instructions on when and where to report the following day.

Laura flew back to the lobby, waving at the receptionist who'd helped her, before heading outside.

I did it. Miss Emma helped me get hired at Centurion, but I got this job by myself.

Laura sat down on a bench just beyond and to the side of the hospital's front door. Her cheeks ached from smiling. She pulled a packet of papers from her purse and leafed through the stack looking for one with a list of nearby apartments and hotels.

Several possibilities were near the hospital, but she crossed off the first three as unacceptable. Two of the apartments cost more than she could afford. One small rooming house had both men and women as residents, and she knew that wouldn't be comfortable for her. She feared having men nearby would bring back her nightmares, especially if they looked anything like the ones who'd tormented her. She decided to spend one hour walking the neighborhood, before she had to catch the trolley back to the YWCA. Maybe she'd see something. Twenty minutes later, she was getting worried, then spotted a large yellow Victorian-style house with a discrete sign over the double doors that read "Thompson's Hotel for Ladies."

She entered and crossed her fingers for luck as she approached the woman sitting at a large mahogany desk just inside a small lobby.

"May I help you?" the redheaded woman behind the desk said, as she looked up from her magazine and waved her cigarette holder around to clear the smoke. A small sign on the desk read "Miss Hathaway."

"I hope so," Laura said. "Do you have a vacancy? I start work tomorrow at the hospital, and your hotel looks perfect for me."

"You're in luck. A resident left yesterday. Haven't even had time to make a sign yet." The cigarette pointed straight at Laura. "The rent runs three dollars per week or ten dollars per month and includes breakfast and supper in the dining room. If you're not there on time, you don't eat. We lock the doors at nine-thirty p.m. If you're late you won't get in."

Miss Hathaway paused. When Laura made no comment or objection, she continued. "No men upstairs. They're only allowed in the parlor on the first floor. You share a bathroom with three other women, but we supply fresh towels and washcloths weekly. You're responsible for keeping your room clean, and also for helping keep the bathroom clean." Miss Hathaway stopped to take a deep drag on her cigarette, then blew out a grey cloud from the side of her mouth. "The room's furnished and we provide clean bedding every other week. If you want it, we require payment in advance."

"Sounds perfect."

"Then follow me and see if you like it."

Laura followed Miss Hathaway up a steep, narrow staircase to the second floor, then down a hallway to the second door on the left. She peeked inside and saw a small, shabby room with a bed, a four-drawer dresser with a square mirror, a single chair, and a tiny closet. The one window had both a shade and thin curtains. Laura stepped inside and compared this room with the one at the YWCA. It had less room, but the dresser was larger. She took four steps to the foot of the bed and sat down. The mattress was a little soft, but not bad.

"I'll take it," Laura said.

"Good. There're some papers to sign, then I'll take your money and give you the key."

They finished the process at Miss Hathaway's desk. Laura put the key inside her coin purse, deep in her pocketbook. "Thank you," she said. Laura wanted to cheer and jump up and down but walked out the door, her emotions revealed only by the huge grin on her face.

When she returned to the YWCA, Laura planned to take her suitcase and hurry back to her new place. Once she sat down, the day caught up with her and she changed her mind. Maybe it'd be better to settle up with the manager tonight, get a good night's sleep and stop at the hotel before work in the morning. It wouldn't be much of a detour, and she could put her things away after her shift ended. Or, she could find a bank first, then go home and get settled in.

"Hey, girl." Laura recognized Ruby's voice outside the door. "Thelma and I are heading for the diner. Want to come with us?"

"No, thanks. I need to wash my hair." She knew they meant well, but she didn't feel up to talking about what had happened. And nobody needed to know where she'd gone.

Laura waited until the hallway was silent, then slipped out the door. She crept down the stairs, making sure there were no sounds before she turned at the landing. It felt wrong to sneak out like this. They'd been good friends to her. She blinked her eyes and pulled her shoulders back. Didn't matter, she needed to make a clean break.

The YWCA manager accepted Laura's story about needing to leave for personal reasons. Her only concern was making sure Laura understood she wouldn't be able to come back without going on the waiting list again. That settled, Laura signed a form and promised to leave her key at the desk when she left in the morning.

CHAPTER FOUR
I Don't Want To Die

Laura was up the next morning long before anyone else, having set her alarm more than an hour early. Purse in one hand and suitcase handle in the other, she made her way to the trolley stop, then got off near her new hotel. Once in her new room, she stowed her suitcase under the bed, then headed to the hospital.

She punched the time clock in the basement, stowed her handbag and coat in her assigned locker, then closed and padlocked it. She dropped the key into an inside pocket of her new white smock, and headed up to the third floor where she'd been told to report.

At the head of the stairs, she bumped into a nurse starting down. She started to ask the nurse where H3 was, but before she could, the nurse pointed behind her toward a doorway with H3 posted above it.

The door opened just before Laura's fingers touched the doorknob.

"Get on in her. No time to waste on this floor." A tall, bone-thin woman who stood in the entrance smelled like ammonia-scented cigarette smoke. "I'm Miz Marston, Housekeeping Supervisor. This is the housekeeping room where we keep all our supplies. The deep sinks in back are where you'll empty the buckets and clean everything."

"Yes, ma'am," Laura said. "I'm Miss Cavanaugh."

"Okay, Cavanaugh, let's get started."

The next few hours were a blur. The third floor contained four wards, each with four beds and a tiny bathroom in one corner. Laura cleaned floors and the bathrooms, collected and disposed of trash, and did whatever the nurses and doctors asked of her. She helped adjust pillows and raise the beds to make the patients more comfortable, but she wasn't supposed to socialize with them. If they asked her to bring them something, like food or pain medicine, she had to get permission from their nurse first.

"What are you doing, Cavanaugh?" Miz Marston stepped out of Ward A, straight into Laura's path.

"I'm taking fresh bedding to Ward D. Mr. Whipple made a mess in the bed, and his nurse sent me to get clean sheets so she can remake it."

"Fine, but you need to take your dinner break as soon as you're done. Do you remember how to get to the cafeteria?"

"Yes, ma'am, on the first floor." Laura hurried on her way to deliver the bed linens, then headed for the stairs.

Laura stared at the menu items on the chalkboard. She settled on a bowl of chicken noodle soup and water. After paying the cashier, she headed to an empty table in the corner.

She couldn't believe she had to pay fifteen cents for a bowl of soup, when a whole chicken only cost twenty cents. She tasted a spoonful, then ate slowly, relishing every swallow. It tasted so good.

Laura returned to the third floor with renewed energy but was exhausted when she clocked out. The work was much harder than working in the file room. I'm done wore out all over. Think I'll ask Miss Hathaway about a bank close by and go there tomorrow.

Bbrrrinnnnggg, the Baby Ben rocketed Laura awake the next morning, still groggy, but excited to start her second day. She slammed her hand down on the alarm clock, fearing everybody on the floor would be awake after that racket.

Laura stood, stretched, and grabbed a small bag containing personal items. Twenty minutes later she was downstairs, ready to join the three women already seated at the breakfast table.

"Hi, you must be the new girl," a short, blond girl with large hazel eyes said. "I'm Abby, and I have the room across from you."

"Nice to meet you, Abby, I'm Laura."

Abby sat at one end of the rectangular table in the center of the room. The dining room had two doors. One led into the kitchen and the other the parlor. A tall glass-fronted cherry wood hutch filled with dishes was against one wall, and a matching sideboard hugged the opposite one.

The other two girls at the table introduced themselves as Barbara and Katie. Barbara, curvy and short, had light brown, shoulder-length hair curled around her heart-shaped face. Katie was tiny, with shiny black hair and olive skin.

"The other two on our floor are Minnie and Grace, but Grace never eats breakfast with us," Abby said. "You'll meet her tonight." She was filling her plate from platters of eggs, potatoes, and ham as she talked. "The food's really good here, and there's plenty of it. Don't be late for supper though, or you won't get any. It's first come, first served, and the first ones don't worry about leaving any for latecomers."

"Thanks for letting me know." Laura followed Abby's lead by placing a biscuit on her plate and spooning some scrambled eggs.

Just as Laura finished serving herself, two more girls entered, chatting as they took their seats.

"Good morning everybody. This is the new girl," Abby sang out, pointing at Laura. "Laura, meet Minnie and Jane."

Laura smiled. She had a lot of new names to remember.

The girls resumed laughing and talking. They reminded her of a flock of prize chickens, lots of bright colors and noise.
Laura didn't say a word as she ate.

"Guess what?" Katie leaned forward, grinning. "Morris invited me to share Thanksgiving with his family. And I think he'll pop the question at dinner."

While the others shrieked and congratulated Katie, Laura tried to keep smiling. It hurt to hear the word Thanksgiving.

"Excuse me, I need to go." Laura stood and glanced around the table. "It was nice meeting you all, but I've got to get to work." She grabbed her purse hanging off the back of the chair and headed out the door.

Laura's eyes stung as she stomped toward the hospital, weaving her way through slower people on the sidewalk. She figured those girls at the hotel probably thought she was rude or crazy, maybe both. She wished she could afford to live alone.

Miz Marston waved at Laura from the housekeeping supply room when she arrived. "You're early. You can start working if you want, but you don't get paid overtime unless it's authorized in advance." Miz Marston stood by several stacks of cartons full of cleaning materials. "You need to unpack all these boxes."

"Doesn't matter, I'd rather work than sit around waiting."

Laura felt the supervisor's gaze cover her face, with a speculative look. "Well, since you're here, go get 3C ready. The bed needs fresh linens. Don't forget to replenish the patient supplies on the table by the bed. We've got a new admission coming up in a few minutes."

"Yes, ma'am." Laura grabbed one of the housekeeping carts and started loading it.

When Laura took her dinner break, she was shocked at how fast the morning had gone by. She stretched her legs out under the table in the cafeteria and rolled her neck and shoulders around to loosen the muscles. That felt good. As she ate a toasted cheese sandwich, she wiggled her toes and flexed her feet. Old sourpuss Mrs. Ellsworth was looking pretty good now, compared to slavedriver Miz Marston.

Licking bits of melted cheese off her fingers, Laura leaned back in her chair and studied the other people in the cafeteria. Some ate their meals in small groups. A few solitary diners were like herself, others ate from brown paper bags or lunch boxes. Conversations and laughter drifted around the room, adding to the pleasant atmosphere.

Dinner break was all too short. Back on the third floor, Laura cleared meal trays from the patient's bedside tables.

"Cavanaugh," Miz Marston called, leaning around a privacy drape. "Get a wiggle on, girl. Watson just went home sick, so you're it for the rest of your shift."

She finished clearing Ward B, then started in C. She could see the outlines of two women inside the drape surrounding bed 3.

"Too bad, isn't it," one hushed voice said. "He's young, and a looker too. Well, I think he would be if the side of his face wasn't so bruised up."

"I know. The doc's pretty sure he won't make it." The second voice sounded sad.

Laura stopped with three dirty trays in her hands, wanting to hear more of the conversation, but feeling guilty eavesdropping.

Metal curtain rings screeched as they slid on the rod. Two nurses stepped out and left the room without a backward glance. Laura followed them into the hallway. She carried the dirty dishes to the bin for the kitchen staff, then looked for Miz Marston.

She decided to check 3C in case he needed something on her way to Ward D. The privacy curtain was still open, so she stepped to the head of the bed and looked down at the doomed patient. His facial muscles were slack, but Laura had no sense of a peaceful sleep. Dark hair lay tangled and dirty, below bandages that covered the top of the man's head.

All of a sudden, Laura saw a quick flash of him stepping off a trolley and getting hit by a speeding car. He'd bounced off the hood to the road, landing on his head, then another car hit him. Her vision was but an instant, but she knew she'd seen the details of what had happened.

Poor man. No wonder they didn't think he'd make it.

"No, don't say that. I don't want to die!" The words screamed in her mind, full of panic and pain. The man's facial expression never changed. His mouth remained closed, lips soft and peaceful looking, and the long dark lashes didn't even tremble.

Laura's heart hammered, the pulse reveberating throughout her body. She looked around. Had anyone else heard the voice? She recalled her sister Ruth warning her not to talk about visions or voices because people would think she was possessed or crazy. She remembered the contempt on Bruce's face when he threw her own history against her as an excuse for his proposition. Her face burned with shame as she turned away from the bed and left the room without a word.

The rest of the day passed in a whirlwind of activity without a moment of rest, but Laura couldn't get the unconscious man out of her thoughts. His voice had been clear, and his fear overpowering. Guilt filled her heart for leaving him all alone after hearing his cries for help. After clocking out, she headed back to the third floor. She wondered if he needed anything. She trudged back to Ward C on leaden feet, then stepped around the closed curtain to the side of the bed.

The man looked as if he hadn't moved at all since she'd last seen him. She reached out and touched his hand, but he didn't respond.

She heard him whisper in her mind. "Help me, please, help me."

Laura jerked her hand back and felt her body turn to ice. "I can't. I'm so sorry but I just can't." She turned and raced out of the room, choked by silent sobs.

Laura held the tears back until she pushed through the hospital doors, then let them stream down her cheeks on the way to the hotel.

What was wrong with her? What kind of horrible person was she to ignore someone in so much pain? It's not like he could tell anyone she'd heard him.

When she reached the hotel door, she wiped her face and pasted a smile on her lips before stepping inside.

CHAPTER FIVE
My Name is Phillip Dunn
Six Days Later, Thanksgiving 1923

Laura tightened the coat around herself and hunched her head down against the cold wind. The streets between her hotel and the hospital were almost deserted. Looked like everybody was sleeping in or staying warm and cozy inside for the holiday celebration.

Her empty stomach growled since she'd missed breakfast to avoid conversation with the other girls. Laura's fingers tightened around an apple nestled in her coat pocket. She was early and had time to eat the apple before heading to the wards.

The hospital hallways were as empty as the streets. All patients who could go home had been discharged the day before, and staffing was minimal. Laura clocked in, then sat on a bench to eat her apple. She was poised to throw the core into the wastebasket, when Miz Marston blew into the room like a storm cloud.

"Cavanaugh, thank goodness I can count on you. Watson called in sick again with another lame excuse and I fired her, so you'll have the floor to yourself. Shouldn't be any problem today, but if you run into something you can't handle, you might have to come find me down on one of the other floors." Miz Marston paused and took a breath. "Any questions?"

"No, ma'am, not that I can think of." Laura's mind stuck on the unexpected praise.

"Good, I'll be in my office on the second floor for the next thirty minutes if you need me." Miz Marston headed out the door.

The patient load was light, but they were the sickest and seemed needier than usual. Laura did her best to make each one feel better, fluffing pillows and adjusting blankets, even running down nurses to convey special requests.

Miz Marston returned just before Laura's supper break. "I'll cover the floor for you. The cafeteria staff cooked a free Thanksgiving meal for the employees. Go now while everything's fresh."

Laura appreciated the news. Wonderful smells greeted her when she arrived in the cafeteria -- turkey and ham, sweet potatoes, apple and pumpkin pies. She tried, but she couldn't eat more than a few bites in spite of her empty stomach. Thanksgiving reminded her of when she learned the truth about Bruce's feelings for her. His invitation to go away with him for the Thanksgiving weekend still hurt. Her queasy stomach felt tied in knots. She kept her smile for the people who wished her a Happy Thanksgiving, but let it vanish on her way up the stairs to her floor.

All three shift nurses stood at the nurses' station, laughing and talking. As she passed by, Laura noticed several plates with home-made fudge and divinity, and a box of See's Candy. She waved to them, then ducked into the housekeeping supply room.

She spent the afternoon going from ward to ward, making sure the patients were comfortable. Each time she entered Ward C, she glanced at the curtained-off section around bed 3, but didn't step inside the closed area. With no other chores to do, Laura decided to unpack some boxes of cleaning products in the housekeeping supply room.. She passed a doctor leaning on the counter at the nurse's station, chatting with the two nurses.

"How's our John Doe doing, ladies? Any changes?" He held a chart in his hands but stared at one of the nurses.

"Haven't noticed any changes today. Is there anything you want done for him?"

"No. Just keep him comfortable and let nature take its course."

Keep him comfortable? Just let him die? Laura clenched her fists as she continued on to the housekeeping room. She couldn't concentrate on restocking the shelves, so she gave up and sat down, leaning her head on her hands. Maybe the doc was right, but nobody should have to die all alone.

She stood and went straight to Ward C, making sure no one was paying attention to her. She slipped inside the curtain and pulled the visitor's chair close to the head of the bed. He looked the same as before. Not even the slightest hint of movement as he breathed. Laura placed her hand on top of his, half afraid it would be cold and stiff. She wondered if they knew his name.

"Phillip Dunn. My name is Phillip Dunn." The voice was clear in her mind, quieter and more resigned than before. "Don't know how you can hear me, but I'm glad you can."

Laura squeezed his hand. "Phillip Dunn, that's a nice name." She slipped her other hand underneath his, closed her eyes, and concentrated on the warmth of his skin next to hers.

She felt a change in the energy around them and opened her eyes. His face looked the same, but his eyelids popped open. He stared at a corner of the ceiling, the corners of his mouth lifting a tiny bit.

"Mama," he whispered out loud in a raspy voice, "Mama, I've missed you so much."

Laura's eyes flashed to where he was staring, but she didn't see a thing. She turned her attention back to Phillip's face and felt his spirit leave. To her surprise the room filled with warmth and peace. She felt no sensation of loss or fear, just joy.

Phillip's mouth opened as his flaccid jaw muscles collapsed toward his chest. His open eyes remained fixed in place as if staring at the ceiling corner, but began to lose their luster. Even the hand she held felt different as his muscle tone disappeared, leaving it limp. She couldn't bring herself to let go, so she continued sitting with him.

"I hope you're at peace now, Phillip Dunn. Just wish I could have done something to help you."

"You did help him, Laura. You heard him and stayed with him at the end. He's safe on the other side now." The comforting voice was her ma's, filling her mind and her body with tranquility. Laura's eyes filled with tears. She hadn't heard her ma's beautiful voice in a long time.

"I thought I heard you talking to someone." A hand rested on Laura's shoulder, then the nurse leaned in toward the bed. "Did he wake up and talk to you before he passed?"

Laura smiled. "Just to tell me his name was Phillip Dunn. Then he was gone."

At least he wouldn't be buried as John Doe.

"That's good news. I'll let administration know." The nurse pulled the sheet up over Phillip's face and smoothed it over his forehead. She turned her attention back to Laura and smiled, patting her on the shoulder.

"Losing your first patient is tough. The day's almost over, so why don't you clock out." She put her hand up to stop the expected protest, then continued. "I'll let Miz Marston know I sent you home. And don't worry, we can handle a mop if we need to."

"Are you sure?"

The nurse nodded, then gave Laura a hug.

Nearly overwhelmed with gratitude, Laura soon found herself out on the street headed home. Once in her room, she couldn't bear to stay there alone. She went downstairs, but when she heard loud conversation and laughter coming from the dining room, she slipped into the parlor instead.

Laura focused her attention on the piano in the corner. It had been so long since she'd played at Miss Emma's. And it looked like the poor lonely piano hadn't been touched for a long time.

She sat down on the scarred wooden bench and raised the dusty cover from the somewhat yellowed keys. She flexed her fingers a few times, placed them in position, and began to play the first song she'd learned. "A B C D, E F G, H I J K, LMNOP..." She sang along, smiling at the image of a 20-year-old woman playing the alphabet song. How thrilled she'd been the first time Miz Gibson played that tune in school. Her fingers rested a moment as she remembered. Was Miz Gibson still teaching? Laura would love to tell her how much her music had meant to her.

Laura closed her eyes, letting her fingers move through Amazing Grace, America the Beautiful, then Old Man River. She was surprised to glance up and find herself surrounded by a small crowd, who all began to clap and compliment her on her playing.

"Don't stop," Abby said when Laura started to push back from the piano. "Please play some more."

"Are you sure? I didn't mean to interrupt your party." Laura was shocked to see five of the other residents and four young men around her, all smiling and urging her on.

"Alright, if you're sure." Requests came one after another, and everyone sang along with her music. She played an eclectic mix, from hymns to popular songs like, Yes, We Have No Bananas, Who's Sorry Now, and Carolina in the Morning. She even played a few Christmas carols.

"May I join you with my harmonica?" A quiet voice came from Laura's right. She glanced up into a nice looking masculine face with brown eyes and sandy colored hair. "I'm Glen Webber and I'd love to join you."

"Glen's my brother, and I asked him to share Thanksgiving with us," Barbara said. "He's really good on the tin sandwich, I promise."

Laura shrugged her assent, remembering the fun of playing with other musicians at Miz Emma's place. Now they sang along to Ain't

Misbehaving, My Blue Heaven, Sonny Boy, and
other popular tunes. Nobody wanted to stop,
but the men had to leave before the landlady
locked the doors at nine-thirty.

Laura stayed at the piano while everyone
else walked to the door to say their goodbyes.
Glen was the last out the door, but turned to
wave at Laura after giving Barbara a hug.
"Thanks, Laura, it was fun making music
together." His gaze lingered, and he smiled
before stepping outside.

Barbara had never mentioned a brother
before. He was nice, and a good musician. Laura
hoped he'd come again.

CHAPTER SIX
Sharing Music
Two Weeks Later, December 1923

Laura hesitated, her hand on the doorknob, not wanting to leave the cozy, warm room. The weather had turned nasty, but she had to get to work. She wished she could wear men's trousers and flannel shirts like she did at Miz Emma's.

Each step Laura took in her heavy rubber galoshes was slow and careful as she made her way toward the hospital's front doors. Once in the foyer, she stamped the snow from her boots, then took off her coat and gloves. Patting her hair into place, she headed for the basement. She wondered what it would be like to live somewhere where there was no snow?

As soon as Laura entered the housekeeping room, she found Miz Marston and a rosy-faced, round figured woman with a cap of unruly dark curls.

"Laura, this is Agnes Murphy. She'll be working with you. I've shown her around, so now it's up to you to teach her the job." Introduction over, Miz Marston breezed out of the room.

"Nice to meet you, Laura. I've been cleaning in the kitchen for the last couple of months but never worked on any of the wards. I'll try not to be a bother if you can show me what to do." Laura couldn't help but grin as Agnes smiled at her.

"Not a lot to it," Laura said. "Why don't you come with me for awhile and I'll show you the ropes. You can ask questions as we go."

Soon Agnes had caught on to the routine, so Laura could work one side of a room while Agnes did the other. In what seemed like minutes Laura and Agnes clocked out for dinner.

"Are you going to the cafeteria to eat?" Laura said as she led the way down the stairs.

"No, my husband works at a little shop across the street. He stores our bag lunches in their back room, and we eat there each day with the other employees."

Laura was glad she didn't have to go out in the cold for dinner. She got a steaming bowl of beef stew, then looked around for an empty table.

"Laura," a voice called out from across the room.

She was surprised to see Glen waving his arms. He sat at a table in the back of the room. Laura didn't want to seem rude, so she threaded her way toward him.

"Thank you." Laura placed her tray down and sat across the table from him. "Looks like not many people are going out of the building for dinner today," Laura said. I've never seen you here before. Do you work for the hospital?"

"I work part-time for groundskeeping. Been shoveling snow since early morning."

Laura could see his red, chapped skin. "That sounds miserable. But I was sure happy to see the walkway cleared when I arrived this morning."

"Glad it helped, but you still need to be careful. Last year one of the doctors took a nasty spill and ended up with a broken back. After that, the hospital doubled the groundskeeping staff."

"Poor man, how awful that must have been. Ice on the walkway can sure be tricky."

"It's nasty out there, but at least it's work. No gardening or mowing in the winter, so snow shoveling is one of the few jobs the boss calls us in for." Glen wrapped his hands around his coffee cup and sighed. "It sure feels good to hold something warm. After a couple of hours outside you get chilled clean through your bones."

Laura nodded in agreement and the conversation ended there. She enjoyed the silence, with no personal questions or expectations, just the simple sharing of a meal.

Christmas dawned bright and cold. The sun shone on a blanket of snow, but the clear sky was a deep blue for the first time in days. Several of the girls were spending part of the day with family or friends, but they all planned to share a special supper. Miss Hathaway and the cook had the day off, so the kitchen belonged to the residents for the holiday. Before leaving on Christmas Eve day, Miss Hathaway had issued dire warnings of potential retribution if they left a mess, but gave them permission to let guests stay until ten that evening.

The girls planned the meal together, but Barbara, Grace, and Jane prepared it. Laura admitted to not being a good cook, so she ended up relegated to basic chores like peeling potatoes, chopping vegetables, and setting a festive table.

By the time the food was ready, everyone had arrived. Minnie and Katie each had their boyfriends, Morris and Thomas, with them. Barbara had invited Glen too. The three cooks basked in the compliments while everybody refilled their plates.

"That was fantastic," Sarah said. "The cooks can stay out of the kitchen while the rest of us clean up. And you guys can start by clearing the table."

"You tell 'em, Sarah. I like the way you think." Barbara plopped down on a sofa, followed by Grace and Jane."

Laura, who didn't consider herself one of the cooks, started for the kitchen.

"Oh, no you don't." Sarah blocked her path. "You helped with supper and you're our piano player, so go sit down with the others and rest your fingers."

"Yes, ma'am." Laura gave Sarah a mock salute and headed for an empty armchair. "Didn't know you were so bossy, but I won't disobey those orders."

With everyone working together, it seemed like minutes before they all trooped to the parlor, carrying the dining room chairs and setting them up in a circle around the piano. Laura fished through the music books in the piano bench while Glen placed his harmonica on a side table near the piano. He took a somewhat battered violin out of its case, while Morris tuned the strings of his guitar.

The energy, enthusiasm, and musical style of the three performers blended well, and Laura's fingers never slowed as she set the pace for the others. Morris and Glen both played with her, then set off on wild riffs to cheers and laughter. Everybody sang with gusto whether on key or not. Laura couldn't remember ever having so much fun just through the joy of sharing music.

All too soon the evening ended and the men were ready to leave. "Wait fellas. Laura, can you play one more?" Grace said, "I'd love to hear Swing Low, Sweet Chariot."
Ending the day with the familiar melody was a great choice. The men left after hugs all around.

The girls put the chairs back in place around the dining room table, then headed to their rooms. Laura started for the stairs, but went back to the parlor to put the music books away. When she opened the bench, she saw a small box wrapped in gold foil, tied with a red velvet ribbon. She held the gift while she read the attached card.

To Laura. Just thought you might enjoy being able to make music wherever you go. Merry Christmas, Glen. She pulled the ribbon and paper off. The top of the box had a picture of a harmonica.

She lifted the lid off and slid her finger across the shiny silver surface of the harmonica. That was so sweet of Glen. She raised the instrument to her lips and blew. Oh my goodness. That sounded more like a raspberry than a music note. Without a doubt, she would need some lessons.

She thought of the way Glen held his harmonica tight against his lips, using his mouth and hands to create music. He always seemed so patient and kind. Such a sweet gift. She'd have to catch him at work in the morning and thank him. She'd ask him if he would teach her how to play. Laura smiled all the way up the stairs to her room, thinking about how much she enjoyed making music with him.

Once in her room, Laura sat down on the bed and stretched out her legs, resting her back against the headboard. She closed her eyes and remembered the last Christmas at home before her ma had died. After Pa had gone out to the barn to tend to the animals, her ma had sung and danced around the room with Laura in her arms, while the other children twirled around them. The dancing hadn't lasted long because

Pa would have had a fit if he'd caught them but the memory was lovely.

A wave of homesickness hit Laura and almost doubled her over. She didn't miss where she'd grown up, but ached for her sisters. Ruth's letters were wonderful, but she'd love to hear her voice. She knelt down and pulled her suitcase out from under the bed. Opening it, she reached for a packet of letters tied with a pink ribbon.

"Now to find the one with Ruth's telephone number," Laura said. She untied the ribbon and spread the letters out on the chenille spread. "I've about memorized these after reading them so many times. I think the one with the number came on my birthday."

Ruth had given her their telephone number, so Laura could call them. She'd have to ask someone how to make a long distant call. Laura pawed through the letters until she found the right one.

Laura rushed through work the next day, her thoughts focused on calling Ruth. After supper was over and cleared away, she settled in the parlor holding a note Miss Hathaway had given her on how to make a long-distance call. She reread it three times, then put it on the little table next to the telephone in the dining room. The Black Bakelite telephone, which had letters and numbers printed in white circles under each hole in the rotary dial, sat next to its ringer box.

"What am I waiting for?" Laura grabbed the handset and dialed the operator to start the process. Almost unable to breathe, she waited for the operator to finish routing the call.

"Hello, Carpenter residence," a man's voice said.

"Paul, is that you?" Laura's voice quivered. "This is Laura."

"Laura? Oh, my goodness, I'm so glad you called. Hold on a minute and let me get Ruth. She'll be so excited."

Laura heard the phone bang on something, then some noises in the background.

"Laura? Is it really you?" Ruth's voice sounded shaky.

"Merry Christmas, Ruth. I've missed you so much, I had to call." She held the phone so tight her knuckles turned white. "I'm sorry to call collect, but the hotel won't let us make long distance telephone calls."

"We don't care about that. It's just so good to hear your voice."

"Yours, too." Tears poured down Laura's face, making it hard to talk around the huge lump in her throat. "How was Christmas? And your little boys and Paul, how are they? What's happening with Lizbeth and Becca? Has Lizbeth had her baby?"

Ruth, then answered each of Laura's questions one by one. She got so caught up with listening she was stunned to glance at the clock and see that five whole minutes had passed.

"Oh, no," Laura said. "It's been five minutes already. This will cost a small fortune. We'd better get off. I love you."

"I guess you're right, but we'll talk again, soon. Give me the number before you leave so I can call you."

Laura gave Ruth the number.

"Okay, I'll call soon, I promise."

Three days later, Laura was surprised when Ruth called.

"Is something wrong?" Laura said. "Has something happened? I mean, it's wonderful to hear from you so quick, but we just talked."

"We're all fine, but Paul had a wonderful idea. What days of the week do you have off?"

"Tuesday and Wednesday."

"Well, what would it take for you to have a Monday and Thursday off as well and come here on the train? You'd spend two days traveling, but we'd have two whole days together."

Laura's whole body trembled hard just thinking about such a trip. She dropped onto the chair next to the phone table. Before she could say a word, Ruth started talking again.

"Don't you say one word about the cost or anything else. We'll make all the arrangements for the tickets and send them to you. You'll travel from Tulsa to Oklahoma City, then to the station here in Ardmore. All you have to do is arrange for the time off and we'll do the rest."

"I can't believe it. Seeing you and Paul and the little ones would be incredible. And maybe Lizbeth and Becca, too?" She blinked back tears. "I've only been on the job a month, so I might not be able to come for awhile."

"It doesn't matter when. In fact, it'd give us all something to look forward to." Ruth paused a moment, then said. "Just promise you'll ask your boss and let us know."

"I can't believe this. Of course I'll ask. Heck, I'll beg." Ruth's laughter rang in Laura's ear. "I'll let you know as soon as they give me a date." Laura gulped and cleared her throat. "And Ruth, thank you. Thank you so much."

CHAPTER SEVEN
Seven Years

Laura had to wait until Monday to talk to Miz Marston about getting time off for her trip. "Miz Marston, can we talk when you have a few minutes?" Laura sounded shaky, and her hands pressed against her thighs. She'd been waiting for Miz Marston to appear on the floor and caught up with her a few steps away from the stairs.

Miz Marston stared at Laura. "Might as well do it, now." Lips pursed, she led the way to the housekeeping supply room. Once there, she crossed her arms and scowled. "All right, let's hear it."

"Well, my sister, Ruth called me yesterday and invited me to come visit the family. I haven't seen my sisters in years." Laura licked her lips, stalling as she tried to find just the right words. "She and her husband want to buy a train ticket for me to come visit." She waited, but Miz Marston didn't respond. "I know I've only been here a month, but..."

Miz Marston shook her head and tapped her fingers on her other arm. "That's right. You've only been here a month, but I thought I knew what kind of person you were. I've depended on you." She shrugged. "I never expected you to leave like this."

"Leave? I'm not leaving. Well, I want to leave for four days when I can arrange it, but that's only two extra days. I even told Ruth I'd probably have to wait a few months before I could get the time off."

"Time off? You only want time off? Horsefeathers. I thought you were resigning to go back to your family."

"No. I like my job. I want to see my sisters, but I'd never move back there." Laura shuddered at the mere thought of even seeing her pa and brother, much less living near them.

"Oh, well, time off is a different thing." Miz Marston's posture relaxed. "You need to talk to Mr. Armstrong, but I'll see if I can arrange a time for you to meet with him today."

Miz Marston sent Laura to see Mr. Armstrong not long after her dinner break since it was quiet on the floor. He sympathized, but couldn't give her vacation days until she'd been working for six months. They agreed on her being off from May 12th through May 15th. When Laura thanked him, he let her know he'd received glowing reports about her work and that he expected her to continue doing well at the hospital.

"Thank you, sir. Thank you so much." Laura shook hands with Mr. Armstrong, her hand disappearing in his giant fist. "You're welcome," he said with a big smile. "Just don't forget to come back or Miz Marston'll be mighty disappointed."

Laura rushed back up to the third floor. She saw Agnes disappear into the supply room and ran after her. "Agnes, you'll never guess what's happened."

"Well, slow down and tell me," Agnes said.

"I just got permission to take time off in May. I'm going to see my sisters. Ruth, the oldest, is sending the train tickets. I last saw her when I was sixteen and haven't seen the others in seven years."

"I'm so happy for you." Agnes hugged Laura tight, then held her shoulders when they pulled away. "Seven years? Why so long?"

"Uh, it's a long story." Laura's mood changed as she remembered the consequences of revealing too much. Bruce had been the first and last person she'd told about her Indian heritage and about being raped by her father. She'd felt safe with him, but he'd turned her words against her. "And a boring one too, but seeing them again will be terrific. Now I've got to be patient until May."

Only once before the trip did her intuitive sense engage. Laura sat with an elderly woman who drifted in and out of consciousness. She held Laura's hand until she stopped breathing. The words "It's so beautiful here." whispered in Laura's mind, full of wonder and a sense of peace. Laura didn't talk about the experience with anyone, doubting they'd believe her.

Music made waiting easier and making music was even better after Glen taught Laura how to play the harmonica. Then he started teaching her to play the fiddle. They often performed together at the hotel, and sometimes at a small dance hall that featured local musicians.

On the last day of April, Laura received the tickets in a letter from Ruth. In twelve days she'd be on a train to see her sisters. She sat on the edge of her bed, staring at the tickets in her hand. They'd even sent meal vouchers so she could eat during the trip.

Her mind raced, wondering how Ruth and the others had changed and what her nephews would look like. Four years had passed since Laura'd seen Ruth at Emma's place, and seven years since she'd seen the others. She'd missed her sisters every single day. Laura hoped she wouldn't run into Pa or Ben. She never wanted to see them again.

The twelve days crawled by. When the big day came, Laura was surprised to find Glen waiting at the bottom of the stairs in the lobby. "What are you doing here?"

"This vacation is mighty important, and you don't want to start by getting lost in the crowds at the train station," Glen said. "There's a taxi waiting, and I'll deliver you and your bag right to the gate. No fuss, no muss."

"But I..." Laura looked at the pleased expression on Glen's face. She could see he was trying to do something special. It would be mean to hurt his feelings. "I had no idea."

"That's the point. I wanted to surprise you."

"You did, that's for sure. Thanks for a lovely surprise." Laura handed him her suitcase as they walked toward the door.

Glen helped Laura into the back seat of the waiting taxi while the driver stowed the suitcase in the trunk. In minutes they were underway through the early morning traffic. Laura was acutely aware of Glen's arm stretched out behind her shoulders on the back of the seat, but his delighted smile kept her at ease.

"You're going to wear out the snap on your purse. I think you've opened and shut it a dozen times since we've been on the road," Glen said.

Laura chuckled, a little embarrassed. "I know the tickets are safe in my purse, but I can't seem to stop checking them. Don't think I'll believe this is happening until I see Ruth again." She snapped the purse closed one final time and tucked it under her arm.

"Seven years since you've seen your family?" Glen said. "Don't mean to pry, but that's a long time."

"Yes, it has been. What about you? Do you have any brothers or sisters other than Barbara?"

Glen's lips tightened as he looked down. "We had a brother, but he passed away during the war. He died in France during the Battle of Cantigny."

She placed her hand over his and squeezed his fingers. "I lost my youngest sister. I know how much that hurts."

"Nobody seems to understand how the pain hits like a punch in the gut, even though it's been years." He turned his hand over, clutching hers. "Don't think anyone gets it unless they've lost someone."

Laura's fingers tingled from the pressure. "What about your parents? Do they live near?"

"They're gone, too. Barbara and I are all that's left of our family."

The taxi pulled into a parking spot near the front of the train station. "We're here, folks. I'll get the suitcase, ma'am."

Both Glen and Laura jumped out of the cab. He paid the driver, picked up the suitcase, then gave her a tour of the station before leaving her at the departure gate for her train.

"Thank you," she said. "I enjoyed your company."

"You're welcome." He surprised her by leaning close and kissing her cheek. "I'd best get going. I'll meet your train when you get back."

Laura picked a window seat at the back of the car, tucking her suitcase between her knees and the seat in front. She rubbed her hand back and forth on the soft, maroon material covering the bench seat.

She stared out the window on her left, watching the scenery race by at an astonishing speed. Everything flying by so fast made her dizzy.

After a short while, she leaned back against the seat and closed her eyes, relaxed by the train's motion. Her thoughts turned back to Glen and their conversation in the taxi. The pain in his voice when he talked about his family worried her.

All of a sudden, she saw Glen running next to a young man she knew was his little brother, both of them slumped down as far as they could, rifles cradled across the front of their bodies. The vision surrounded her, the sight, sounds, and smells terrifying. Heavy, dark smoke filled the air, burning Glen's nose and throat. Fiery flashes of light pierced the dark, followed by deafening explosions of noise and earth spraying high into the air. Gunfire exploded all around, sometimes so close he could feel the rush of air on his face and hear the buzzing sound as the bullet passed.

Glen's focus was split between the stand of trees he'd been ordered to reach and his brother next to him. His heart was hammering so hard it felt ready to fly out of his chest. Then his brother fell, face first, to the ground.

Glen dropped to his knees, a scream caught in his throat, "Bobby, get up, Bobby." He shook his brother's shoulders, then turned him over. He saw a bullet hole, surrounded by a ring of bright red blood, on the left side of Bobby's chest. "No. No. You can't die out here. Get up, Bobby, please."

Glen collapsed over his brother's chest, deep guttural sobs tore through him.

"Come on, soldier, he's dead. You can't help him." A sergeant grabbed Glen's arm and tried to pull him away.

"He's my brother. I can't leave him out here." Glen stroked Bobby's dirt-encrusted face.

"I'm sorry, son, but there's nothing you can do. If you don't get up, you'll end up dead, too."

"I don't care."

"Get up soldier. That's an order."

A sharp tone, together with insistent pulling, got Glen to his feet. He resumed running through the smoke and bullets with the sergeant.

"Miss?" A voice, that didn't belong, intruded into Laura's vision. "Excuse me, miss." The porter's voice snapped her back to the train. "We'll be bringing lunch in a few minutes. Would you prefer a hot beef or turkey sandwich?"

Disoriented and sick at heart from what she'd seen, Laura mumbled. "Turkey, thank you," just to get him to leave.

"Are you okay?" From the expression on his face, the porter seemed alarmed.

"I'm fine."

He hesitated a moment, then moved to the passengers behind her.

Oh, my god, poor Glen. Laura's whole body trembled as she wrapped her arms around herself, filled with the pain she'd witnessed. His brother killed right next to him and then having to leave him there in the middle of all that.

She squeezed her eyes shut to escape the suffering she'd seen, but found herself thrust into a different scene.

Glen was limping down a quiet road lined by identical small houses. It looked like mid-morning after everyone had already left for work and school. He turned into a path that led to a bright blue front door. His sister Barbara burst out the door before he reached it.

"Glen, thank goodness you made it in time." She embraced him, tears running down her face.

He held her tight, his eyes glistening. "How is she?"

"Bad. The doctor didn't think she'd hold on for you to get home." Barbara looked up into her brother's face. "She got sick right after we heard about Bobby. It's like she just gave up and didn't even care. I did everything I could, Glen, believe me, I tried."

"It's not your fault, sis, don't blame yourself."

The two went into the house. The interior was dark and smelled stale. They walked, still holding on to each other, to the back bedroom where their mother rested on a narrow bed. Quilts covered her body, but her bone-thin arms rested outside the covers. Her eyes were closed and the raspy sound of her breathing filled the small room.

Barbara grasped her mom's flaccid hand.
"Mama, Glen's home."

"I love you, Mama. I missed you so
much." Glen whispered in her ear as she
wheezed with every breath.

"She knows you're here. I think I felt her
hand squeeze my fingers a little."

Barbara's words were kind, but neither
she nor Glen saw any movement from the bed.
As they stood watch, the breathing slowed,
became irregular, and stopped.

"She's gone. Mama's gone." Barbara burst
into tears and buried her face against Glen's
chest.

"I know, sis, I know." Glen held her close,
patted her back, and pressed his cheek against
the top of her head. Then he whispered, his
voice too low for Barbara to hear over her sobs.
"Please forgive me, Mama. I promised to bring
Bobby home, and I tried. I really did."

The vision slipped away, morphing back
into the countryside slipping past the train
window. Laura rubbed her tearful eyes and
coughed to clear her throat.

She saw the food tray on the seat next to her, and wondered if the porter had attempted to get her attention before putting it down. Embarrassed, she hoped he'd decided she was just asleep.

She reached out and touched the sandwich, surprised by sudden hunger pangs that cramped her empty belly. She started to eat, but couldn't get the visions out of her mind. Poor Glen, how awful for him to feel responsible for the deaths of both his brother and mother. No doubt he thought Barbara blamed him too.

She felt so bad for him, and was sure he had nightmares just like she did.

She hoped someday Glen would feel safe telling her what happened to his brother and his mother because she could never let him know what she'd seen.

CHAPTER EIGHT
Back To Ardmore

The train station at Ardmore was a lot smaller than the one in Tulsa. It was a neat-looking single-story building painted white with dark brown trim, and a false-front facing the tracks. Big letters spelled out Ardmore just above the first story windows and door. A wrought-iron fence that separated the walkway and parking area from the tracks had a large gate to let passengers board and exit from the trains.

Laura wasn't worried about getting lost, but she didn't know who'd be there to pick her up. She started waving her arms as soon as she saw Paul. He looked so different, a handsome man instead of a boy.

"Laura, is that you? My goodness, you're all grown up."

She didn't have time to reply before he grabbed her in a bearhug, lifted her off her feet and swung her around. "Put me down. People will think you're crazy."

"Don't care." Paul laughed but put her back on her feet. "But if I don't get you home fast, Ruth will shoot me." He grabbed her suitcase and pointed the way out of the terminal.

They threaded their way through the crowd, then to a Ford Model T in the middle of the parking lot. "Come on. Hop in, and we'll be on our way."

"How could you tell which one was yours?" Laura looked around at a sea of black Ford Model Ts.

"Got to remember where you parked, and look for your stuff inside on the seats." Paul opened the rear door, then pushed a small wooden toy car out of the way before placing her suitcase on the seat. "Up you go," he said after closing the rear door and opening the front passenger door. "Oops, forgot Aaron's blanket. Just push it out of the way or toss it in the back."

Paul got in and closed his door, turned the key to the battery position and stepped on the starter while grabbing the throttle.

Laura picked up the bright quilt and held it on her lap. "This is beautiful. Love the little rocking-horse design squares. I've never seen anything like this before."

"Becca made it." Paul looked out the windshield and then the side window as he started to ease the car out of the parking lot. "Lizbeth bought her a new quilting frame for Christmas, and she's been experimenting by designing all kinds of patterns."

"I never would have imagined she had it in her." Laura folded the bright colored blanket, then stroked the soft material. Ma would be so proud. She always loved pretty things and tried her best to brighten the house up, but they had nothing as nice as this.

Conversation flowed between the two as Paul navigated the streets into the center of town, then parked.

"Oh, my word." Laura stared at the new, three-story building that filled an entire city block from one end to the other. The bright sign

above the double-wide front doors said,
"Carpenter Mercantile." She jumped out instead
of waiting for Paul to open her door.

"Laura, Laura."

Laura turned around on the sidewalk,
trying to locate the voice.

"Laura, up here."

Laura looked up and saw a woman
waving out of an upper-story window.

"Ruth, is that you?" Laura jumped up and
down, shading her eyes from the sun with one
hand while waving the other.

The woman disappeared from behind
the curtains.

"Let's get you upstairs before your sister
busts a gasket." Paul wrapped one arm around
Laura's shoulder and grabbed her suitcase
handle in his other hand. After they entered the
store's lobby, Paul guided her toward the
elevator. He used a key to unlock the grill, then
opened the inner door. Once inside, he pressed
the button for the third floor.

The minute the elevator doors opened,
Ruth squealed and opened her arms. Laura ran

into her sister's hug, where they laughed and cried as they held each other.

"I can't believe you're really here." Ruth stood back, still holding Laura's hands. "You're so pretty, and I love your hair." Without waiting for a reply, she pulled her sister through the door into the living room. "Come on in. Supper's on the table. Paul's folks have the boys settled in their places at the table. They can't wait to see you."

Laura's heart hammered and her breathing sounded like she'd just run a footrace. She stopped in the doorway into the dining room, greeted by smiles from two adults and two small children seated at the table.

"Hey, Miz Martha and Jake, she made it," Ruth said.

"Laura, it's so good to see you again." Martha was a petite woman with blonde hair and hazel eyes, and a round, almost plump body. She stood behind a small boy who sat in a wooden highchair pulled up to the dining room table. Jake, an older version of Paul, tall with thick dark brown hair and brown eyes, got up from his seat next to the highchair.

"It's good to see you too." Laura took a deep breath, then looked back and forth between the couple at the table. "I owe you two more than I can ever express. Without your help, I could never have gotten away from Pa. Thank you so much."

"It was the right thing to do." Jake moved around the table toward Laura, then put his arms around her in a tight hug. "We're so proud of you and what you've accomplished. And we want you to know that we're always here if you need us."

Tears stung Laura's eyes, but she brushed them away and took a deep breath. "Ruth is so lucky to have you in her life."

"Enough of that. Our boys have waited long enough for supper, and I'll bet you're hungry, too." Ruth motioned toward an empty chair.

Laura sat between Paul and Ruth. The youngest little boy, Aaron, banged his spoon on the highchair's wooden tray with one hand and stuffed a piece of bread into his mouth with the other. Miz Martha sat between Aaron on one side and Elliot on the other. Elliot also held a piece of buttered bread, and stared at Laura's face. Jake sat between Elliot and Paul.

Platters and bowls of food covered the table. Fragrant steam drifted from the dishes.

"Let's give thanks first," Jake said, reaching out to Paul and Elliot.

Laura grasped Ruth's and Paul's extended palms and bowed her head.

"Lord, we give thanks for so many blessings today. We're grateful for our family and for this wonderful meal. Most of all, we thank you for taking care of Laura and bringing her here today. Amen."

Everyone began filling their plates and passing the food around the table. Their conversation was easy, and everybody chimed in. Even Elliot and Aaron spoke up now and then, sometimes provoking laughter and smiles with their comments.

As evening stretched on, it became clear that Aaron was getting tired. He started to throw himself side-to-side in his highchair, wanting down. Before Ruth could stop him, he threw his arms out and knocked his glass of milk to the floor.

Laura tensed and held her breath when Paul stood up.

"Okay, little man, time for you to go to bed."

Miz Martha grabbed a rag to clean up the mess on the floor, while Ruth cleared the tray.

"I've got him," Paul said. "Ruth, you stay and visit."

Aaron started to kick and cry but calmed down as Paul carried him out of the room.

"I want down, too," Elliot said. "I'm all done."

Ruth looked at his messy face and a plate that was still half full. "Finish that last little bit of meatloaf and eat two spoonfuls of peas, then you can get down ... after you wipe your face and hands."

"Yes, ma'am." The bites disappeared, then Elliot rubbed the napkin over his face, and ran after his father and brother.

"The boys love having their pa get them ready for bed." Ruth squeezed Laura's hand. "I told you he's a different kind of father than we grew up with."

Laura couldn't imagine Pa ever holding any of them or helping them to bed. Ben might have turned out different if he'd had a Pa like Paul.

Jake left to help Paul, while the women cleared the table and did the dishes. Miz Martha and the two sisters took to the sofas in the living room when the work was finished. A pair of damp looking men and two pajama-clad boys soon joined them. The children made the rounds, passing out goodnight hugs and kisses, then Paul escorted them to bed.

Laura kicked off her shoes and sat sideways on the divan, her feet tucked under her. Ruth was such a lucky woman, two beautiful boys and a husband who loved her and their children. When she and Ruth were little, they never had a family supper where everybody talked and laughed, happy to be together. And nobody yelled when Aaron spilled the milk. Pa would have used a belt on him and threatened anyone who tried to interfere.

"Martha, don't you think it's about time we went home? We have to be up early, and I think Ruth and Laura need some quiet time together to catch up." Jake put his arm around his wife's shoulders, then kissed her on the forehead.

Paul entered the room just as his parents stood, ready to leave. Ruth and Laura walked with him to the door and thanked his folks for making the evening one of the nicest ever.

"You two need some time alone, and I need to head for bed." Paul patted Laura's shoulders, kissed his wife, then left the room.

The sisters returned to the living room and curled up on the big sofa, facing each other. "You have no idea how much we've worried about you. If not for Pa, Jake and Martha would have taken you in since Paul and I hadn't gotten married yet." Ruth's eyes glistened, and her voice quivered. "But you were so young. The Sheriff would have made you go back."

"I know. But it's Pa's fault both of us left home the way we did. I'll never forget him beating you with that horsewhip. And I didn't dare stay after he raped me." It was hard for Laura to choke down the fear and anger that threatened to overflow.

"You're right, but look at us now," Ruth said. "No telling what would have happened if we'd stayed home with him."

Sobered by the truth in that statement, they sat together, quiet, lost in their memories.

"Do you see Pa often?" Laura said, finding it hard to even mention him.

"Not too much. He buys his supplies and his wife, Mary, sells her butter and eggs at the other stores in town." Ruth interlaced her fingers in her lap. "He also spends time with his friends at a couple of bars, playing darts and pool."

"He has friends?" Laura snorted. "Can't imagine anyone dumb enough to be friends with him. He was mean and nasty to everybody."

Ruth chuckled and shrugged her shoulders. "You'd be surprised. He plays the big man, and there're lots of men who believe his stories. Of course, nobody who's known him for long is fooled, but there're lots of newcomers in town that think he's a tough guy."

"How can you stand seeing him? And your babies. Surely you don't let him talk to them." The thought of Pa near Aaron and Elliot was terrifying.

"I cringe inside every single time I see him. Can't help it. I'm filled with rage and fear at the same time." Ruth leaned close to Laura and stroked her shoulder. "He's seen the boys, but never spoken to them. Paul and Jake would beat him to a pulp if he ever came near us, and Pa knows it."

Talking about Pa drained the joy out of the room, leaving the sisters deep in thought. Laura yawned, her body heavy and tired. "It's been a long day. I think I'd better go to bed before I fall asleep here on the sofa."

Ruth stood and pulled Laura to her feet. "Come on. I'll take you to your room." When they reached the bedroom door, Ruth wrapped her arms around Laura in a fierce hug. "Sleep well. We love you and are thrilled you're here."

CHAPTER NINE
Reunion

Laura woke up to the sounds of whispers and scuffling outside the door.

"Wanna go in." The voice was high-pitched and sweet, but determined.

"No, you heard Mom. She said Aunt Laura's tired, and we're not supposed to wake her up."

Something thumped against the door, and the doorknob rattled. "No, you don't. I'll tell."

"It's okay, boys, I'm up." Laura pulled a long robe over her nightgown and stepped into warm slippers. Sunshine poured in through soft-green, sheer curtains and highlighted the wallpaper covered with pink roses and dark green leaves.

Before she reached the door, it burst open and two little bodies hurtled through the opening.

"Good morning." She knelt down to be on the same level as the bashful boys. "Did your mom send you to get me?"

Elliot stumbled a half-step forward when Aaron dove behind his back. "We're supposed to take you to the kitchen after you wake up."

"Then lead the way."

Together Elliot and Aaron pulled her through the living room to the kitchen.

Laura enjoyed breakfast with her sister and the boys, helped clean the kitchen, then watched Ruth assist the children as they washed and got dressed.

"Is there anything else I can do for you before I get dressed and ready?"

"Not a thing. Just don't be surprised if you get curious company. You're the most excitement they've had since Christmas."

Taking that advice to heart, Laura locked the bedroom door, then the bathroom door as she washed, brushed her teeth, and fixed her hair. Sure enough, two huge smiles greeted her when she opened the bedroom door.

Those two are incredible, like a pair of wiggly puppies that never stopped talking, and never slowed down. How did Ruth do it?

"Okay boys, Aunt Laura needs a break. Go play." Ruth ignored the protests and shooed them outside to the wide porch that ran along the entire back of the building.

"Do those two ever slow down?" Laura rested her elbows on the table.

"Not really." Ruth pulled her apron off, then sat next to her sister. "You've won them over for sure, so they might try sneaking back inside."

"I wouldn't mind. But how on earth do you get anything done with them underfoot? You used to send us off to do chores or to play in the yard, but that doesn't work in the city."

"It's harder, but there is a yard in back of the store where they can run and play when one of us can take the time to watch them, and on the porch, they can play alone. Thank goodness for Miz Martha's help."

"I'm happy for you, but tell me, how are Lizbeth and Becca?"

Ruth's face split into a huge grin. "You can judge for yourself tonight. We're having a big family supper in your honor and they'll both be here."

Laura's sudden, loud cheer brought both boys racing through the door, just to make sure she was okay.

"I can't wait. This will be the first time we're all together since you escaped seven years ago." Laura's smile disappeared, wiped away by the memory of Ruth's bloody back, torn by Pa's whip.

The rest of the day passed in a blur of preparation, as Laura helped Ruth and Miz Martha cook and arrange the porch furniture for the celebration supper. By the time Paul and Jake came upstairs from the store, full bowls and platters, each draped with towels to hold in the heat and keep insects away, covered two long trestle tables. Elliot and Aaron chased each other in a continuous game of tag, back and forth from one end of the porch to the other, winding their way between the wooden benches and tables, and around the Adirondack chairs scattered along the wall and porch rails.

Once everything was ready, Laura excused herself and sat on the bench in the foyer near the elevator, eager to see her sisters the minute they arrived. When she heard the elevator clank and groan its way upstairs, she jumped to her feet, bouncing on her toes right in front of the door, breathless.

The solid door opened, and there they were, Lizbeth and Becca, hidden only by the elevator screen. All three sisters shouted each other's names until the screen slid aside, then flew into one another's arms.

"Oh, my goodness, I've missed you so much."

"You look wonderful."

"I can't believe you're here."

Their words covered each other, all expressing the same emotions. The three-way embrace held tight.

"Uh, would you ladies mind moving so I can get out of the elevator?"

The embrace broke apart with apologies
and giggles, then Lizbeth reached for the man
standing in the back of the elevator. "Laura, I'd
like you to meet my husband, Roy. And our
baby daughter, Lily."

"Your daughter?" Laura was entranced at
the sight of the infant cradled in the crook of
her papa's arm. She wanted to touch the perfect
little face, capped by a fuzzy crown of dark hair.
"Can I touch her?"

"Of course. Would you like to hold her?"
Roy's kind voice matched the expression on his
face.

Laura hesitated a moment, but when Roy
lifted the sleeping baby toward her, she accepted
the warm, sweet-smelling bundle. "Thank you."

The baby stretched, opened her tiny
mouth in a pink yawn, then settled against
Laura's body. "She's beautiful."

"Are you all going to stay out here in the
foyer or come inside?" Ruth asked, a huge grin
on her face.

Everyone trooped in, Laura holding Lily,
Lizbeth and Becca each with canvas bags slung
over their shoulders. Ruth snagged the baby,

then led the way to the tables on the porch. Once there she relinquished Lily to Miz Martha, who sat down with the little one cradled on her lap.

Conversation and laughter filled the room as everyone took their places. The little boys seated together this time, poking each other and making faces.

"Papa, would you say grace so we can get started?" Paul said. With their bowed heads and closed eyes, Jake began the prayer by giving thanks.

While keeping her head bowed with respect, Laura peered around the table. She caught Elliot's, then Aaron's, eyes wide open. She shook her head to stop them from saying something and giving her away, but she couldn't resist grinning back at them.

With the prayer over, cheerful conversation circled the table. The boys were so happy and carefree, what would it be like to grow up in a home like this, never having to be afraid of being hit for a wrong word or a smile?

Lily woke up and started fussing as the adults finished eating. Lizbeth took her from Miz Martha, and said, "I need to feed and change her. She's slept longer than I expected."

"Could you use company?" Laura stood and followed her sister out of the room.

"Sure. Would you mind grabbing my bag?" Lizbeth pointed at her colorful canvas bag resting on a wing chair in the living room. "We can have some privacy and quiet in the parlor."

As soon as they settled on the sofa, Lizbeth put Lily down on the empty center cushion and unwrapped her blanket. "She'll fuss like mad, but I like to make sure she's dry before she nurses since she always falls asleep once she's full."

"I've never spent time with little babies. Everybody I'm around is single, except at the hospital." Laura watched Lizbeth change the baby's wet gown and diaper, place her on a fresh wool pad, then she wrapped a blanket around the baby. "I wondered if you'd be nursing your baby. Lots of women in Tulsa are using bottles of cow's milk, but the doctors are saying it isn't as good."

"It's a debate here, too, more about convenience for the moms than what's best for the baby. Roy and I talked about it, and decided to stick with nature's way." Lizbeth opened the buttons on her dress and guided Lily to her nipple. The hungry baby latched on and worked her tiny fingers against her mom's skin.

"Does it hurt?"

"Sometimes she chomps so hard it feels like she's got a full set of teeth. I was awful tender at first, but it's better now."

Both sisters watched Lily suckle, her little eyes closed and fingers moving open and closed like a kitten's paws.

"Are you happy?" Laura scrutinized Lizbeth's face. "I know you needed to get away from Pa, but I couldn't believe it when Ruth told me you'd married old Mr. Perkins and taken over the care of his four children."

"Old Mr. Perkins?" Lizbeth chuckled. "I'd forgotten that's what we used to call Roy.

"I'm sorry, it's hard to think of him as Roy. He seems like a good man, but what happened?"

Lizbeth glanced down at Lily's face, stroked her cheek, then looked back at Laura. "When we woke up and discovered that you were gone, Pa went into a rage. He told Ben and me to take care of the chores, and left." She hesitated, sighed, then continued. "When he came back without you he was worse than I've ever seen him. We were all terrified and did our best to stay out of his way."

"A few days later," Lizbeth said, "I took eggs and milk to town to sell, then collapsed on the road. I sat in that wagon seat and cried like a baby. My face hurt from where Pa had backhanded me that morning, and I couldn't face going back."

"I'm so sorry," Laura said, shaking her head. "It wasn't fair for him to take his mad out on you."

"It wasn't your fault." Lizbeth transferred the baby to her other breast and readjusted her dress. "Roy saw my wagon stopped on the road and asked if I needed help. I don't know what came over me, but I just cried harder. He was so sweet. He suggested we move the wagons off the road a ways and take a little time to settle down.

We drove to a small group of trees, tied the horses, and sat down on the ground. He didn't push or anything, but all of a sudden I told him everything. The whole story of what Pa did to all of us, and how Ruth had to run away, and how you'd disappeared a few days before."

"Oh, no, Pa'd kill you if he knew you'd told someone our family business. You must have been terrified."

"I was. Roy told me I mustn't go back, that we had to think of a way to keep me safe. All of a sudden, he sat up straight and said I was an answer to his prayers. He was out of his mind trying to run his farm and take care of four small children since his wife died. If I'd move in with them, he could take care of the farm again and Pa couldn't touch me since I was of age."

"And you agreed?"

"No, of course not. I told him it wouldn't be proper, not even to get away from Pa. So, he said he'd marry me if I'd agree." Lizbeth chuckled and shook her head. "You should have seen him blush, then he said I didn't have to worry about him, he wouldn't do anything but give me his name for protection. Kind of like a business agreement." She stopped a moment, stroking her sleeping baby's head.

"So what happened? Did you go home and tell Pa?"

"No, we went to the church looking for the preacher because I feared my courage would fail me. We found him in the rectory and asked him to marry us right away. His only question was whether my swollen face was because Roy had hit me. I guess my shock and instant denial convinced him, so he called his wife out to witness the ceremony and married us on the spot."

"How did you tell Pa? And how did the business arrangement turn into a true marriage?"

"Hold on a minute." Lizbeth moved Lily up to her shoulder, burped her, then buttoned her dress. "We drove the wagons to Pa's place, but he and Ben were both out in the fields. Becca and Bonnie were in the chicken coop and came running to find out what was going on. I'm such a coward, not strong like you and Ruth. Terrified, I just ran inside and grabbed some of my stuff and threw it into Roy's wagon. Then I told them I had married Mr. Perkins and left."

"And?"

"And that was it. I took care of the kids and the house, working harder than I'd ever worked. But Roy was so patient with me, a perfect gentleman. In time we learned to care for each other. My only regret was leaving Becca and Bonnie, but Pa married Mary within a week and moved her in. I guess he got the idea from us, but at least it took the pressure off Becca since she and Mary became good friends." Story told and baby fed, Lizbeth rose to lead the way back to the porch.

"Hold on a second." Laura waited for her sister to stop moving. "Thank you for telling me. Every single day since I left, I've felt guilty. Knowing you're both safe and happy makes a huge difference." The sisters embraced, Lily between them.

"I'm happier than I've ever been, but what about you?" Lizbeth stared into Laura's eyes. "You didn't share much during dinner, except to talk about your job at the hospital and to tell stories about the women you live with at the hotel. Is there someone special in your life? You're smart and pretty. Any guy would be lucky to have you."

Laura turned away. "Nobody special."

"You're hiding something," Lizbeth said. "Come on, I won't tell anyone if you don't want me to."

Laura's thoughts turned to Glen, surprising her. "Well, nothing serious, but there is a sweet guy I like to spend time with. His name is Glen. He loves music and is great to talk to. Glen drove me to the train station so I wouldn't get lost." Laura felt her neck flush. "His sister Barbara lives in the hotel so he's around a lot."

"He sounds like a nice man." Lizbeth led the way back toward the living room to rejoin the rest of the family. "I won't say a word."

Conversation flowed in waves, but the silences were just as pleasant as the adults relaxed on the porch. Elliot and Aaron played with their toys on a throw-rug, until they fell asleep surrounded by wooden houses and cars. Paul and Jake picked the boys up and put them to bed.

"Did they brush their teeth and wash up," Ruth asked.

"Nope, they were both so tired we took off their shoes and tucked them in." Paul dropped into the chair next to her.

"Honey, they were grubby as can be."

"They'll survive." He took his wife's hand and scooted lower in the chair.

"I hate to break up the party, but we better get on our way." Roy stretched, then stood and turned to Laura. "It was a pleasure meeting you after hearing so much from your sisters."

"My pleasure, too." Laura hugged him and whispered in his ear. "Thank you for saving my sister."

The goodbyes and hugs continued all the way to the elevator. When the doors closed, and the car groaned its way down, Laura felt tears collecting in the corners of her eyes and a lonely ache in her heart. She wished they didn't live so far apart.

Paul kissed his wife and headed for their room, leaving Ruth behind.

"Come on, join me for a cup of tea before we call it a night," Ruth said. "I'm too wound up to sleep."

"Sure, but let me fix it. You've done enough."

Ruth agreed, sat down and stretched her arms over her head. Then she watched Laura fill the kettle with water and set two cups on the table.

"Sure is quiet with Paul and the boys asleep," Laura said. "So different from having a whole family sleeping on the floor." She chuckled, remembering. "Between Pa's snoring, Ben's passing gas and the sound of so many people breathing, it was never quiet."

"You're right. Getting used to sleeping in a room all by myself was hard, much less on a bed instead of a floor pallet."

"I felt the same way. But I'll take being alone in a quiet room, feeling safe, any time over sharing a room filled with fear."

CHAPTER TEN
Two Cemetery Markers

"My turn first," insisted the young voice that got louder with each word.

Here they are again. Much sweeter than a Baby Ben alarm clock, but with no off button.

"Hang on boys, I'm awake." Laura slipped her arms into her robe as she stood. "Give me a few minutes and I'll be ready." It seemed impossible that this was her last day there.

"Good morning," Laura sang out, led into the kitchen with one little boy on each side. Breakfast was a fast affair since Ruth had scrambled eggs, bacon, and toast ready and waiting.

The boys climbed into their chairs, then reached for the plates Ruth handed to them. "Manners, you two. We're not in a race." She handed each of them a glass of milk, then joined

Laura at the table. "How would you like to go to the cemetery this morning? We could take a picnic lunch and then spend the afternoon in town walking through the streets around the town square."

"That's a wonderful idea, but won't the boys get bored?"

"No. We'll take a couple of big quilts, one they can use to play on when they get tired of running around, and one for us to sit on. We can even take flowers for Ma and Bonnie."

Laura's smile faltered a moment at the thought of Bonnie's grave. "I'd like that." Would she ever stop feeling guilty for leaving Bonnie behind? If she'd taken Bonnie with her, Bonnie would still be alive.

Ruth climbed into the driver's seat after making sure Elliot was comfortable in back behind Laura, with the blankets and an overflowing picnic basket beside him. Two large bunches of flowers wrapped in paper cones had been tucked between the picnic basket and one side door. Another basket full of toys was stowed on the floor next to Elliot's legs. Aaron sat on Laura's lap in front, where he bounced up and down with excitement.

"Everybody ready?"

"More than ready," Laura said. "Just for fun, would you tell me what you're doing as you start up? I'd love to learn how to drive."

"Sure." Ruth said, reaching for a tall lever on the floor by the driver's door. "First, make sure the emergency brake is all the way back. Next move the spark advance lever all the way up to retard position. Removing her hand from the emergency brake, she grabbed the lever behind the steering wheel on the left side of the steering column and shoved it up. Then her right hand reached for a similar lever on the right side.

"Mom, Aaron's making faces at me," Elliot said.

"Hush, we'll leave in just a minute." Ruth rolled her eyes. "Next step, move the throttle lever about a quarter of the way down."

"Enough, I'm lost already. Maybe you can show me things later when I can check them out one at a time."

"Good idea." Ruth laughed, as she drove the Tin Lizzie onto the road.

Elliot and Aaron kept up a running commentary, pointing out places of interest along the way. They didn't slow down until their mom turned the car onto the cemetery road.

"Do you remember when you brought me here for a picnic when I was eight?" Laura asked.

Ruth nodded and smiled.

"That's one of my favorite memories."

Ruth parked near a small stand of trees. They grew inside a wrought iron fence that surrounded a family plot with one large double headstone and four smaller ones. She turned the engine off and opened her door. Laura put Aaron down on the ground as Elliot burst out his door, then took off running and jumping around the markers.

"So much for our helpers." Ruth reached inside and pulled out the baskets, quilts, and flowers. "Can you carry half or do we need two trips?"

"No problem." Laura wrapped one blanket around her neck and carried a basket and pink phlox and black-eyed-susans from Ruth's flower beds. Her purse was draped over her neck and shoulder, just like her sister's.

She followed Ruth, then slowed her steps when she saw two wooden crosses where she remembered seeing only one. They were close together with a rock border outlining a rough rectangle around them. A huge lump blocked her throat and made it hard to breathe. Oh, my god, Bonnie was really there. Laura knew Bonnie was dead, but seeing this made it real, and final. She stared at the two cemetery markers that memorialized her ma and baby sister.

"I know what the words say, Aunt Laura." Elliot, who had just returned to her side, pointed at her ma's cross and said, "Vera Cavanaugh, eighteen seventy-six to nineteen ought-seven. She's my grandma." He directed her attention to the other cross. "Bonnie Cavanaugh, nineteen ought-six to nineteen eighteen. She was Mom's baby sister, but she died when she was just a little girl."

"Great job, Elliot. Thanks for reading those to me." Laura found it hard to keep her voice even, and a smile pasted on her face. Sobs threatened to burst from her throat.

"You two go play hide and seek while we get the picnic ready." Ruth sounded a little shaky, but the boys didn't notice. "Come on, let's get everything arranged, Laura. We can have a little quiet time before they're ready to eat."

"Look what we found." Aaron announced a short time later when the brothers returned. "I found it, but he picked it up."

Elliot held a large snake with a yellow stripe on either side and a black checkered pattern between the stripes.

"Can we keep it? It's really pretty, and Papa can build a box for it to live in. We'll catch mice and bugs for food. Please, we'll take good care of it, we promise." The snake wound around Elliot's arm, as the brothers extolled its virtues as a pet.

"It's a real beauty." Ruth stroked the snake's back, confident that the garter snake wasn't a threat. "But it needs to be free to take

care of its own family. Why don't you put it
back where you found it. Thank you for
showing it to your Aunt Laura and me."

Together the women spread out the
blankets, put the toy basket in the middle of
one, then arranged the picnic on the other. They
carried the flowers to the wooden crosses, where
they arranged them in two flower containers,
one at the base of each memorial.

The picnic was a lively affair, with the
boys talking about the snake they'd caught and
released. When they finished eating, the
brothers dumped out the toy basket and started
to play.

"You're such a good mother." Laura
patted Ruth's hand as they sat together, just a
few feet from the crosses. "A good daughter,
too. I can only imagine how hard it must have
been for you to take over when Ma died. Twelve
is much too young to take on the responsibility
of five little kids and all the household chores."

To Laura's surprise, Ruth teared up. "Ma
was a wonderful mother, but I didn't realize that
until it was too late. Sometimes I hated her. I
always loved her, but I hated how she never said

a word when Pa was beating us with his belt. And when he used his fists on her, she never, ever fought back or said anything." Ruth brushed the tears away from under her eyes, then gazed into Laura's face. "I thought she was a coward and even called her that once. She looked so hurt. I wish I could take those words and thoughts back, because now I know she was protecting us the only way she knew how."

Before she could answer, Aaron pulled on Laura's shoulder. "Aunt Laura, I've got to go potty."

Laura giggled and heard an answering snicker from her sister, their somber mood gone.

"Go behind one of the big headstones." Ruth swept her arms out towards some large monuments several yards away. "Elliot, you go, too, since we need to pack up and go. Don't get your clothes wet."

"You don't think they'll pee on their clothes, do you?"

"Most likely. They're little boys. They'll play silly games about how far they can spray and somehow it'll just happen. That's why I packed extra clothes for each in a basket."

Once back in Ardmore they dropped the tired boys off with Miz Martha, put the baskets and blankets away, then headed out for the town square. Laura could see trees scattered throughout the expanse of lawn and bright-colored flowers planted along the walkways. The sidewalk was wide, with planter boxes full of shrubs and vivid annuals about twenty feet apart next to the street. Most of the people walking by seemed focused on their thoughts, seldom glancing at the trees or flowers, Laura noticed.

"I don't remember any of these shops from before. And wasn't the original Carpenter General Store on the other side of the square?" Laura linked her arm through Ruth's as they walked.

"Most of these places are new. Yes, we were on the other side in what used to be the heart of town. Some of the old places are still there, but the number of businesses has exploded."

A few yards down the street on their right, two men came out of a door, turned, and walked in their direction.

Laura's body froze when she recognized the man in the lead. Oh, my god, it's him. Her pa didn't recognize her at first, then his eyes widened as he looked back and forth between the two sisters.

Pa, just as big and mean looking as she remembered in her nightmares, stopped about ten feet away. He glared at Ruth first, then stared at Laura.

"Well, well." he sneered, eyes slitted and meaty fists resting on his hips. "Looks like my lucky day. The half-breed whore come back to visit her harlot sister." His laugh was ugly and threatening.

Ruth grabbed Laura's arm and tried to guide her across the street. "Come on, he isn't worth a second of our time."

Laura shrugged away from Ruth and stepped closer to him, burning with a powerful, righteous rage. "Watch your mouth, old man. I'm not the scared little girl you raped on the riverbank years ago." Her voice was loud and strong, not a hint of fear in it.

Pa's eyes widened and his face turned brick red. He glanced at his friend, then back at Laura. He raised his clenched right fist and cocked it back. "Shut up, you bitch. You look just like your ma. I didn't stand for her backtalking me, and if you keep it up I'll..."

"You'll what?" Laura stepped even closer, toe to toe, staring up at him. She curled her lip in disgust, repulsed by the smell of alcohol, bad breath, and stale sweat. "Go ahead, hit me you disgusting bully. Or am I too old for you now? Afraid to face a grown woman instead of a little girl, you filthy coward?" Every fiber in Laura's body quivered with fury. Her lips pulled tight against her teeth as she spat out the words.

"Come on, I'm not afraid of you." She curled her fingers, daring him forward. "I'll have you arrested for assault and rape the second you touch me. Don't think I won't, and don't think the sheriff won't believe me." She stood still, body vibrating with ferocious anger, daring him to make a move. She stared him down for almost a full minute before he dropped his fist and turned away.

"Come on, Tom," Pa said to the man with him. "Don't listen to that crazy bitch. Nobody's gonna care about what she says."

The two men walked away and never looked back.

Ruth wrapped her arm around Laura's rigid waist. "You're incredible, that was the bravest thing I've ever seen."

"I was scared to death, but I'll never let him touch me again."

"You backed him down. Never, ever thought I'd see that happen," Ruth said. "And that guy with him heard what you said. Now he knows Pa raped his own daughter, and I'll bet by this time tomorrow lots more people will know."

"Let's go back. My legs are kind of shaky." Arm in arm the sisters turned around and walked back the way they'd come.

CHAPTER ELEVEN
It's Good To Be Home

Laura woke long before the alarm was set to go off. She didn't remember having any nightmares, but the twisted bedclothes and a pounding headache were evidence of a night spent thrashing about. Just seeing Pa again ruined her sleep, but it felt good standing up to him.

Laura dressed and finished packing, doing her best to ignore the throbbing behind her forehead. She pasted a smile on her face, then joined Paul and Ruth in the kitchen.

"Sit down." Ruth handed Laura a plate with a steaming stack of pancakes, butter dripping down the sides. "Careful, it's hot."

"Thanks. It sure is quiet without the boys. I'll miss them." Laura poured syrup on the pancakes, then took a big bite. She moaned with pleasure and saluted Ruth with her fork as Paul handed her a cup of coffee.

All three dug in and the plates were almost empty when the front door opened after a soft knock. "Good morning," Miz Martha said as she joined everyone at the table. "Laura, Jake had to open the store, but he wanted me to say goodbye for him, and to tell you how much he'll miss you."

"Thank you so much. Let him know I'll miss him, too," Laura said.

Miz Martha handed her a paper sack. "Here's something to make the trip easier."

The bag contained two paperback books, So Big, by Edna Ferber and The Plastic Age, by Percy Marks. "Wow. A Pulitzer Prize winner and a book that was banned in Boston." Laura looked from one cover to the other. "It'll be hard to choose which to read first."

"I hate to say it, but we've got to get going," Paul said, interrupting.

"Where are you going? I want to go too." Pajama clad Elliot stood in the doorway, rubbing his eyes. A scant minute later, Aaron appeared behind him.

"Sorry son, not today," Paul said. "You and your brother have to stay with granny."

Laura hugged both boys and promised to send them letters, but still needed Miz Martha's help to peel their arms from around her neck. Once in the elevator with Paul and Ruth, her feelings vacillated between relief and regret. Relief that the tearful goodbyes were over, and regret for leaving the little boys behind.

The street was quiet and just beginning to become pink with dawn. Paul brought the car around from its parking spot in back of the building, tossed Laura's suitcase inside and held the doors for both women.

"Elliot and Aaron will miss you something fierce." Ruth twisted around in the front seat of the car so she could talk to Laura in the back. "And so will we."

"I'll miss you all, too. I love those little scamps."

"You could move back and see them all the time. Heck, you could stay with us until you found a job and a place of your own." Paul said, with a glance at Ruth. "We'd love to have you, and the boys would be thrilled to death."

"Move back here?" An icy jolt shot down Laura's spine, and her headache pulsed with renewed strength. An image of Pa's angry face flashed before her eyes. "Uh, that's awful nice of you, but I've got a good job and friends in Tulsa."

"Would you at least think about it?" Ruth said. "The whole family misses you. Please?"

Laura's heart raced, but she managed a slight nod and a shaky smile. "Okay, I'll think about it." Never could she live in that town, wondering when Pa would appear. Ruth had made her peace, thanks to emotional support from Paul and his family, but Laura couldn't do it.

The rest of the trip was quiet, punctuated only with small talk and smiles until they arrived at the train station. Paul parked the car, jumped out, and ran around to the passenger side to open the doors. After both women stepped down, he grabbed the suitcase and led the way into the station.

"There's your gate." Ruth said as they walked through the station. "Looks like they're about ready to start boarding."

They stopped at the gate for a tight, three-way hug. Ruth and Laura's eyes glistened as they let go.

Laura was once again settled next to a window of the train with her suitcase secured under the seat in front. Her purse was next to her on the seat, with the tickets tucked inside the flap.

Laura wished there'd been more time with her sisters since their four days together had passed so fast. If Pa didn't live there, she'd move in a minute. And they hadn't even talked about Ben. She shuddered at the thought of her vicious, manipulative brother. Ruth had told her he'd fought with Pa and moved to another town, but that didn't mean he'd never come back.

While the train was stopped in Oklahoma City, a stout, older woman plopped down next to Laura, interrupting her thoughts.

The matron placed a large crocheted bag next to Laura's purse and pulled out what appeared to be half a child's bright red sweater threaded on bronze knitting needles. Smoothing out the yarn that snaked out of the bag, she started knitting and staring at Laura.

"Hello, dear. I'm Mrs. Holloway. I'm on my way to visit my son and his family in Fayetteville, Arkansas. What about you?"

"Laura Cavanaugh. I'm headed home after visiting my sisters."

Laura's reply unleashed a torrent of nosy questions from Mrs. Holloway, which she didn't feel like answering. When single syllable answers failed to stem the flow, she pulled one of the books out of her purse. "Excuse me, I don't mean to be rude, but I've been dying to read this book." She glanced at the cover. "The Plastic Age is supposed to be an amazing story."

"Oh, my word, how can a proper young lady read such trash. Don't you know that book was banned in Boston? You should be ashamed." Mrs. Holloway dropped her knitting and pulled a Bible out of her huge purse, shaking it in front of Laura's face. "This is the only book you need to be reading."

"No, ma'am, I'm an atheist." Laura was shocked to hear the words come out of her mouth, but gratified by their effect.

In less than a minute, Mrs Holloway shoved her knitting and the Bible back into the bag. She then marched down the aisle, muttering under her breath.

Laura was sure glad she'd said what she did. It worked. She settled down to read. The rest of the trip was much more peaceful, since she had the seat to herself all the rest of the way.

When the train pulled into the Tulsa station, Laura was over half-way through the book. She tucked it into her purse, then secured the shoulder strap across her chest. It didn't take long to exit the train with the other passengers. As the crowd thinned, she saw Glen leaning against the wall, a huge grin on his face.

"Welcome back." He wrapped one arm around her shoulders and squeezed, then picked up her suitcase.

"You're a sight for sore eyes." He let go of her, but stood close and stared, as if memorizing her every feature.

"It's good to be home." Laura said, surprised to realize she meant it. "Anything exciting happen while I was gone?"

"Just the usual." Glen paused for a minute. "Minnie and Morris got engaged, but that's not really a surprise. They've been going together a long time, but he waited to pop the question until after he talked with her father. Fact is, he gave her a ring the day after you left."

"I can't wait to see it."

The easy conversation continued until Glen hailed a taxi. After they settled into the back seat, he asked, "So, how was the visit? It must have felt strange to see your family after so many years."

"It was fabulous. I spent time with all three of my sisters. Ruth and her husband, Paul, have two adorable little boys. Lizbeth and her husband, Roy, just had a baby girl named Lily. We used to call Roy old Mr. Perkins, but he's a very nice man who loves Lizbeth and treats her well. Becca doesn't have a family of her own, but

lives with Lizbeth where she's an important
member of the household."

"They all live in the same town? I thought
you grew up on a big farm. How did they end
up moving to the same place while you ended
up so far away?"

"My pa is a vicious, horrible, cruel man.
We all left the homestead to escape him."
Laura's tone was harsh. "I just ran farther away."

Laura waited for questions from Glen,
questions about what Pa had done to them and
why she'd traveled a much greater distance than
her sisters. To her surprise, Glen shook his head
but didn't say another word.

When they arrived at the hotel, Glen
walked Laura inside. They found Grace, Abby,
and Barbara lounging on the sofas in the living
room. The three girls greeted Laura with squeals
of excitement, demanding a day-by-day
accounting of the time she'd been away. She
told them all about it, except for the ugly scene
with Pa. When the conversation lagged, she
learned that Glen had left without saying
anything.

She was ashamed to not have noticed. She'd have to apologize if she saw him tomorrow.

"Oops, it's getting late and I've got to be at work early tomorrow." Abby stood and started toward the stairs.

Laura grabbed her suitcase from its spot near the front door and headed toward her room. "Me too, and I need to unpack first."

It didn't take long to put everything away. Soon Laura settled in bed for the night. The room seemed too quiet and lonely after having Ruth, Paul and the children close by for the last three days. She remembered how tender and sweet they were together, sharing hugs and kisses, so comfortable with their affection for one another.

Lizbeth and Roy were a little more reserved, but their glances at each other were warm and loving too. She wondered if she'd ever have someone look at her like Paul and Roy looked at Ruth and Lizbeth.

CHAPTER TWELVE
Won't Anyone Help Me

The traffic congestion seemed louder and noisier than usual to Laura as she walked to work the next day. Ruth's house was so peaceful except for worrying about Pa turning up. And she missed the boys' hugs and kisses even if they were sticky most of the time. Still, she was happy to be home.

After clocking in at the hospital, Laura hurried to the third floor, where Miz Marston met her near the stairwell.

"Glad you're back, Cavanaugh, but you might not feel the same when you see what's waiting." Miz Marston led the way to the housekeeping room at a fast trot. "Grab a bucket and extra rags. Got a bunch of folks upchucking all over today."

"What happened?" Laura grabbed a cleaning cart and loaded it with supplies, including a mop and bucket.

"Well, the story is that there was a party at a dance hall and everyone got sick from bad food -- most blamed the potato salad -- right before the cops raided the place. Funny thing though, the folks all stink of cheap hooch, and what I've been mopping smells like pure, rotgut alcohol. The cops arrested everyone they could catch, but the paddy wagon ended up at Charity Hospital instead of jail because the whole drunken bunch started puking their guts out. From what I've heard, the Charity staff heard the same spoiled food story we got, but they don't believe it either."

The morning hours raced by without a spare minute between the needs of one patient to another. By the time Laura escaped to the cafeteria for lunch, she was dead on her feet. She filled her tray with a large green salad and a cup of soup, then headed for a corner table where Glen was waiting.

"You look beat." He pulled her chair out for her, then sat down.

"Gee, thanks." Laura's raised eyebrows and sarcastic tone made Glen stammer a quick apology.

She waved it aside with a grin and slipped her shoes off under the table, groaning with pleasure. "We've got a whole floor of people sick from moonshine. Course, they aren't admitting drinking at a big party over at Danny's Place last night. They all insist they ate spoiled food."

"Lots of stories about Danny's Place," Glen said. "The front part is just a dance hall, but the big back room's a speakeasy. The door's hidden, but plenty of people know about it." Glen shook his head. "I know the temperance folks had good intentions when they passed prohibition, but I think telling someone they can't do something just makes them more determined to do it."

Laura nodded in agreement. "Listen, I'm sorry I didn't thank you last night for picking me up at the station and taking me home. The girls and I started talking and we didn't notice when you left."

"No problem. You were all cackling away like a bunch of hens. I figured I'd never get a word in edgewise." Glen smiled, then reached out and patted Laura's hand. "I was happy to help. Hey, do you want to go to the Fifty-First Street Club tonight? It'd be nice to dance and play some jazz."

"Sounds great. I think music is the perfect thing to turn this day around."

By the end of the week, Laura's trip felt almost like a dream. Routine ruled the following days, weeks and months. Work at the hospital ranged from controlled chaos to mind-numbing boredom. Life at the hotel depended on what was happening with the social lives of the residents. Plans for Minnie's wedding was the major topic, but Laura didn't get involved with the preparations. Instead, her greatest pleasure came from playing music and dancing with Glen. Every Friday and Saturday night they'd spend hours together at different dancehalls in the city. That pattern continued through the summer, right until her birthday in August.

Laura was glad nobody knew it was her birthday. She headed downstairs for breakfast, not in the mood for a fuss. She couldn't help thinking about her previous birthday with Bruce when he'd been charming and attentive. He'd taken her to a beautiful park where they'd had a picnic, then gotten her to talk about her family history, the same history he'd used against her during the horrible break-up months later. She shook her head to clear the memory and took her place at the table.

"Laura, there's a phone call for you," Jane said, as she walked into the dining room. "I think it's your sister."

"Thanks," Laura said. That was a safe guess since nobody else ever called her.

"Ruth?"

"Hi, I hope it's okay to call this early."

"It's fine," Laura said. "I have a little time before I have to leave for work. What's happening?"

"Well, first, I wanted to wish you Happy Birthday. Can't believe you're twenty-one and all grown up."

Ruth's voice sounded so warm, Laura wished she could reach through the phone and hug her. "Thanks. That number sounds old, but I've felt grown up for a long time."

"I know. But just think, you'll be able to vote this year," Ruth said.

"True, but you voted last time in the first election when it was legal for women to participate in a national election. You're one of the true pioneers."

Ruth sighed. "You're right, but it's shameful how few women voted. I hope it'll be different this time."

"I know," Laura said. "Miss Emma told me that women would have the vote one day. I thought she was crazy, but now it's happening." Laura paused, remembering Miss Emma and all the things she'd learned from her. "I'm reading newspapers every day and learning all I can about the candidates and the issues. No excuse to not get educated and make our votes count."

"Good for you. Sometimes I want to grab a bunch of the women in town and shake them. They just parrot what their husbands say instead of using their own brains." Ruth paused for a minute, then continued. "But enough about politics. I have wonderful news to share. Paul and I wanted you to be the first to know we're expecting another baby ... in April."

Laura shrieked and twirled, wrapping the phone cord around her shoulders. "That's fabulous. Maybe you'll have a little girl for Paul. What do Elliot and Aaron think?"

"Ow, I think I'm deaf in one ear after that screech," Ruth said, laughing. "We'll tell them tonight when Paul gets home from the store. Everybody will know in the next day or two, but we wanted you to be first since you're so far away."

"Thank you, but I'd better get off. Calls are expensive, and I need to leave for work."

The sisters said goodbye, but Laura stood in place for a moment, rubbing the receiver in its cradle. She remembered the feeling of holding little Lily in her arms, and the sweet smell of the baby's hair. Someday she'd love to hold her own little one.

Laura shrugged her shoulders and headed back to the dining room. "Stop feeling sorry for yourself," she muttered under her breath.

"Is everything alright with your sister?" Jane asked.

"Better than okay, she's having another baby." Laura glanced at the dark wooden clock that hung on the wall, its brass pendulum swinging back and forth. "Oops, I've got to go."

She slung her purse over her shoulder but stopped when Sarah called out. "Hey, everybody, look at this picture. Bruce Erickson is engaged to Gwendolyn Harcourt. The banker's son is marrying the daughter of the guy who owns the biggest textile company in the state."

"That's not a marriage, it's a merger," Sarah said, leaning in for a better look at the picture that filled the top half of the society page.

Laura looked too, telling herself that they'd think something was odd if she didn't.

Bruce looked as handsome and dapper as ever
in a gray suit and a Panama hat, one arm
wrapped around the waist of a short, blonde
woman wearing a stylish silk dress, a pendant
trim hat, and a double-loop string of pearls.
"You're right, Sarah. I'll bet it's all about
money."

The picture stayed in Laura's mind as she
walked, much faster than usual, to the hospital.
He was such a snake. He got what he wanted, a
rich woman to please his parents. She wondered
if he had another woman on the side, somebody
dumb enough to believe he loved her.

Laura, stopped on the sidewalk and took
a few deep breaths to calm herself. Passing
pedestrians gave her curious looks, but she
ignored them.

She hated Bruce and never wanted to see
him again. Why should she care if he married
some high society woman? She held her head
high and resumed walking, never slowing again
until she entered the hospital lobby.

Agnes and Laura climbed the stairs together after they clocked in. Miz Marston saw them arrive and waved them over.

"Listen, we have a special situation in D-two. A young woman, Clara Miller, is dying, and her husband, Asa, has been with her all night. According to the doctor, there's nothing that can be done to save her, so all the nurses can do is make sure she and her poor husband are comfortable."

"What's wrong with her?" Agnes said. "Was it an accident?"

"No, kidney failure has got her all swelled up like a balloon. I haven't seen the chart, but heard the nurses say it's kidney failure from diabetes." Miz Marston crossed her arms and turned to glance at the door to D ward. "It's so very sad. Her husband is all broken up, and there's a one-year-old baby at home. She's only twenty-three, much too young for this to happen." She paused a moment, then looked back at Agnes and Laura. "Just do whatever you can to help them. There aren't any other patients in the room right now, and the nurses have promised to keep it that way if possible."

Laura checked on Clara throughout the morning as she worked and always asked her husband if he needed anything. Asa declined each time until she returned from her dinner break.

"Miss, could you do something for me?" He asked as Laura entered the room.

"Of course, if I can." The poor man looked half dead from exhaustion and worry. His eyes were sunken in dark pits and his skin was gray.

"I need to go home and change and check on the baby. My mom is with her, so I know she's alright, but I'd feel better if I could see her."

Laura reached out and touched his arm. "No need to explain. I'll keep an eye on your wife until you get back. Take your time. If you could take a nap, I'll bet it would help a lot."

"But can you stay with her? They say she won't wake up again, but if she does, I don't want her to be alone." His voice broke, and

Laura could see his eyes glistening with tears that threatened to overflow.

"Don't you worry. I promise to stay with her until you return. Just give me a minute to let my supervisor know."

Laura went straight to Miz Marston and got permission, then returned to the room. "Take your time," she said. "And don't worry, I promise I won't leave her side until you get back."

"Thank you." He started to say more, then blinked back tears and left the room.

Laura settled into a chair next to the bed and looked at the still figure covered with a blanket up to her chest. "My word, she's all puffed up like dough that's through rising," she said aloud. Dark hair fanned out on the pillow around her distorted face. Swollen flesh surrounded her closed eyes and her cheeks, and her chin had lost all definition.

Not knowing what to do, but needing to do something, Laura reached out her hands and placed them on the pale, puffy arm that rested outside the covers. Clara's skin felt warm but too soft. Laura closed her eyes to pray but found herself transported to a gray, misty place. Clara was there and her body looked normal, but she was frantic and crying. "Help me, please," she begged. "I've got to get back to my husband and baby. They need me."

Laura jerked her hands back, opened her eyes, and heard a familiar voice filling her mind. "Don't think, just open your heart. You'll find the right words for her. Just trust what you feel and share with her."

"Ma?" Laura looked around the room, knowing no one was there, but checking anyway. "Ma, she's so afraid. I don't know what to say."

"No one knows, but the words will come to you, I promise. Just trust yourself and let them come through."

As the voice faded, Laura was enveloped in a peaceful warmth and was no longer afraid. She scooted back to the edge of the bed and slipped her hand under Clara's with their palms together, clasping the bloated fingers. Then she stroked Clara's arm, just below her elbow. She took a deep breath and closed her eyes.

"Please, help me. Why won't anyone help me?" The thick mist swirled around Clara, who clasped her hands together as she cried out.

"Listen to me," Laura spoke in her mind and knew Clara could hear her. "Your body is failing, but Asa and your little girl will be fine. He loves you so much, and will make sure she grows up loving you."

"No, no, please don't say that. I need to stay. I don't want to leave them. I can't leave now, it's not fair."

"I'm so sorry. You're right, it doesn't seem fair, but you must trust God and move on into heaven with him. I wish it was different, but your poor little body is shutting down and can no longer sustain you." Laura didn't question the words that poured out of her and knew that Clara could feel the truth in them.

"But I love Asa and Zoe. How can I turn my back on them?"

"You're not turning your back on them. You'll still be able to see them and send your love. They'll sense you around them always and know you're watching over them. All you need to do is accept what's happening. You're still connected to your body, but your spirit can reach out and explore the other side right now."

Clara didn't say another word.

"Thank you, Ma, for helping me. I think, I hope, it made a difference." The words inside Laura's mind were almost like a prayer. She felt tranquility instead of fear when she opened her eyes.

Laura leaned back, crossing her arms. Clara's face looked the same, but her breathing was slower. As Laura's gaze moved down the still body, she was horrified to see deep impressions in Clara's swollen flesh. Oh no, if Asa sees those indentations he'll think I was hurting her. She didn't know her fingers were sinking into Clara's skin like that.

Laura stayed in the chair and watched as the marks filled in over the next hour, almost disappearing just before Asa returned. She stood so he could have the chair by his wife and left them together.

That night Laura had a hard time going to sleep. She hated to admit she was jealous of her sisters' happy families. But she was also grateful to be alive and surrounded by people who cared. Perhaps falling in love and having children meant taking a risk of losing everything, like poor Clara.

CHAPTER THIRTEEN
Dead Is Dead
August, 1924

Chatter about Gwendolyn Harcourt upcoming wedding to Bruce Erickson dominated breakfast the next morning. The newspaper called it the biggest social event in decades.

"Did you see the picture of her ring?" Grace pointed at three pictures under the headline Erickson and Harcourt Nuptials. One was of the betrothed couple grinning at each other during a family celebration. The second was the bride's engagement ring, and the third a beautiful mansion. "I'll bet that ring costs more than any of us makes in a year. And this gorgeous house? Her parents are giving it to them for a wedding present. I'll be lucky to get a set of china from my folks when I get married."

"Must be nice." Sarah snorted and shook her head.

"No kidding," Katie said, leaning in to get a better look at the newspaper pictures. "He sure is a looker. She's one lucky girl. And no one can call her a gold digger with all her daddy's money."

"He looks too slick to me," Laura said. "Just another swell in love with himself. I'll bet he cares more about her family's money than her." As soon as the words left Laura's mouth, she knew they sounded too harsh. Sure enough, conversation stopped as the others stared at her with surprised looks on their faces.

"Wow, sounds like you know something we don't," Grace said. "What makes you think he's like that? Have you ever met him?"

Laura shrugged her shoulders. "How would I know somebody like that? Maybe I'm all wet. It could be just the way he looks in the picture, all smirky and self satisfied. He's probably okay." She stood and grabbed her purse. "See you all later. I've got to go."

Laura didn't look back as she strode to the door. Why hadn't she kept her mouth shut?

Nobody would have thought anything of her staying quiet. She never intended to tell a soul about her relationship with Bruce. Falling in love with him was the dumbest thing she'd ever done.

Right after Laura reached the third floor of the hospital, Miz Marston took her aside. "Listen, the patient in D two is even weaker today. In fact, her doctor told the nurses he doesn't expect her to make it past tonight."

"That's so sad," Laura said. "Her husband's having an awful hard time."

"I know. He stayed here all night by her side. If he asks you for help again, just let me know. In fact, whatever he needs, let's help him all we can."

Laura agreed and made D2 her first stop. She found Asa still sleeping in the chair next to Clara's bed with his long legs stretched out and his head leaning to the side on two bunched pillows. His sallow skin looked puffy and dry, and the dark circles were obvious even with his eyes closed. Clara's breathing was louder and irregular.

Her body looked even more swollen, almost like a single touch would cause her skin to collapse like a fallen cake.

Laura eased her way out of the room. She hoped Asa could rest a little longer in spite of the noises coming from the busy hall.

In a repeat of the day before, Asa asked Laura to stay with Clara while he went home to clean up, change clothes, and spend time with his baby girl. Minutes after finishing lunch in the cafeteria, Laura found herself alone with the dying woman. She dragged the chair close to the bed, closed her eyes, and rested her hands on the blanket.

"Not getting anything," she said to herself. "I can feel you pulling at my mind, but nothing is clear."

Laura took a deep breath. then touched Clara's body and her mind filled with a joyous sensation of Clara smiling.

"I'm so glad you're back and that you can hear me." Clara's voice was clear in Laura's mind. "I want to show you something."

The scene changed. Laura found herself next to Clara in the side-yard of a white, two-story house, staring at Asa and a young woman as they rocked back and forth on a porch swing. The couple was unaware of Laura and Clara's presence. They laughed and clapped as they watched a little girl who looked about three years old, play ball with a puppy and a young boy about five.

"You see, everything will work out fine." Clara's voice filled Laura's mind. "I was scared yesterday for Asa and Zoe because I knew the doctor couldn't make me well. The thought of leaving them was terrifying."

"But now you're not?" Laura said. "I don't understand."

"I moved to the light like you told me. Then an angel showed me the future so I could stop being afraid. Look how happy and beautiful Zoe is."

"But who's the woman with Asa? And the little boy?"

"That's my sister Deborah and her little boy, Zeke. Deborah's husband died in the war while she was pregnant. Asa and I spent lots of time with them," Clara said. "Don't you see? The people I love the most end up as a family."

The vision came to an abrupt end as a nurse entered the room. She checked Clara's heart rate and respiration, smiled at Laura, then left the room.

Laura couldn't feel Clara anymore, but she knew she'd never forget the lovely picture Clara shared.

Asa looked rested and clean when he returned. The minute he came through the door, his face turned to Clara. He leaned down, whispered in her ear, and kissed her forehead.

"Thank you for staying with her," Asa said, turning to Laura, who had moved away from the bed.

"You're welcome. Your wife is a lovely lady and I'm pleased to help in any way I can." Laura picked her words with care, not wanting to make things harder, or seem too forward.

Asa nodded and sat in the chair. "You'll think I'm crazy, but I keep talking to her even when I'm at home, telling her how much I love her."

Laura didn't want to interrupt him, so she just tilted her head and smiled.

"And I tell her it's alright to go, that I'll always love her and make sure our baby grows up knowing all about her, and that her mom is watching from heaven."

"You're a good man. I've no doubt Zoe will grow up and make both you and Clara proud."

Asa started to shake his head in response, then stopped. "How did you know our daughter's name? I never told you."

"I, uh, I guess I must have heard it from someone." Laura edged toward the door.

"Heard someone? I don't hold with folks gossiping about my family." He crossed his arms, no longer smiling. "Who was it."

"I'm sorry, but I don't remember. I've got to get back to work." Laura scooted out the door and raced to the housekeeping room.

How could she have done that? If he made a complaint, there was no way to explain. Laura vowed to herself to stay out of Asa's sight for the rest of her shift, and hope he didn't say anything.

Laura's luck held for the rest of the day. The next morning, Miz Marston sent her to the second floor to work. When she returned to the third floor after lunch, the first thing she saw was Agnes carrying an extra chair into room D. An elderly man was holding the door open, and the murmur of voices drifted into the hallway.

Thank goodness it was over for Clara. Laura was grateful she didn't have to face Asa again.

Laura kept thinking about Asa and Clara that day at work, and then when she returned home. She didn't want to be alone, so she joined Barbara and Glen in the parlor after dinner, curling up in the corner of the sofa with her arms wrapped around her knees. Otto Gray and his Oklahoma Cowboys were playing on KUFR, the most popular radio station in Tulsa, but she found it hard to pay attention to the music.

Barbara, seated at the other end of the divan, leaned forward and rubbed Laura's arm. "Is something wrong? You've been so quiet all evening. Looks like you're a million miles away."

"I'm sorry," Laura said, glancing up to see both Glen and Barbara staring at her. "I can't stop thinking about a patient who died last night. She was only twenty-three and left her husband and their year-old baby."

Glen, seated in a chair next to his sister, said, "No wonder you're so quiet. Somehow you've got to learn to leave those cases at the hospital or they'll break your heart."

Laura smiled in agreement. "That little girl will never get to know her mom. Her father will tell her stories, but it's not the same." She paused to organize her thoughts. "Do you think it's possible for someone who's passed on to communicate with their loved ones?"

"Course not." Glen crossed his arms. "Dead is dead. No coming back from that."

"Sometimes I wonder." Laura averted her eyes and picked at her fingernails. "There was a girl in school who swore her grandmother sometimes talked to her and sang songs. She said nobody else in the family could hear it, but she was positive it was her granny's voice."

"Glen's right," Barbara chimed in. "Nobody hears voices or songs from the dead. Most likely she wanted attention from you and made up some tall tales."

Laura unwound her feet and arms, then stood up and stretched. "I guess you're both right. Her stories sure seemed real, though." The words sounded hollow in Laura's ears. "I'm worn out. See you tomorrow." She headed for the stairs.

Ruth and Miss Emma were right. If She told anyone about Ma talking and humming inside her head, or about the visions that Clara showed her, she'd end up locked in a rubber room.

CHAPTER FOURTEEN
Marry Me
November, 1924

The months after Clara's death were lonely for Laura. She was careful at the hospital, even though several times she connected with dying patients. Nurses often asked her to sit with the difficult cases. No one seemed to know why that helped. She never revealed the conversations that took place in her mind when she sat with them.

Outside the hospital, she avoided all the excited discussions about Bruce's wedding, scheduled for Wednesday, December 10th, in accordance with The 1903 White House Etiquette guide's recommendations -- Mondays were for wealth and Tuesdays for health. Wednesday was the best day of all, Thursdays were for crosses, and Fridays for losses. Saturday for no luck at all.

Instead of thinking about all the society fuss, Laura focused on the Presidential election, determined to make her vote count. Too much infighting and mudslinging took place between the contenders of both major parties and the independents before the primaries. Most of Laura's friends supported Republican Calvin Coolidge for a second term, but she preferred Democrat John Davis. Both major party candidates were conservative. The progressive candidate, Robert La Follette, campaigned on gradual nationalization of the railroads and increased taxes on the wealthy.

Voting Day, Tuesday, November 4th, was crisp and cold. Laura had the day off but got up early to cast her vote. Ten people were lined up outside the door at her polling place, the Public Library four blocks from the hotel, when she arrived. Laura noticed there was only one other woman in the line, an older one who looked like her feet hurt. When the door opened, everyone scooted inside to escape the cold.

When it was Laura's turn, she hurried inside the narrow wooden space and closed the curtain behind her. The booth was dark wood on three sides. The open top let in the light, illuminating the narrow shelf below the voting machine. Each candidate was listed on an upright board, with metal levers next to the names.

Laura pulled a piece of paper out of her pocket and smoothed it on the narrow shelf. Good thing she'd brought her list, or she might not remember her choices for all the positions. After she made her selections, Laura felt so proud and sure she'd remember the day forever.

"Phone call, Laura," Sarah called up the stairs on Thanksgiving morning.

"Be right there." Laura slung her purse, scarf, and coat over her shoulder and headed down the steps. She was surprised to hear Lizbeth's voice instead of Ruth's on the phone.

"Happy Thanksgiving, Laura. How are you?"

"I'm fine. How are Roy and Lily? Is everything okay? You've never called before."

"Sorry to worry you, but I've got news to share." Lizbeth sounded breathy with excitement. "Becca got married three weeks ago."

"What? I thought she'd be with you forever. Tell me everything."

The story was a sweet surprise. Angus Freeman had worked in a pastry shop in Norman, Oklahoma for years, but when the bakery down the street from the Carpenter's store was put up for sale, he bought it and moved. Angus and Becca bumped into one another in the store and were smitten before he finished apologizing. They hadn't wanted to wait, so got married at the church as soon as they could make the arrangements. She moved into Angus's house on the edge of town, and they spent every possible minute together.

"That's amazing. I'm thrilled for her. Give them my best and be sure to put her address in your next letter. I want to send them a wedding present."

After hanging up, Laura headed straight to the hospital. She'd agreed to work the holiday, so the married staffers could have the day off. Becca's married? And in love with a baker? I'm happy for her. I am.

She tried hard to stay focused on Becca's happiness, but she couldn't drown out a whiny little voice inside her head that wondered why all her sisters found love, while she was still alone.

The floor was almost empty when Laura arrived, since everyone who could go home had been released the day before. Even Miz Marston took the day off, leaving Laura alone with only a list of duties for her in the housekeeping room.

"Nothing new on this checklist. Guess she wanted to make sure I wouldn't forget," Laura realized. She left the note where she found it and loaded a cart for cleaning the rooms.

The day was slow, no new admissions and no patient problems. The nurses and doctors let her know there were cookies and candy at the nurses' station, but Laura didn't feel like joining them. She skipped the holiday spread in the cafeteria too, munching on a sandwich in the housekeeping room, instead. It felt like a week had passed before she could clock out.

"Hi, missed you at lunch," Glen said, surprising Laura when he joined her at the time clock.

Laura jumped at the sound of his voice. "You startled me. I wasn't in the mood for the whole holiday thing, so I just bought a sandwich and ate it in the housekeeping room." She pulled her coat on and wrapped a long gray scarf around her neck. "I didn't know you were working today."

Glen nodded and pushed away from the wall where he'd been leaning. "Want to go to dinner at that new diner across from the hotel? I skipped lunch too, so we both could use a good meal."

"Mom's Kitchen? Sounds good."

A nasty, wet wind pulled at the door as they stepped out of the hospital. Laura tucked her chin into the folds of her warm woolen scarf and tried to protect her eyes against the wind, taking shallow breaths of the icy air. She planted each foot on the slippery pathway with care, bracing herself against freezing gusts.

"Here," Glen said, holding out his bent arm.

"Thanks." Laura took his arm.

He placed his gloved hand over hers, holding her close. They supported each other as they made their way down the windy street.

Warmth and delicious aromas surrounded the two as soon as they entered the restaurant.

A small woman with a big smile and a round body, testament to years devoted to good food, greeted them. "Welcome, folks. Let me take your coats and scarves while you find a table."

Glen led the way to the back corner of the room where he pulled Laura's chair out before sitting next to her.

The hostess joined them in minutes. "My name's Mabel and I'll take good care of you tonight. Do you two want our traditional Thanksgiving dinner?"

Glen and Laura looked at each other. "No, ma'am. I think we'd prefer something as far away from turkey and all the fixings as we can get," Glen said, glancing at Laura.

"Alright then, I've got a scrumptious pot roast with new potatoes, carrots, and thick slices of hot bread. Then we can follow that with a big piece of chocolate cake. How does that sound?" Mabel directed her words first to Glen, then to Laura.

"That sounds perfect," Laura answered for both.

"Good. It won't take long. Let me know if you need anything else."

The food lived up to Mabel's promise. Glen and Laura dug in with relish and didn't slow down or start a conversation until their plates were half empty.

"You looked kind of down at the hospital, and it seemed like more than just Thanksgiving was on your mind. Is something wrong?" Glen stopped eating.

"I was, a little, but I feel selfish talking about it." Laura stared at her food rather than looking at Glen. "Lizbeth called this morning to tell me that Becca got married almost a month ago. Becca fell head over heels with her new husband when they met, and he felt the same. I was thrilled for her, but then I felt bad because all my sisters have husbands who love them and families of their own." Laura looked at Glen, surprised at how intent his focus was on her. "I shouldn't complain because I have a good life, but someday I'd love to have children and a family of my own."

Glen cleared his throat, then said, "Don't feel bad, I understand." He paused a moment. "I have some good news to share. I got that job with the city I told you about, starting in two weeks, and I'll make almost twice my hospital salary."

"Congratulations. That's great news."

He hesitated, looking down, took a deep breath and squared his shoulders. "Laura ... we've known each other over a year now and spent a lot of time together. We both love music and dancing, and we've talked about everything under the sun. I feel the same way about wanting a family and children as you do." He stopped again, swallowed hard, then continued. "Laura, would you marry me?"

Laura stared, speechless. Had she heard him right?

"I know I'm no Valentino, but I promise to take care of you and our family." Glen took her hand and held tight. "I'm a hard worker. I'll do whatever it takes to make sure you have a good home and everything you need."

Laura interrupted him. "Yes"

"I ... Yes? Did you say yes?"

"Yes, I'll marry you." Laura smiled and ignored the question that screamed in her head. What in the world had she just done?

Glen jumped out of his chair, pulling Laura up with him, and hugged her tight as Mabel approached the table.

"My food's good, but I've never had folks jumping up and down over it," Mabel said.

"She said yes. We're getting married." Glen didn't move his eyes from Laura's face.

"That's wonderful," Mabel said with a smile almost as big as Glen's. "Did you give her a ring?"

"Oh, I forgot. Hold on." Glen reached into his pocket and pulled out a small velvet box. "This belonged to my grandmother." He opened the lid and handed it to Laura. "When Pa died Gram gave it to Mom to hold for me."

Laura looked at the narrow rose gold band with a small round diamond in the center and three diamond chips on each side. "It's beautiful, just about the prettiest ring I've ever seen," she said.

Glen took her left hand and placed the ring on her finger. She noticed his hands were shaking almost as much as hers. The roaring in her ears made it hard to hear his words.

"Laura, I promise I'll make you happy. I love you."

"I love you, too," Laura said, wondering if it might be true.

Without another word, Mabel waved off Glen's money and left to get their coats. When she returned, Laura saw tears in Mabel's eyes, and a huge smile.

* * *

The cold outside was a shock, but Glen held Laura close to his side as they made their way from the diner to the hotel. The lobby was deserted when they darted inside. Laura started to disengage from Glen's arms, but he held her even closer, stroked her cheek and kissed her.

His lips were so warm and soft. Laura realized she might not be in love with him, but being with him felt so good. She'd never felt so safe in her whole life.

CHAPTER FIFTEEN
You May Kiss The Bride

The next morning Laura reached for the ring as she woke up, half thinking she had imagined the entire proposal. It was real. She watched the diamonds sparkle in the light from her window. It was real, and she was getting married just like her sisters.

The ring was small, but it captured the eyes of everyone when she went down for breakfast.

"Oh, my god, that's gram's ring," Barbara shrieked when Laura settled at the table. "Glen asked you to marry him?"

Laura started to nod, but Barbara put her arms around Laura before she could finish.

Everyone joined in with congratulations, hugs, and advice. The madness continued at the hospital, with all the nurses and other staff complimenting the ring and wishing her well.

The best attention was from Glen, though. Most evenings he had supper with her at the hotel since the cost was less than going out to eat. Glen's apartment had a small kitchen, but they never cooked together unless Barbara was included, since it wouldn't look proper for them to be alone there. After eating, they'd play cards —- Stop Thief, Canasta, or Black Jack were the favorites —- or dominoes and listening to the radio in the parlor.

Once Laura got used to the idea of getting married, she and Glen began making plans. They decided to wait six months and save all they could for a nest egg, rather than spending money on a fancy wedding. A simple ceremony at a Justice of the Peace was all they needed, and Wednesday, May 20th appeared to be the perfect date.

"Today's my wedding day," Laura repeated the words to herself, pacing around the room in her robe. She stared out the window at a few wispy clouds, which still had a faint pink tint of dawn, as they drifted across the sky. "Better get started."

She waited until Abby, Barbara, and Grace had finished in the bathroom so she could take her time. Laura stared in the misty mirror. She needed to hurry since the car would arrive to pick Barbara and her up in about an hour.

Tightening the robe belt, she left the bathroom and slipped down to the kitchen. She wasn't hungry but knew she'd better eat something. Laura smeared two biscuits with honey, poured herself a tall glass of milk, and then carried the food up to her room.

"Hey, are you ready?" Barbara knocked on the door.

"Not quite, but I'm getting there."

Barbara came into the room and wrapped her arms around Laura, then took the brush from her hand. "Let me help, that's what sisters are supposed to do for each other."

Laura sat on the edge of the bed and sighed. "My sister Ruth used to do my hair when we were little girls. I about drove her crazy by getting my braids all knotted up."

"No braids today. This bob looks wonderful on you." Barbara pulled the remaining bobby-pins out of Laura's hair, then brushed through the pin curls. When she finished, Laura's side-parted hair was a mass of curls that wrapped down over her ears and framed the sides of her face. The back was shorter than the sides and tapered toward the top of her neck.

"Thanks for your help. I'm all thumbs today."

"Of course you are," Barbara said. "Stand up and turn around so I can see how you look."

Laura's make-up consisted of mascara, a little blush, and pale lipstick. Her dress, a simple white cotton shift with cap-sleeves, had lace around the scoop neckline and two long, lace edged ribbons down the front. She wore low-heeled white pumps with an eyelet design on the toe.

"You look beautiful. My brother is one lucky man." Barbara looked around the room, then grabbed the suitcase that sat by the door. "I'll carry this for you. We don't dare forget your honeymoon suitcase."

Laura waited for the Justice of the Peace
to call her into his office, holding a bouquet of
six red roses wrapped in white ribbon. Barbara
had insisted that every bride should make a
proper entrance and march to her groom even if
it wasn't a formal church wedding.

When the clerk opened the door, Laura
walked at a careful, measured pace to Glen's
side. He looked solemn, but so handsome. She'd
never seen him dressed that way, in a dark blue
suit, white shirt, and a navy blue and white
checked tie.

Glen reached for Laura. She passed the
flowers to Barbara, then stepped forward with
Glen. All Laura remembered later was Glen
placing the wedding ring on her finger, the
words "You may kiss your bride," then him
saying "... Mr. and Mrs. Glen Webber."

Laura held tight to Glen's arm, her
thoughts a jumble as they ran to the car. When
they arrived at the Mariemont Hotel, a
uniformed bellhop opened the door and took

their suitcases. In minutes they stood at the door to room 520.

Glen unlocked the door, took Laura in his arms, carried her over the threshold and kicked the door closed behind them. Once inside, he put her down but kept his arms around her, kissing her harder and longer than he ever had before.

"Look at this room." Laura pulled away and turned around with her arms outstretched. "It's even prettier than the pictures. Look at the view." She leaned against the windowsill, her heart pounding.

Glen moved up behind her, then wrapped his arms around her waist and nuzzled her neck. "You're prettier than anything out that window."

"Thank you," Laura said. "That's sweet. You know what I'd like to do? Let's have dinner in that restaurant by the lobby. Since we only have one night, let's explore the hotel shops. We can take all the time we want. It'll be fun."

Glen pulled his lips away from her neck and sighed. "If that's what you want, that's what we'll do."

Dinner was perfect. Glen let the waiter know they were newlyweds, so the staff treated them like royalty. The shops sold a wide variety of finery, but Laura wasn't paying close attention. This was her wedding day, and she knew Glen was not interested in shopping.

"Come on, honey, we've seen every single store. Let's go back to our room."

Laura could only smile and let him lead her to the elevator. There was no way to keep stalling.

Once they were back in the room, Glen tossed his jacket on a chair and took off his tie. "Let's get more comfortable."

Laura kicked off her shoes. "I'll turn on the radio. Maybe we can find some dance music."

"Only if there's something romantic. I want to hold my new wife."

Glen was gentle but insistent. They danced, but he held her against his body like never before and teased her mouth open with his. Laura responded, enjoying the new sensations until he began unbuttoning her dress and guiding her over to the bed.

"Wait," Laura said. "I'm not ready."

"It's okay, we're married. I'll go slow, I promise." Glen's voice was throaty, and his lips never left her face and neck.

Laura found herself on her back with Glen's weight pressing her against the mattress. When his hand pushed her dress up between them, the horror of Pa on top of her slammed into her mind. "No, no, stop," she cried. "Please stop." She shoved hard, rolled out from under Glen's body and burst into tears.

"I'm sorry. Did I hurt you?" Glen knelt on the floor in front of Laura. "You mean everything to me and I want you to be happy. I didn't mean to scare you."

Laura cried even harder, knowing she could never make him understand. She also knew that it was much too late to tell him what had happened in the past. "I'm okay, really. You didn't hurt me." She took a deep breath. "Please, just give me a few minutes to wash my face and calm down."

Much later, after Glen had fallen asleep with his arm still holding her close, Laura relaxed and let the tears flow. She couldn't bear having Glen on top of her, so he had rolled them on their sides, lifting her leg over his. He had tried to be gentle, thinking it was her first time, but his movements sped up with his passion. She kept her emotions in an iron grip, only able to escape what was happening to her body by holding on to the memories of baby Lily in her arms.

CHAPTER SIXTEEN
Marshmallow Man

The sound of snoring near her ear startled Laura awake. Her instant of panic eased when she looked at Glen's face on the pillow next to her. Thank goodness she hadn't screamed. Sleeping with him would take some getting used to.

She stared at her new husband's face. He looked so peaceful and sweet. He'd probably been a cute little boy.

Laura eased her way off the edge of the bed and crept across the room, one slow step after another. She opened the drawer inch by inch to get her clothes, then slid it closed without a sound. She tiptoed to the bathroom, slipped into the small, dark space, then locked the door behind her. Only then did she turn on the light.

She was a married woman now. No more
sleeping alone or sharing a bathroom with only
women. Laura leaned closer to her image in the
mirror over the sink and examined her
reflection, turning her face from side to side.
The mirror image didn't look any different.

She'd better get a move on or he'd be
knocking on the door wanting in. The thought
of his company in the bathroom mortified her.
She rechecked the door, then wedged the chair
from the dressing table underneath it. A sense
of urgency stayed with her as she got dressed.

"Laura." Glen's voice rang out while
Laura was putting the chair back in its place.
"Sweetheart, are you about done in there?"

Laura reached for the doorknob and
caught sight of the two rings nestled together
into a single unit on her hand. She'd wanted to
marry a man who loved her. She got him, so
she'd better treat him right. "Coming right out."

Glen was sitting on the edge of the bed in
his underwear when Laura stepped through the
bathroom door. A huge grin creased his face.
He got to his feet as she walked toward him.

Laura burst into giggles, and the more she tried to stop the harder she giggled.

Glen's grin disappeared "What's so funny?" He put his hands on his hips and squished his eyebrows together.

"I'm sorry." Laura did her best to get herself under control. "It's just that you look so funny."

Glen crossed his arms and tilted his head to the side. "Funny?"

"Your face and neck and your forearms and hands are dark, but the rest of you, especially your legs, are white as marshmallows."

The grin came back. "I guess you'll just have to get used to being married to a marshmallow man."

Glen reached Laura in two quick steps, gathered her in his arms and kissed her. "I love you, Mrs. Webber."

"I love you, too." Laura smiled as she said the words she knew Glen needed — and deserved — to hear.

"We'd better get a move on to beat the check out time." Glen nuzzled Laura's neck, gave her another quick kiss, then moved away to scoop clean clothing out of his open suitcase. "Why don't you pack our bags while I shower and shave, then we can head down for breakfast."

"Okay." Pack our bags? She'd never packed for anyone else before. After gathering her things from the drawer and closet, she folded them into her case, placing the small canvas bag with her toiletries and makeup on top. She moved her suitcase next to the door, then sighed and looked for Glen's.

His bag was open on the floor, so she moved it to the bed to make it easier to pack. Glen's dirty clothing was strewn around the room. His jacket draped over the back of a chair, and his shoes lay on their sides several feet apart near the door. She left his shoes, but gathered all the other items and folded each piece before placing it into the suitcase. Touching his things felt weird. Handling his socks and underwear seemed even more intimate than what they'd done the night before.

Breakfast in the restaurant was a treat and checking out of the hotel was uneventful. When the taxi deposited them in front of Glen's, now their, apartment building, Laura knew her life would never be the same.

"Hold on," Glen said, putting the suitcases down outside their door. He turned the key in the lock and pushed the door open. With a huge grin, he scooped Laura in his arms and carried her inside, as he pressed his lips against hers.

Once inside the room, Laura pulled away from the kiss and pushed against Glen's chest to get down. She smoothed her skirt, then patted her hair, needing a minute to get her breath back under control. She touched Glen's arm and smiled, then glanced around the room.

Laura pointed to a pile of boxes on the table in the living room. "Look at this stuff." She walked into the room and plucked a piece of paper off the top box. "It's from Barbara. She says Minnie and Morris helped her bring all my things over and put some of them away."

"That was nice of them." Glen carried their bags inside and closed the door. He joined Laura, peering over her shoulder at the note. "Hey, they filled the icebox and the pantry so we won't have to worry about shopping for awhile."

"They didn't need to do that, but it sure was thoughtful of them."

Glen chuckled. "Yes, but then that sister of mine finishes up by reminding me we need to get a car of our own, now." He took the paper from Laura and put it on the table. "She's right, you know. I'll have to start looking for a decent used one we can get for a good price."

Nodding in agreement, Laura looked around the room. "You were lucky to find this place last month. Your old apartment would have been super crowded for the two of us."

"With all your clothes and stuff? No kidding."

Laura snorted. "All my things? You had tools stacked on the kitchen table and clean laundry all over the living room."

It didn't take long to put everything away. Throughout the next few weeks they moved furniture around and added decorating touches that turned the apartment into a home. The strangeness of living together soon turned into a comfortable routine, with days centered around their jobs and evenings spent together in the kitchen for supper. When the meal was over, they did household chores and listened to the radio.

After living in a residence hotel for years, it was strange for Laura to have her own kitchen, complete with a gas stove, oven, and modern icebox, and to share a bathroom with only one person. She had to master using the wringer washing machine outside in the wash-house, and to get used to hanging the clean clothes on the lines in the yard. Laundry, cooking, and cleaning were her responsibilities, but Glen took care of the heavy work including the car, paid the bills, and budgeted to build a savings account.

Laura enjoyed Glen's company, even though it took a lot to get used to sharing a home with a man. The toilet seat was always left up, the dirty clothes never quite made it to the hamper, and globs of toothpaste hardened in the bathroom sink. At first she nagged him, but gave up when his promises to do better never made a difference.

The biggest adjustment to married life was sleeping together. Laura discovered, to her surprise, that she enjoyed Glen's affection, the little pats when she walked past him, the warm hugs, and his habit of kissing her goodbye whenever he left to go out and again upon his return. But when he turned to her in bed, her stomach always knotted up inside.

Glen's mouth would cover hers, open and probe deep as his touches became more intimate and insistent. Laura's heart would race, which he interpreted as rising passion. She fought to keep her attention on him and not let her nightmare memories intrude. She couldn't bear having his body pressed flat on top of her, and would start fighting him. Glen learned to turn them on their sides or to pull Laura on top, unaware that the cessation of her struggles just meant she was able to keep the bad memories at bay. He never asked how she felt or what brought her pleasure, and she never told him the reason she fought.

The bedroom held other secrets as well because Laura wasn't the only one with nightmares. Many times Glen would thrash around and cry out in his sleep. She could see his nightmares in her own mind and felt his pain each time he relived the awful scene of his brother's death over and over, drowning in the torment and helplessness. Sometimes her touch would soothe him, but he refused to talk about the nightmares, insisting she was wrong. He even accused her of making it up because of her own bad dreams. Laura admitted to having nightmares of her own, but always insisted that she couldn't remember them. She had to keep lying or risk telling him the truth about what Pa had done to her, and that she couldn't do.

The secrets festered under the smooth surface of their relationship. Glen and Laura almost never argued, established comfortable routines at home, and enjoyed their time out at the movies and local dance halls. But in spite of Laura's gentle attempts to talk about family, Glen was steadfast in his refusal to discuss the loss of his father, his brother's death, or his guilt for breaking his promise to his mother. Those subjects were locked away. Laura had seen everything in her visions, felt the turmoil and horror of each nightmare, but couldn't ease his suffering. She didn't view her secrets in the same way, however, since she was sure her silence was for the best.

CHAPTER SEVENTEEN
Tulsa to Seminole
July 1926, Fourteen months later

Laura cut up the chicken she'd pulled out of the icebox, rinsed each piece, dried it off, and dipped it in a beaten egg. She made her fried chicken just like Miz Mary taught her, but it never tasted quite the same. Laura dredged the pieces in a seasoned bowl of flour. Thank goodness Glen wasn't too fussy about his food.

The flame under the cast-iron skillet was on high, melting the white mountain of Crisco that floated in the pan, almost ready for the chicken.

"Honey, come see what I've got," Glen called out as he entered the front door.

"Can it wait until after supper? I'm just getting ready to put the chicken in the pan."

Glen popped into the kitchen, reached around Laura and turned the burner off. "Supper can wait. I've got a huge surprise for you." He gave her a quick kiss, grabbed her hand, and pulled her toward the door.

Once outside, Laura stared at a pickup truck parked at the curb. "Isn't she a beauty? I traded our car straight across with a guy at work whose wife just had twins. The truck has lots of room for us, and I can earn extra money doing hauling jobs."

Glen stroked the shiny front fender, then led the way to the back. The pickup was a delivery style, with a large enclosed box behind the cab. He opened the rear doors so Laura could see the space. "The guy threw in the cargo straps and dollies since he won't need them. Isn't it great?"

"Great?" Laura crossed her arms. "Great? I don't know. I could drive the car, but I can't drive this thing. We never talked about this."

Glen's wide smile disappeared. "It just came up today, and I decided before somebody else got it. I can teach you to drive the truck. It isn't much different." He slammed the back doors closed. "I thought you'd be excited, too."

"I'm sorry," Laura said. "You surprised me, that's all."

Mollified, Glen followed Laura inside. They didn't talk much through supper, but after Laura finished the dishes, he said, "Sit down. We need to talk."

"Okay. You sound awful serious. Is something wrong?"

"No, but I've got an idea." Glen planted his elbows on the table and cleared his throat. "I want us to move to Seminole."

"What?" Laura gasped, rearing back from the table. "But we're ..."

"Just listen." Glen said. "You know the news has been filled with stories about the oil strike in Seminole, and today there was another one. People will be flooding there for jobs, and if we move now, we can beat the rush."

"But what about our jobs here? And where would we live?" Laura's voice was shrill, her eyes wide. "You don't know anything about working in an oilfield."

"No, but I'm a great mechanic, and they'll need people who're good with machines. You can always get a job in a hospital or office. We need to get there now, though, before the town fills up with people trying to get their share of the money from the oil." He paused and took a breath. "And the truck will be perfect to get us moved. We can even camp in it until we're settled in a new place."

Thoughts whirled through Laura's mind. Could he be right? Their lives were comfortable now. Should they take such a huge risk? She remembered running away -- twice -- and starting over to escape bad situations. Both times had worked out for the best for her. Would this be the same?

"Honey, look at me," Glen said. "We can do this. I'm thinking of our future."

Laura shook her head, then sighed and said, "Okay, but let's plan everything out."

Two weeks later found them on the road, headed out of Tulsa. The smooth hum of the truck motor filled the cab, a testament to Glen's careful attention and mechanical skills. Laura's legs tilted toward her door, sharing space in front of her seat with a box that contained six apples, two mason jars of water and ice, several waxed-paper-wrapped sandwiches, and a tin full of cookies. A folded map lay between them, with a well-marked route visible for quick reference.

"It should take just under an hour to get to Sapulpa on highway seven." Glen was grinning like a child under the Christmas tree. "We can make a quick stop to check everything in back, then we head south on twelve to Beggs."

"I know." Laura laughed and grinned back at him. "I've got the route memorized too, you know. We'll pass through Kiefer and Mounds, where we can stop to check our gas and oil and maybe find a restroom."

The good news in Sapulpa was that nothing had shifted in the back of the truck. The bad news was in front of them, just past where they left the pavement. Clouds of dust covered the road and the people in the vehicles waiting in line for their turn since the road was closed to a single lane, and that was just the beginning. The entire length of the road between Sapulpa and Beggs was a nightmare. They drove on surfaces that were often scraped dirt and endured constant delays, waiting for their turn to pass road crews and paving equipment. Dirt and the heavy smell of asphalt filled the air, making it hard to breathe, and road debris was everywhere.

Twice they had to stop to fix a flat tire. Glen had planned well, having brought two extra tires and innertubes, and a flat patch kit. Both times they were lucky and patching was all that was necessary, but the process took time.

When they reached Beggs and drove through the main street, Laura and Glen were exhausted, dirty, and sticky with sweat.

"Look," Laura said, pointing at the road ahead just past the business district. "Pavement, beautiful pavement again."

"Do you want to stop first? That's the last paved section between us and Seminole. When it ends in Henryetta, the rest of the way is gravel, construction, or dirt."

"We're so far behind now, I'd just as soon stop there." Laura rubbed her sunburned cheek.

"And let's see if we can find a place to spend the night instead of sleeping in the truck. I'd kill for a bath."

"Probably do us both good. Henryetta, here we come."

The tiny hotel they found in Henryetta was next door to a small cafe. Glen parked the truck, pulled out their suitcases, and padlocked the doors closed. Once registered, they headed to their room, which was clean, had a decent bed, and a large claw-foot bathtub. They were both famished but decided washing off layers of dirt was more important than eating.

"You go first," Glen said after dropping their suitcases next to the bed. "Just make it quick since the diner's supposed to close in two hours."

Laura nodded as she leaned down and started the water running. She closed the bathroom door, took off her filthy clothes and stepped into the tub.

"Oooohhhhh," she moaned and lowered herself into the steamy water. She closed her eyes but didn't dare keep them closed or she might fall asleep. "Oh, well, as soon as we get scrubbed we can eat, then head straight to bed," Laura mumbled, grabbed the soap and washcloth and got started.

The food at the cafe was plentiful and hot. Neither Glen nor Laura paid much attention to the taste. They were both exhausted from the day, and on the edge of passing out at the table. No one at neighboring tables seemed to notice them, so they finished in silence and headed back to their room. In minutes they were undressed and in bed, covers pushed off while a sluggish fan stirred the air over their sleeping bodies.

The unwelcome ring of the alarm clock woke Glen the next morning, but Laura pulled the pillow up over her head and groaned.

"Come on, sleepyhead," Glen said. "We've got to get going."

"Okay, okay." Laura rolled over, put her feet on the floor, and rubbed the sleep from her eyes.

In less than fifteen minutes they'd stowed their bags in the back of the truck and refilled the box of provisions in the cab from the cold box in the back of the truck. The mason jars of water no longer had ice though, and they'd have to make peanut butter sandwiches when they stopped. More apples and cookies rounded out the food, just like the day before. The map, refolded to show the way, was spread on the seat between them.

"This is it, babe. A little over ninety miles and we'll be in Seminole." Glen started the engine with a roar, and they pulled out of the hotel parking lot.

What would have taken between four and five hours on good pavement ended up taking ten grueling, sweltering hours. Gravel roads were interspersed with construction zones as they passed by little towns with exotic names —- Okemah, Weeletka, Wehumka —- on their way to Holdenville. Only one town, Wewoka, was left before Seminole, and they spent the night there so they could be fresh when they rolled into the city that would be their new home.

CHAPTER EIGHTEEN
We're Having A Baby
November 1927,
Sixteen months later

Laura peeked out the window, holding the frayed, heavy brown curtains open just enough to see through. The street, a mere twenty feet from the front of the house, was filled with traffic, cars, and trucks mired half way up the tires in sticky mud. Horns honked, men cursed and yelled, and teams of horses worked to pull the vehicles free.

"Wonder how long before Glen gets home," Laura murmured. "Might have worked late again, or he might be caught in this mess." She stepped back and pulled the curtain closed, not wanting to be seen. Rowdy crowds of men, often drunk and lonely, made it dangerous for a solitary women in Seminole, even in her home.

The room was cold in spite of the fire behind the black mesh fire screen. The flames popped and flickered as they devoured a fresh log, bending with each gust that found its way down the chimney. "Don't know how the last tenant managed without a screen in front of the fireplace," Laura said. She glanced at the dark char marks on the floor in front of the grate. "It's a wonder this place didn't burn down." She tightened the shawl around her shoulders as a strong gust worked through the narrow gaps around the windows and door. "That might be a good idea, if there were any other places to live in this town."

Laura heard Glen's key open the lock, and turned to greet him.

"Doggone, it's cold and nasty out there." He sat on the bench just inside the door, pulled off his mud-covered boots, and tucked them under the seat. Then he shrugged off his heavy overcoat and tossed it on the coat tree. He headed to the fireplace in damp socks to warm up.

Before Glen reached the hearth, someone tried to open the front door, rattling the doorknob, then banging on the wood panel. "Open up, Doc, my friend's hand is cut bad. We need you."

Cussing, Glen walked back to the door, but didn't open it. "The doc is in the house next door on your right. You've got the wrong place."

"I know it's a bad time, after hours and all, but we need your help." The voice was loud, the words slurred. "Come on, he's bleeding all over the porch."

"Damn it," Glen swore, opening the door just enough to let himself out. The voices were too low for her to understand, but Laura had heard the same conversation numerous times over the past year.

She shook her head, then went to the kitchen to fill their plates, and pour two glasses of milk. She heard the door open and slam shut minutes before Glen joined her.

"Those guys were too drunk to listen or figure out what I was saying. I've got to get a sign made with arrows pointing to the doc on one side and the lawyer on the other." He gave Laura a quick kiss and hug, then plopped into his chair as she placed his plate, heaped high with food, on the table. "I think a crossbar for the door would be a good idea too, since they could have broken in if they'd had a mind to."

"You've talked about those same ideas before," she said, taking a deep breath. She felt a huge smile stretch across her face. "But I think now's the perfect time to get them done." She put her fork down and steepled her hands on the table. "I mean, now that we're going to have a baby's safety to think about."

"What did you say?" Glen's eyebrows tightened, then lifted into his hairline. "A baby? We're having a baby?"

When Laura nodded, beaming at him, he pulled her out of the chair into his arms and swung her around. "Oh my goodness, we're having a baby." He stopped twirling and steadied her in place. "Oh, no, what am I doing? Did I hurt you? Honey, you should sit down. Can I get you anything? Do you want to put your feet up?"

"I'm fine. In fact I'm fantastic." Laura laughed, waving Glen back to his own place. "It's not due until next summer."

"Next summer? That's perfect. But we've got so much to do before the baby comes." Glen jumped up to fish a piece of paper and a pencil out of the top drawer under the counter, next to the icebox. "Better start a list."

By the time they settled into bed, Glen's list had grown to include door signs, security bars on the front and back doors, porch stair repairs, caulking around the door and all the window frames, and lots more. First item on the list, though, was having Laura quit work. He was adamant, insisting she needed her rest, although he did agree that she could do projects around the house to get ready for the birth.

"Promise you'll quit today," Glen said, holding the door open before he left the next morning.

"I will." Laura pulled her robe tight against the cold draft from the door. "I sure hope Mrs. Prescott is in this morning. I'd be embarrassed to tell her husband why I'm leaving."

"If she's not, just tell him I want you to stay home. There are so many people looking for work, he won't care." Glen grabbed the doorknob. "Gotta get that crossbar put in tonight when I get home."

Laura chuckled at his parting words, confident that after months of procrastinating about fixing the doors, now it would get done.

"No problem, dear," Mrs. Prescott said. "Wonderful news. We don't hold with women in the family way working here in our store, so appreciate your letting us know. I'll get your check ready."

In less than fifteen minutes Laura was walking the two blocks back home. That was fast. She guessed it was a good thing she quit, or Mrs. Prescott would have fired her when she figured out Laura was expecting.

Laura threaded her way through knots of people on the sidewalk and tried to stay next to the buildings to avoid being splashed with mud from cars passing in the street. She didn't think she'd ever want to live in a city again after staying here in Seminole. And what rotten surroundings for raising a baby, so different from her sisters' homes in Ardmore.

CHAPTER NINETEEN
Just Call Me Mouse
April 1928, Five months later

Laura rubbed slow circles around and over her mounded middle. She sat in one of the kitchen chairs, her feet up on the chair in front of her, holding the telephone receiver.

"I don't know how we'd have made it without your help. The clothes you sent me, especially the maternity corsets and the baby things are such a help."

"Since Lizbeth, Becca, and I can't be with you, sending things you'll need seemed like the least we could do. Uh, oh, hold on." Ruth banged the receiver down. "I'm back. Maggie always wants to follow the boys, but sometimes they want to play alone."

Laura smiled, thinking about Ruth's rambunctious little daughter. "She sounds like such a sweetheart."

"She is that. Where's Glen? I called today because I was sure we'd catch you both home on the Saturday before Easter."

"You'd think so, but business here never seems to slow down. Glen is off on a hauling job today. He's working hard to build up our savings. He never wants to be caught short, and he's trying to accumulate as much as we can before the baby arrives."

"What does your doctor say? Will you deliver at home or in a hospital?"

"I don't have a doctor," Laura said. She dropped her feet to the floor and stood up. "Glen wants me to use the doctor next door, but I can't stand the thought of him touching me. He stinks of cigars and I hate the creepy way he looks at me. I sure wish Miz Dobbs had a younger sister who lived here."

"Have you heard about any midwives in town? That's what you want."

"No. There aren't many women in town, and none of the ones I know are pregnant or have babies."

Laura swayed back and forth, twisting the phone cord in her hand. "How can I find out about midwives?"

"I've got an idea." Ruth sounded excited. "Tomorrow's Easter, so most likely there'll be lots of visiting after church services. Look for some of the oldest women and ask them if they know of a midwife. Church matrons know everything that's going on in town. If there's a midwife around, they'll know."

The conversation ended when Maggie started crying and banging on the door to go out on the porch with her brothers. After a hasty goodbye, Laura hung up the receiver and sat back down.

Ruth's idea sounded good, but could she do it? Getting Glen to church would be hard enough, but approaching a bunch of women she didn't know to ask about midwives?

A hard kick up under her ribs brought Laura's attention back to her belly. "You're right, little one. It doesn't matter if it's hard for me, I have to do what's best for you." She closed her eyes for a moment, hands cupped under the swell of her stomach, imagining what it would be like when the baby was born. Her swollen midriff moved to the side, a tiny bump poking out and sliding under the skin. "Not too much longer," Laura said, pressing her fingers on the roving bulge. "I know it's getting crowded in there."

With a sigh, Laura leaned forward and pulled herself upright. "So much for resting. Can't believe I need the bathroom again. That I won't miss."

Laura convinced Glen to take her to the First Methodist Church since it was the oldest church congregation in town. The new building, a gothic brick two-story, had been completed for only a year. Laura loved the arch that framed the wide front doors and the stained glass windows high above them.

Glen wasn't happy and fidgeted throughout the sermon. After the service ended, he hugged Laura and wished her good luck, then joined a group of men standing near the parking lot. Laura wandered around introducing herself to the church ladies.

Ruth was right on all counts. After church, most of the parishioners gathered outside to visit at tables arranged under huge old shade trees that dotted the lawn. Four elderly ladies, all wearing stylish hats and short gloves, sat together under the biggest tree and beckoned Laura to join them.

The ladies were eager to learn all about her and asked lots of questions, including when her baby was expected. That was a natural opening for Laura to ask if there was a good midwife in town. She told them she was afraid they might not have enough time to get to the hospital in Wewoka, and would feel more comfortable with a local midwife.

"Honey, there's only one in town we'd trust. She delivered my babies and my grandson," said Miz Anderson, leaning forward to pat Laura's hands.

"She's right," Miz Bellwether chimed in. "My daughters both used her."

By the time Laura said her goodbyes, she had the midwife's name and address, and more interesting gossip about the history of Seminole than she'd ever imagined.

Glen leaned against his truck talking to three men when Laura found him.

"Let me know if you need any hauling on weekends." Glen shook hands with the men, then turned to his smiling wife. "I guess you got what you wanted," he said.

Laura nodded as she climbed into the truck.

Glen said, "So, tell me about her."

"She's an old woman who's been delivering babies for years. In fact, all four of the ladies I talked to either know her or about her from their families and friends. They think we should go to her house, now, since she's most likely at home."

"Does she have a name?"

"Everyone just calls her Mouse, and she lives at the edge of old town"

"Mouse? The edge of old town?"

"Yes. They said her family called her
Mouse when she was little, and it stuck. She
grew up in old town and never left."

"Wait a minute, that sounds like she's
Indian. Old town was first settled by the
Seminole tribe, and most of the old ones stayed
there." Glen turned to Laura, lips in a tight line.
"You'd rather have a dirty old Indian woman
deliver our baby than a modern doctor? We
need to talk to Doc Gunderson next door before
we go to some crazy old Indian woman."

Laura reared back as if she'd been
slapped. Her face flushed as she clenched her
fists. "Glen Webber, I've gone along with your
decisions from the day we got married. But not
this time. I'll deliver this baby by myself before
I'll let that smelly, disgusting old lech touch
me."

Glen stared back, nostrils flared and eyes
slitted. Then he started the truck and slammed
it into gear. "I hope you know what you're
doing," he muttered under his breath as they
lurched into the traffic.

Laura stared through the windshield.
What would Glen say if he knew her ma was an

Indian? He'd never talked this way before. Miss Emma's warning to never reveal her Indian heritage rang in her ears. Would it have mattered enough to keep Glen from marrying her?

Neither of them said a word until they reached the oldest section of town, when she gave Glen the directions she'd received at church. They pulled into a narrow dirt road next to a huge black walnut tree with lightning scars on one side of the trunk. Glen stopped in front of a tiny clapboard house, weathered to a silvery patina, and shaded by an ancient dogwood tree. Though the building was old, the flowers and herbs growing in clay pots on the porch looked bright and well cared for. Laura could see a butterfly resting on a deep green leaf, like a gemstone brooch against an emerald blouse.

Glen parked near the porch steps, then hurried around to open Laura's door. "I'm sorry, but you know I worry about you." He helped Laura down from her seat and closed the door. He stroked her cheek. "Look, I'll come pick you up in about an hour. I'd just be in the way here.

I'll be at that little cafe we passed a mile or so back." His fingers touched her lips. "I love you."

"Thank you, I love you, too." Laura watched him drive away, then turned toward the house.

"Hello, dear." The tall, slender woman with gray hair smiled at Laura. "I expected you earlier, but come on inside now that you're here."

"Expected me? I only learned about you this morning." Laura's voice rose. She climbed the two stairs to the porch and followed Mouse through the open screen door.

"Let's sit at the table. Would you like a cup of tea? I've got some nice peppermint brewing."

"I've never tried peppermint before, but it sounds good." She folded her hands on her belly. "The ladies from the Methodist Church told me about you and said everyone calls you Mouse."

"That they do." Mouse brought two cups to the table and joined Laura

Laura looked closely at Mouse. She had expected a Seminole woman, but Mouse's complexion was much darker and her silver hair had crinkles in it.

Mouse laughed, a soft, pleasant sound. My ma was just a little girl when she was sold, together with her ma, to a rich Seminole. He purchased them in the South, then brought them here. When Mr. Lincoln freed the slaves, they were freed, too."

"I didn't know Indians had colored slaves," Laura said.

"Oh, yes. Most of the slaves were captives from wars with other tribes, but when white people came and brought colored slaves, Indians started buying them, too." Mouse poured more tea into their cups. "Ma was a grown woman when she was freed but had no place to go. She married a Seminole man, and they lived in Wewoka. When my pa's body was found in a ditch by the main road, shot to death, Ma took all the cash they'd hidden away and brought me here. She bought this land, and I've lived in this house ever since."

"That's quite a story, Miz Mouse. I didn't want to ask, but ..."

"It's just Mouse. I thought you should know since you understand what it's like to be of mixed blood." Mouse put her hand up to stop Laura from speaking. "Your ma told me all about what you've been through and made me promise to take good care of you."

Laura felt a chill creep over her body and wrapped her hands around the warm cup. "Ma told you I was coming?"

"She sure did. I was washing up some dishes, watching the birds through the window. When I turned around, she was sitting right where you are now, plain as day."

"You saw her," Laura's voice squeaked like a rusty hinge. Her eyes opened wide, and her hands flew up to her chin. "I've heard her speak since I was a little girl, but I've never seen her."

"I often see spirits. You hear her and see visions in your mind, but the second sight is different for each person."

Laura didn't know how to respond, so she took a deep breath, placed her hands on top of her belly, and said, "Well, I guess we should talk about the baby. Will you come to our house?"

"No, I've got all my stuff here. When your time comes, your husband needs to bring you to me. Then when you and your little one are both rested and ready, he can take you home."

"I know Glen will ask me what it will cost, even though I feel funny talking about money."

"Of course he will, as he should. The hospital in Wewoka costs seven dollars per night, plus extra for the baby, and they'd keep you about three days. You can tell him I'll charge four dollars for the delivery and your overnight stay with the baby, plus an extra two dollars if you need to stay another day."

"Okay," Laura said. "That'll make him happy. I'm thinking my delivery date will be around the end of June."

"No, last week of May or the first week of June."

"How do you know? You haven't asked any personal questions or examined me?"

Mouse smiled again and brought the cup to her lips. "Your baby is healthy and strong. Just starting to get cramped inside. Don't need to touch your belly to feel her."

"Her?" Laura cupped her fingers under the precious mound. "We're having a girl?"

"Yes, a fine little girl. I think you need to leave that out of your report to Glen. He'll have enough trouble dealing with all this."

Laura agreed, thinking this secret would join the many others between them. She turned her attention back to Mouse and listened to instructions about what to expect for the rest of the pregnancy.

When all Laura's questions had been answered, Mouse stood up and reached into a cabinet. "I've got two jars of tea leaves for you to take home. One is peppermint with a little lavender. Brew it early in the day to help you feel more relaxed and to help your digestion. The other is chamomile. Drink a cup of that in the evening so you will sleep better."

Mouse handed Laura the small jars filled with dried leaves, then said, "We'd better go on out to the porch. Your man will be here soon, and he'll feel better seeing us all smiles, relaxed, sitting in the rockers, when he arrives."

CHAPTER TWENTY
You Must Leave
July 1929, Thirteen months later

The midwife's predictions were right. After an easy labor, June Alice Webber was born on Friday afternoon, June 1st, 1928. Laura picked out the name June because of the birthdate, but Glen chose Alice because he wanted the baby's initials to spell a word.

Right after the baby was born, Mouse brought Glen inside a tiny bedroom that served as a delivery room to see his wife and daughter. When Laura reached for him, he knelt by the bed, and held her and the baby.

"Thank you, Miz Mouse. Thank you so much," he whispered.

When Glen's knees gave out from kneeling on the hard floor, Mouse spread a pallet for him next to Laura's bed, so he didn't have to go home alone.

"Honey, that floor can't be comfortable," Laura said when she woke during the night. "Have you gotten any sleep at all?"

"Not much. Seems like I pop up whenever you or the baby move around," he said. "But I'm not going home without you, then we can both catch up on our sleep."

Mouse, who'd just stepped through the door to check on Laura, chuckled and shook her head, "Easy to tell this is your first baby, Mr. Webber. You won't be catching up on sleep for a long time."

From the minute they tucked little June into her cradle at home, she was the center of the household. When he was home, Glen loved to watch her while she slept or hold her when she was awake. His fascination with their daughter astonished Laura. She couldn't believe how different he was from her pa.

"I've got her. She's fine." Glen would say when he noticed his wife's eyes focused on June in his arms, and her body poised to take over. Feeling protective, Laura always watched in case she needed to intervene.

"Can you believe how much June has changed things in just a month?" Laura sat on the sofa with Glen, folding clothes fresh from the line while they listened to the radio.

Glen laughed, holding June on his lap, her tiny hands wrapped around his thumbs. "That's for sure." He leaned forward and cooed at June. "Everything we do now is centered around you, Junebug, and will be for years. And your mama and I love it."

"Glen," Laura said, shaking him awake. "Some guy is on the phone for you."

"Tell him I'll be right there."

Laura went back to the kitchen where June was banging a spoon on her highchair table. She traded a piece of toast for the spoon and grabbed the phone. "Please hold on, he'll be right here."

June gummed the toast, then threw it on the floor. She reached for the spoon instead, but it was just out of her reach. Laura picked her up to keep her quiet while Glen was on the phone.

"Got to go," he said, hanging up the receiver. "Problems over at Fixico."

"On a Sunday? Again?"

Glen leaned down and kissed the top of June's head. "Oil wells don't care about Sunday. See you when I can." He kissed Laura and held both of his girls in a tight hug. "Could you do some mending today? I'm getting kind of low on shirts."

"Okay." Laura followed him to the door. "We'll miss you."

One final quick peck, then he was gone. "Sometimes I wish your papa wasn't quite so good at what he does."

June followed Laura from room to room as she gathered up laundry and tidied up the house. "You, little one, are not helping," Laura said when she redirected the baby's attention from items on the bookshelf to her box of toys in the corner.

The ploy didn't work. June turned right around and returned to pulling books down.

"I give up. Let's go outside for awhile." Laura stacked her basket of mending, the sewing box, and June's toy-box. "Come on, Junebug," she said, leading the little girl to the back door.

The back yard was tiny, the width of the house plus two feet on either side, extending twenty feet from the back of the house. Two old Adirondack chairs squatted against the house on a six-by-six concrete pad outside the back door. A ten-foot-square wash house was tucked into the right-hand corner. Dandelions dotted the sparse green grass, which provided a place for June to play. The wooden fence leaned in places but provided welcome privacy.

Laura put her basket and the toys down while keeping an eye on June, who toddled from one yellow flower to another. "Pick them if you want, Junebug, but do not put them in your mouth."

By the time Laura had organized her sewing, June had returned and spread her toys on the other chair.

"I love my sewing machine, but wish it could do buttons and buttonholes." She spread one of Glen's shirts on her lap and chose a button from her spare button bag. "I swear, he loses at least one button a week, and rips one or two shirts as well." Laura always talked out loud when she was with June, knowing the little girl enjoyed her voice.

June looked up and grinned, flashing two tiny teeth, then went back to filling three small wooden bowls with grass and smashed yellow petals.

"She's such a beautiful baby, you and Glen have done well." The warm, soft voice sounded in Laura's mind, and seemed to originate all around her.

Laura missed the hole in the button and stabbed the needle into her finger. "Ma? It's been so long since I've heard your voice." She sucked the oozing tip of her finger, glanced at June, then continued the conversation in her head instead of speaking out loud again.

"Time isn't the same on this side. I have some important news for you." The tone was different, the words carried a sense of urgency.

Laura's hands tightened on the shirt in her lap. She kept her eyes on June but focused on Ma's words.

"You need to leave Seminole before the middle of August. Serious changes are coming and you need to get out ahead of them."

"Leave? Things are going great here. It'll be darn near impossible to get Glen to pull up stakes again."

"It doesn't matter how hard it is. You must leave Seminole by August 15th. And be sure to take all your money out of the bank before you go. That date will give you time to travel and resettle before the financial crash comes. If you wait, you risk losing everything."

"But where can we go? This is the busiest of all the oil towns, and Glen has established a great reputation as a machinist, besides his hauling business."

"You can't go to another city. You need to find a small town where he has friends or family. He'll know the right place."

"Ma, he won't leave just because I tell him to."

"You must convince him. Do or say whatever you need to, but it's vital for you to leave by the middle of August."

Laura started to protest again, but Ma was gone. How was she supposed to convince Glen? After mending three of his shirts and hemming a new dress she'd made for June, ideas were still chasing around in her head. She folded the clothes in the mending basket, popped the sewing box on top and carried them inside.

When she returned, June was still playing with her bowls and some empty thread bobbins, ignoring the dolls and blocks scattered around. "Come on, baby girl. We need to get you cleaned up and fed before your nap." She picked the baby up, and brushed off the dirt and grass.

Laura washed June's face and hands, changed her diaper and dress, and put her back on the kitchen floor. "Better check the beans before you eat, since you're such a slowpoke."

Fragrant steam escaped the simmering navy beans when she lifted the lid off the cast-iron pot. She stirred the simmering beans, her face enveloped by the warm mist, and worked around the ham hock that bobbed in the bubbling stock. Her gaze fell on the stack of newspapers in a bin by the door. She wondered how long it had been since she'd read one through, front to back, like Miss Emma had taught her.

"There's an idea," she said to June, who had pulled herself up on her feet against a chair. "I can skim the papers for financial stories and maybe find enough to convince Glen, without bringing Ma into it."

She grabbed a stack of papers and turned them upside down on the table so she could look at the oldest ones first. "Come on, Junebug," she said, lifting the baby onto her lap and opened the buttons on her blouse. "Time to eat before you go down for a nap."

June nursed with gusto, her little hands stroking and kneading her mama's skin. Laura smoothed the baby's damp hair out of her face, overwhelmed with love for this tiny being and determined to protect her family no matter what it took. Laura cradled June with one arm and spread the newspaper open with the other.

She read headlines and skimmed stories from over two months of weekly papers and stopped only when it was time to put the sleeping baby to bed.

Glen found her in the kitchen pulling cornbread out of the oven. "How are my girls today?" He leaned in for a quick kiss, then opened the icebox and pulled out a pitcher of cold water.

"Junebug should wake up any minute." Laura cut and moved golden squares from the baking pan to a serving platter. "Go wash up, supper will be on the table when you get back."

Glen nodded and left the room, patting Laura's bottom on the way out. Would his frisky mood make it easier or harder to talk about moving?

CHAPTER TWENTY-ONE
The Second Sight

"What's going on?" Glen said when Laura returned from putting June to bed. "You've been skittish as a long-tailed cat in a room full of rockers ever since I got home. Sit down and talk to me."

Laura started to deny, then exhaled and plopped in her chair across from the sofa where Glen sat. "You're right, I am on edge." She rubbed her hands together, then clasped them in her lap. "When you asked me to move to Seminole because you had a hunch about the oil boom, I said yes. It worked because the timing was perfect. Later, lots of folks had the same idea, but ended up without a decent place to live or dependable jobs."

Glen didn't respond, just sat and stared.

"Well, I think we need to leave now, or at least in the next month." Laura leaned forward and raised her hands before Glen could speak. "The news is full of falling prices for oil, and crop prices have been down for a couple of years. Lately, some of the stories have even talked about a possible stock crash or problems with the banks."

"Come on, those stories aren't new, and we're still pumping oil like crazy. Sure, there've been rough patches, but the stocks have been up for a long time. Why should we pull out now while I'm making good money?"

"We were earning decent money before in Tulsa, but, we moved to get the jump on things. I think we should leave before the boom goes south on us."

Glen stood, hands on his hips. "No, our savings are growing and I'm working almost every day." He walked over to the radio and turned it on. "We'd be fools to leave now. And besides, where would we go?" He twisted the dial to KFGF, then sat down to listen to his favorite Grand Old Opry songs, ignoring Laura.

She was afraid of that. Now he's mad and determined not to listen. Laura stared at her husband, noting his rigid posture and white knuckles. No point saying anything else tonight.

Laura tried for three days to steer the conversation back to moving, but Glen deflected her attempts. On the fourth day, determined to make him listen, she put the baby to bed, marched into the living room and turned off the radio.

"I was listening to that," Glen said. "Turn it back on."

"No, you've been changing the subject every time I try to talk to you about moving. We need to sort this out tonight."

"Nothing to talk about. I told you we're not leaving." Glen sat back on the couch and crossed his legs. His hands rested in his lap, fingers curled into his palms.

"Not this time, Glen. You're going to listen instead of making a pronouncement like some kind of king." Laura felt her voice rise in pitch and volume. "Your decision to come here was right, based on some news stories and your gut feeling. Well, my gut feelings count, too, and it's telling me we need to start our preparations to leave by the middle of August. I followed you here because I believe in you. Now it's your turn to have faith in me."

"I listened to you. I even talked to some of my buddies about what you said, and nobody thinks it's near time to give up yet. Unless you've got some kind of crystal ball to tell the future ... and can prove it ... we're staying right here, and that's final."

"Final? That's final?" Laura stepped closer to the couch, looking down into Glen's face. Blood rushed through her ears. She took a deep breath to calm herself. "I don't need a crystal ball to know things. And I can prove that right now." She stopped, closed her eyes for a moment, then sat down next to him.

"I know how your brother Bobby died. In fact, I saw the whole thing in a vision, and I see it over and over again in your nightmares."

Glen's face flushed. "I told you how my brother died, and I probably talk while I'm dreaming. No magic in that." He leaned toward her and spit out his next words. "But it's pretty low to use his death against me."

"You never told me the details." Laura lowered her voice and reached out to touch his hand, only to have him pull it away. "Both of you were running next to each other through heavy gunfire toward some trees when he went down on his face. When you turned him over there was a bullet hole in the left side of his chest. You fell on top of him, sobbing, but a sergeant forced you to leave his body. You never saw him again."

The blood drained out of Glen's face, changing it from flushed to dead white. He shook his head from side to side in denial and started to stand.

"I saw you when you got home, too, limping down a quiet road to your house. The front door was bright blue, and flowerbeds lined the sidewalk. Barbara opened the door and took you to see your mother. She was in a narrow bed in a back bedroom. You held her hand, but she died minutes after you arrived."

"Stop it. Just stop it." Glen yelled, then dropped his face into his hands. "Barbara shouldn't have told you all this." He shuddered and kept his face hidden.

Laura couldn't help the tears that rolled from her eyes. "Barbara didn't tell me anything, honey. Barbara has never known the details of Bobby's death. And when she cried in your arms after your mother died, she didn't hear you apologize to your Mama for breaking your promise to bring Bobby home safe."

Glen's hands shook as he lowered them into his lap. His eyes glistened with unshed tears. "How can you know these things? It's not possible."

"I don't know how it works and I can't control what I see. I've seen visions and visits from my ma. They're called second sight."

"But your ma is dead. She can't visit you. That's crazy talk."

"I know it sounds crazy, but Ma has talked to me off and on throughout the years, most often when there's something important that I need to know."

The color crept back into Glen's face, but his eyes were still wide. "Is she the one telling you we have to move?"

"Yes. She said we need to leave by the middle of August and must take all our money out of the bank in cash. She said something very bad is going to happen, and we need time to get away from the city and settled in a quiet, safe place."

"But where would we go?"

"She said you would know, that it would be to a friend or family member of yours."

"Laura, tell me the truth. Do you actually believe that your dead ma was here giving you advice for the future?" Glen's voice broke as if it hurt to say the words.

"Yes, honey, I do, without a single doubt."

Glen nodded but didn't say another word. They sat together on the couch, both deep in thought. When they went to bed, Glen curled up facing the edge of the bed, rather than spooning around her body. Neither had any bad dreams during the night, but when Laura woke in the morning, she found him asleep on the couch.

CHAPTER TWENTY-TWO
No Shoes
Seven miles outside of Geddes, South Dakota, August 1932, Three Years Later

Laura moved the rocker as she sat on the narrow porch of their two-room shack. Her left arm tingled from the weight of nine-month-old Jimmy. He was still nursing, but almost asleep. Four-year-old June ran circles around her brother, Raymond, almost two, in the dirt yard a few feet from the porch. Both children were barefoot, dressed in coveralls, giggling as they played. Their feet kicked up powdery dust that filled the air and settled on their faces and hair.

She'd never imagined a place like this when they left Seminole. Glen's uncle Dennis' property was flat and gray, the color leached out of the plants and trees by the wind and sand storms. The silence was profound, since there weren't any neighbors nearby, and even the animals seemed too lethargic to make much noise -- different in every way from the noisy, oil-boom city they'd fled.

Dennis was a gentle, sweet man who made the family welcome. His wife, Gladys, was snippy and brittle, the opposite of Dennis. Laura understood that a family tragedy had drained all the warmth out of Gladys, but still found it difficult to hold her temper around the woman.

The trip had taken five uncomfortable days. Traveling with a fussy toddler meant frequent stops for June to stretch her legs and play by the road, costing extra hours on the road each day. They avoided hotels and restaurants, living on the food they'd packed in an icebox tied down in the back of the truck. They'd slept on the two mattresses they'd piled alongside and covered with blankets. Glen had cut windows in opposite sides of the truck box, complete with screens and shades, so they could have light and air inside.

Glen hadn't wanted anyone to know what they were doing, in part to avoid getting fired when the company learned he was planning to leave, and as a safeguard to prevent their savings being stolen. He withdrew their money in stages to avoid attention and questions, then put the cash in a mason jar and hid it in the crawl space at the back of the house until they were ready to go.

"Mama, look, Papa's coming," June shouted, bouncing up and down.

Laura's attention snapped back to the children dancing in front of her. "Raymond, don't you go running off by yourself."

"Can we go, Mama, please?" June said, hopping from one foot to the other.

"Sure, but hold on to your brother. And don't drag him."

The two children were off, as fast as little Ray's legs could go. He did his best to keep up with his sister, who he adored.

Laura smiled, that boy was the image of his papa. She couldn't imagine life without any of our children, but it sure would have been easier if the boys had been born back in Seminole or even Tulsa.

She shuddered thinking about the difficult births in the shack with only Glen and his aunt Gladys to help her. Glen hadn't known what to do, and Gladys had no softness or compassion in her nature.

Who could have guessed that the only doctor in Geddes would be treating a farmer's broken leg when Raymond was born, then up and died three months before Jimmy arrived? She didn't know what she would have done without Mouse. Mouse's image and voice were clear in Laura's mind, just like Ma's. And just like messages and images from Ma, Laura kept Mouse's presence during the births secret.

Glen was still about two hundred yards away, between his Uncle Dennis and Aunt Gladys's two-story house and the equipment shed he'd turned into a machine shop. A sliver of the barn was visible from the other side of the house. Two additional structures, a large chicken coop and a well-house, were out of sight behind the barn. Both the barn and the house had been painted in the past, but only patches of color remained after the scouring effects of the sandstorms had plagued the area for the last couple of years.

Jimmy was asleep, so Laura buttoned her blouse and carried him inside to his bed. She watched him sleep for a few minutes, then went back outside on the porch. The children closed the distance to their Pa, who opened his arms wide. Glen grabbed them both in a giant hug, then put June down and slung Raymond up on his shoulders, holding Raymond's little legs in place with his right arm. Glen leaned over and picked up June with his other arm. She wrapped her legs around his waist, her arms around his chest.

"Mama, Mama," Raymond shouted from his perch, waving one arm while he held fast to Glen's hair with the other.

"Me, too, Mama, look at me, too." June waved, a huge grin on her face.

Laura waved back, enjoying the sight. She knew Glen adored his children, and they loved his attention.

"Okay, down you go," Glen said when the trio reached the porch. He held the door open

248

after putting the kids on their feet and pointed inside. "Go wash up for supper. June, help your little brother."

Supper was simple -- chicken stock thickened with cornstarch, loaded with chopped potatoes, onions, and turnips. Chunks of bread soaked up the juice on each plate. The meal was seasoned with conversation as each member of the family talked about their day. Even Jimmy chimed in with squeals and giggles after he woke up, moving back and forth between Laura and Glen's laps.

Once the kitchen was clean, and the children were in bed, Laura joined her husband outside. "All three asleep?" Glen said from his seat on the porch swing. When Laura nodded, he scooted over and patted the place next to him.

She sat down, took a deep breath of the evening air, then placed her hand over his. "You're such a good father. Truth is, I never knew a man could be so good with kids."

Glen turned his hand over so their palms were together and squeezed her fingers. "Our family is everything to me."

They held hands and rocked, at peace, until Glen cleared his throat. "Listen, Gladys invited her pastor to supper tomorrow after evening services and wants us to join them."

"The kids, too? You know she doesn't think they should talk at the table."

"They'll manage. And they need to learn to respect rules in other people's homes."

"You're right." Laura sighed and took a deep breath. "If only Gladys wasn't so contrary. I've tried everything, but she seems to hate me and our kids."

"It's not you," Glen said. "Uncle Dennis says that when their twin boys drowned in the cistern ten years ago, the best parts of Gladys died, too. She's still hurting inside and blames him for letting them die."

"I know you're right." Laura wrapped her arms around herself. "And losing both of them at the same time? Can't even imagine the pain." She closed her eyes and shook her head, then looked up at Glen. "Don't know why she blames Dennis, though. Who could have guessed the twins could lift the trap door and fall in?"

"Guess that's why she turned to religion, trying to make sense of it all."

"And chose a church as rigid and joyless as she is." Laura put her hand up to Glen's lips before he could speak. "Don't worry, we'll go for your Uncle Dennis's sake, and we'll make sure the kids are on their best behavior... and I'll be nice to Gladys even if it kills me."

"No shoes, no." Raymond kicked and wailed.

"Sorry, little man. Look at your sister, she has her shoes on." Glen held fast to his son's foot, pushing the shoe in place.

The walk to Dennis and Glady's house was slower than usual since Glen held both June and Raymond's hands while Laura carried Jimmy. Glen promised a rough and tumble play session after supper if the kids were good and minded their manners.

"Remember, best behavior," Laura whispered when the family reached the front porch.

Dennis opened the screen door and stepped aside. "Welcome. Come on in. Gladys and the preacher are already at the table."

Soon everyone sat around a cherry wood table covered with a heavy damask tablecloth and napkins, flowered china, silver cutlery, glass pitchers of water and milk, and a variety of steaming, serving dishes. Glen was between Gladys and Raymond, who sat on an upended cooking pot to raise him up to the edge of the table. Laura, with Jimmy on her lap, was between Raymond and June. Dennis sat next to June, ready to help her if she needed anything, with Reverend Lowell on Dennis' other side.

Gladys tapped her glass to get everyone's attention, then introduced Reverend Lowell to Glen and Laura. Glen stood and leaned across Gladys to shake the pastor's limp hand.

Everything about Reverend Lowell was large -- his doughy, sweaty hands, his wide torso above a belly that strained his shirt buttons, and his round bald head nestled atop multiple chins tucked into his hunched shoulders.

"It's a pleasure meeting you both. Sister Gladys has often talked about your family since you came to live on their farm." Reverend Lowell's chair creaked as he settled into place. "Glen, would you like to lead everyone in saying grace before we begin our meal?"

Glen's eyes widened. "Uh, no thanks. I think it'd be better if you did that, you being a preacher and all."

"It'd be my honor. Let's bow our heads and pray."

The prayer ran on and on. Laura peeked up to catch first June's eyes, then Raymond's, and shook her head at them when they started to fidget. Each time she could feel Gladys's glare.

"Amen," Reverend Lowell said, dropping his hands from in front of his chest. "Sister Gladys, this looks wonderful." He reached for the roast beef platter and started serving himself. "Brother Webber, I've been hoping we'd see you and your lovely family in church one Sunday."

Glen shrugged, "Never was much of a churchgoer. Besides, it's hard to go to church with three small children. Wouldn't be fair to disturb other people."

"True, but children need to learn proper behavior in the Lord's house. The Bible says whoever believes and is baptized will be saved, but whoever does not believe will be condemned to Hell. Mark sixteen, sixteen. I'm sure you don't want to send your little ones to Hell just because you didn't take them to church."

Laura's sharp intake of breath was ignored, as the pastor continued.

"And you're in luck. Sister Gladys is in charge of the church nursery, so you'd never have to worry about your children when they're in her care."

Glen's face flushed, but after looking at Dennis, he stayed silent. Neither Dennis nor Laura said another word during the meal. Reverend Lowell preached on a variety of subjects as they ate. Gladys watched him with rapt attention, only interjecting to ask a question or praise his insight.

When Gladys saw that the pastor's plate was clean, after several helpings of everything, she jumped up. "My word, Reverend Lowell, it is sure a pleasure to serve someone who appreciates good food like you do. I hope you saved room for some berry pie."

"Always room for pie, Sister Gladys."

Laura stood and handed Jimmy to Glen so she could help clear the table and serve dessert. Raymond tried to get up, too, but knocked his milk glass over. He started to cry as the tablecloth soaked up the liquid.

"It's okay, son. Let your mama help you down."

"Okay?" Gladys said. "It's not okay. My best damask tablecloth is soaked with milk, and he could have broken the glass. That boy deserves a good spanking."

"Aunt Gladys, it was just an accident." Glen handed Jimmy to Laura, picked Raymond up, thumbed his tears away and kissed his forehead before putting him down on the floor.

Reverend Lowell jumped in before Gladys could speak. "Spare the rod and spoil the child. A loving father has to be stern to save children from the fires of hell."

"Mama, I'm afraid of fire." June began to cry.

Glen started to speak, but Laura interrupted and said, "Dennis, thank you very much for your hospitality, but our children are upset and I think we need to leave." She put her free arm around June, glanced at Glen, then turned to Gladys and Reverend Lowell. "You need to apologize to Glen. He's a fine man and the best, most loving father I've ever known. My pa beat all of us children with his fists, with his belt, with anything he could get hold of. He even beat my oldest sister with a horsewhip so bad her back is still scarred. That didn't make us better people or teach us to love God. We hated him and escaped from his house as fast as we could." Laura didn't even wait for a response, just marched out the door with Jimmy and June.

Laura didn't get far before she heard Glen's steps on the porch. Her whole body shook with anger, which intensified when she felt tears streaking down her cheeks.

"Slow down, honey," Glen said. "Gladys will get over herself, and both Dennis and I agree with you. And I don't give a fig about what that blowhard preacher thinks."

He put Raymond down, took Jimmy from Laura, and wrapped his arm around her waist. "I'm just sorry you had to grow up with a man like that."

"Shoes off." Raymond plopped down in the dirt and pulled his shoes and socks off. June sat right next to him and yanked hers off, too.

Laura began to protest their sitting in the dirt wearing their best clothes, then gave up when Glen started laughing. He picked up the discarded shoes and socks, tucked them in his pockets, and chased after the kids with his arms wide. How could she stay mad watching him swing one child around after another, all three giggling and laughing the whole way home?

CHAPTER TWENTY-THREE
She Didn't Mean To Harm Them
May 1933, Nine Months Later

As it turned out, they were no longer having family meals with Gladys, and Laura and the children were no longer receiving invitations to Reverend Lowell's church. Glen still worked with his Uncle Dennis though, and often shared the midday meal with him and Gladys. She even gave Glen a Bible, telling him every family needed one to record their history of marriages, births, and deaths.

Then, on a Saturday evening, when they went to bed, Glen told Laura he was going to church in the morning.

"Why? You've never been interested before, especially after that awful meal with her preacher."

"Not really interested, but Gladys asked me to go as a favor to her. Her boys died in May when they were only seven years old, and there'll be a special remembrance during the service." Glen turned to face Laura. "Besides, we should teach the kids about Jesus and the Bible."

"I guess so, but we'll teach them, not that awful pastor."

"He's not so bad. I mean, he's kind of stuffy and full of himself, but he does know his Bible and cares about people being saved."

After that first Sunday, Glen went once a month, always as a favor to Gladys. Dennis often didn't want to go. Laura didn't mind and even encouraged Glen when he started teaching the children Bible stories and saying grace at supper. But then, the questions began each evening, after the children were in bed.

Laura joined Glen on the porch swing one Sunday evening.
"Have you heard from your ma since we moved here?"

Laura tilted her head and stared at him, not sure how to answer. "I could feel her with me when the boys were born and heard her singing afterward."

"You never said anything. Why did you hide it from me?" Glen's voice was tight.

"Hide it? Nothing to hide. She was just sending comfort and love for her new grandchildren." Laura could feel the tension in Glen's body even though they weren't touching.

"Are you sure it's your ma? The devil works in strange ways, you know. His demons are good at tricking people to mess with their minds and turn them against God."

Laura turned her back to him. "I can't believe you'd say that." Her throat closed, stifling the anger and hurt that threatened to spill out.

"Well, it's not normal to say you talk to a dead person. And claiming she's talked to you for years is plain crazy." Glen waited for a response that never came, then he said, "What if you're wrong? What if the devil is talking to you, and will go after the children next? I'm just thinking of them."

She didn't, couldn't, say another word.

Two days later, Glen took June and Raymond with him when he left in the morning. He was planning to build new nesting boxes for the chicken house and said the kids could play near him. Knowing how much they loved being with their papa, she couldn't turn down the chance to have a few hours with just Jimmy underfoot.

The kids danced with excitement as they got ready in the morning. When they stepped off the porch and walked a few steps, Glen grabbed June's hands and spun her around in circles, her legs flying, as she screamed in delight. After enough time to make them both dizzy, he brought her to a stop. "That's enough, Junebug."

"Me, too, my turn," Raymond said, reaching up with both hands.

"I've got a better idea for you." Glen lifted his son up onto his shoulders. "June's too big for this."

Laura watched them leave, not turning away until they had almost reached the big house.

"I thought that boy would never fall asleep," Laura said hours later as she tiptoed out the front door carrying a wooden milk carton.

She emptied the carton, then turned it upside down. She put one of the big metal bowls on top of the carton, then pulled the other bowl into her lap, and tucked a burlap bag half full of potatoes next to her in the chair. Her paring knife slipped under the surface, peeling long strips of potato skin that fell into the bowl in her lap. She tossed the naked tubers into the bowl perched on the carton.

She listened to the wind as she worked, grateful that the house shielded her from the gusts. Her mind flashed to a memory of sitting at her ma's feet on the porch long ago, watching long spirals spinning away from the knife in her ma's hands. "I miss you, Ma, but you'd be proud of how Ruth took care of all of us," Laura said, enjoying the sound of her own voice against the backdrop of the wind. "Guess I'd better take this stuff inside and start preparations for dinner."

As she stood, holding the full bowl of peelings in her hand, she saw Glen and the children walking home. Raymond was nestled across his father's chest instead of on his shoulders. June walked alone, several feet away from Glen, instead of holding his hand.

Panic closed Laura's throat. Something was wrong. Dropping the bowl, she sprinted off the porch toward her family. June saw her coming and ran to meet her, leaving Glen and Raymond far behind.

"Mama, she hit Raymond real hard. I tried to stop her, but I couldn't." June was breathing hard when she ran into Laura's arms.

Laura knelt in the dirt, holding June, and kissed the top of her head. "Who hit Raymond? Take a deep breath and tell me what happened."

June turned her face up, lips trembling and tears streaming down her cheeks. "He didn't do it on purpose. It was just an accident. But she got real mad and started yelling."

"Start at the beginning, honey. What did he do?"

"We were playing tag in the side yard. I went real slow since Raymond's so little. He ran back and forth between the sheets on the line, but he fell." June's tears spilled harder. "He reached for the sheet to keep from falling and it came off the line into the dirt. He fell down anyway, and was sitting in the dirt holding on to the sheet when, when ..." Words gave way to sobs. June buried her face in Laura's neck.

"When Gladys came out and found the sheet on the ground?"

June nodded, but kept her face buried.

"What did she do?" Laura took June's shoulders and moved her back a little, then raised her chin so they were facing one another. "I need to know exactly what happened."

"She yelled about her dirty sheet, then said Raymond needed to be punished for not being more careful. She grabbed a stick from under the oak tree, pulled Raymond up by his arm and hit him."

Laura was shaking now, but with anger instead of fear like her daughter.

"I told her to leave him alone, but she hit him a couple more times." June's face was red and wet with tears. "Then she said somebody better teach me not to talk back and hit me, too. Three times, Mama, she hit me three times. It hurt."

Laura pulled her close again. "I'm so sorry. Gladys had no right to do this." Glen was just a step away. Laura turned her head to face him as she questioned June. "Where was your father while Gladys was hitting you?"

"I don't know. When she threw the stick down, Raymond and me were both crying. Papa came to us then and we started home."

Laura's gaze never moved from Glen's ashen face. He stared down, not meeting her eyes. Raymond clambered down and ran to join his sister in Laura's arms. Glen never said a word.

"Mama, Aunt Gladys said we'll burn in Hell, that we're heathens and heathens burn in Hell. I'm scared of fire. What's a heathen?" June's words ran together in a rush. Raymond nodded in agreement.

"Don't you worry about burning. In fact, don't you worry about anything Gladys said to you at all. She's a sick woman, and I won't ever let her around either of you again."

Laura got her feet underneath her but stayed low to the ground. "Raymond, climb on my back for a horsey ride." She got him situated, little hands clasped around her neck, then stood up. His legs wrapped around her waist. She held them in place with one arm, then extended her other hand to June. "Come on. Let's go home so I can look at both of you."

Glen followed behind them all the way, his steps on the porch the only sound he made.

"Okay big boy, let's take a look at you." Laura sat on a chair and slipped Raymond's coveralls off his shoulders and down to his ankles. "Turn around."

When her son's backside came into view, Laura sucked in her breath and bit her lip. An angry red welt, edged in blue, made a diagonal line across his upper thighs. Part of another welt was forming on his back, sticking out of his waistband. She peeled his drawers down, revealing the rest of the welt that extended down from his back onto one side of his bottom, and another one across both his buttocks. None of the three had bled, but all looked puffy and painful against his tender skin.

"Hold still while I get your nightshirt and the Cloverine Salve." Laura's hands shook, but she kept her voice soft so the children wouldn't be frightened. She took only a minute to fetch the nightshirt and help Raymond slip it on.

She opened the black and white tin with the little green flowers around the edge and scooped some of the thick paste out with her fingers. "This may hurt a little," she said, then smoothed the salve on the welts. "Good boy. Now go lie down in bed on your tummy. I'll bring you something to drink that'll help you feel better after I take care of June."

June, who'd watched the whole procedure, took Raymond's place in front of her mother. She slipped on the nightshirt Laura gave her, then pushed down the coveralls from underneath.

"Do I have to take off my bloomers, too?"

"Yes, Junebug, I need to see your whole backside."

Two angry marks streaked across June's lower back, with a third crossing the flesh just

above the crease of her bottom. Laura struggled
to keep her voice under control. "Hold still
honey, so I can put the salve on these marks. I'll
be as careful as I can."

Laura put away the Cloverine, then
pulled the glass bottle of Konjola Syrup from
the shelf. The bottle was only half-full of dark
brown liquid, which the label described as "A
Medicine of Proven Merit". She shook their
bottle, then gave each child one spoonful to
calm them and soothe the pain. Soon, both were
asleep in their bed.

Laura, every muscle tense, went out on
the porch and stared at Gladys's house. She
crossed arms, and her fingernails pressed into
her palms.

"She was wrong, no question, but she
didn't mean to harm them," Glen said, standing
behind her.

"I don't care what she meant." Laura didn't
turn around, and her voice was as tense as her
body. "She hurt our children, children we're
supposed to protect. I meant what I said before
... she will never see or touch either of them

again." Without a glance at Glen, Laura went back inside, leaving him alone on the porch.

CHAPTER TWENTY-FOUR
Never Again

A long night followed, the bedroom was small and crowded, with two beds and a crib in the tight space, and storage chests full of clothing tucked under each bed. June and Raymond slept through, thanks to the Konjola Syrup, but Laura kept jerking awake. She could see the children and hear their breathing from her bed. She felt compelled to get up and touch them each time.

Jimmy woke and pulled himself up with the crib bars just before dawn. "Good morning, sweetie," Laura whispered, reaching for him before he made a sound. Once she had him clean and dry, she carried him out of the bedroom so he could play while she fixed breakfast.

The food was ready when Glen came out of the tiny water closet, wet hair slicked back, face ruddy from the razor. He pulled a delighted Jimmy up onto his lap and handed him a piece of potato pancake to chew on. "That's good, isn't it, Jimmy boy? Won't be too long until you get a plate of your own."

When Glen finished eating, he headed to the door. Laura followed him, holding Jimmy in her arms. "Glen, you know we have to leave here."

"No, I don't know that." He turned to face her, the door handle in his hand.

"I meant what I said yesterday. Gladys will not see or touch our children again."

"They're my children too, and Dennis is my uncle. Other than Barbara, he's my only kin." He took a deep breath. "I'm as sick at heart as you, but it won't happen again."

"No, it won't, because we are not staying here. You didn't protect them yesterday, so how can we know you'll be able to protect them in the future."

Glen reared back as though she'd slapped him, color draining from his face. "Are you accusing me of hurting my kids?"

"Of course not. You'd never hurt them, but Gladys did and you didn't stop her."

Laura watched Glen's head sink into slumped shoulders, then said, "We can't stay here and take the chance of her hurting them again."

Glen stepped through the door onto the porch. He stopped at the edge, hands on his hips. "Where will we go? If not for Dennis, we wouldn't have had a home since leaving Seminole."

"I don't know, but we'll figure it out."

Voice dripping with sarcasm, Glen said. "We? Or is your dead ma calling the shots with her messages again?"

Laura bit back an angry retort. "The only message I needed was the marks on our children's bodies."

CHAPTER TWENTY-FIVE
Not A Good Night

The Cloverine Salve and Kinjara Syrup did their jobs well. June and Raymond slept much later than usual, waking long after Jimmy was up and fed. Laura heard their voices from the bedroom and turned the heat back on under the cornmeal mush she'd cooked hours ago. She added a little water to the pot and stirred it with a wooden spoon.

"Come to the table you two," Laura said. "If you don't want a bowl full of lukewarm, lumpy mush, quit dallying around."

"Aw, you know I hate cornmeal mush, Mama." June folded her arms. "Can't we have something else?"

"No, you can't, and you know better than whining like that." Laura put two glasses of milk on the table and pulled out June's chair. "Sit down and eat."

June grimaced and sat on her chair, then said. "Ow, that hurts." She stood back up, her hands touching her back.

"Sorry, Junebug. Do you want to sit on a pillow?"

When she nodded, Laura looked at the open bedroom door and called out. "Raymond, get up right now and bring June's pillow. Bring yours too, so you can both sit on them at the table."

"Me, too." Jimmy ran into the bedroom to get his pillow out of the crib. He threw it on the floor near the door and plopped his bottom in the middle. Jimmy's attention turned to playing with a cooking pan and lid, and a pile of empty thread spools.

"You kids have to stay inside, today," Laura said as the children finished their breakfast. "The wind's fierce outside. Not a full-on dust storm, thank the lord, but the doors and windows need to stay shut to keep the dirt from blowing in."

"Awww, it's no fun playing inside," June said, Raymond nodded at her side.

"Well, if you don't want to play, I'm sure I can find some chores for you to do." Hands on her hips, Laura's stare wilted their pouty expressions. "First thing, get changed out of your nightclothes and go wash up. When you're finished, straighten the beds."

The wind whistled outside until early afternoon. The house was stuffy and hot with the doors and windows closed, but fine-grained sand found its way inside, covering the window sills and creating a ridge on the floor in front of the doors.

Laura wished she didn't have to keep the stove going, but the chicken from last night's supper would go bad if it wasn't cooked. She stripped all the meat from the bones of the carcass, and from the partially eaten pieces, then put it into the icebox. The bones and giblets went into a pot of water to boil. A second pot, full of water and beans that had soaked overnight, also simmered on the stove.

All morning, as she cooked and interacted with the children, Laura mulled over what they'd need to take with them when they left. The biggest challenge was not knowing how long they'd be on the road or where they'd end up. She remembered how cramped and uncomfortable the move from Seminole had been, and with two more children, the trip would be even worse.

When the wind died, June and Raymond raced outside, while Jimmy trailed behind. Laura shut off the stove burners and carried a basket of mending to the porch. "Oh, my goodness, it feels good to get off my feet." She sank onto the porch swing and placed the sewing materials beside her.

The children played one game after another, chasing back and forth and around the house -- tag, hide and go seek, ring-around-the-rosies -- while Laura replaced missing buttons, fixed tears and torn pockets, and let down hems and cuffs. Jimmy couldn't keep up with the older ones, so he settled down, with his wooden cars, at the base of the porch steps.

"Mama, look." June pointed toward the machine shop behind Dennis's house. "Papa's coming. Can we go meet him?"

Fine sandy dirt coated all three children's clothes. Jimmy was the worst. He giggled while throwing handfuls of powdery sand in the air, most of which settled back down on his hair and clothes.

"June, you and Raymond can go meet your papa." Laura stood and reached for her grimy toddler. "But you, Jimmy boy, are staying with me and getting cleaned up."

Laura changed Jimmy's clothes after scrubbing his face and hands. She turned him loose just as Glen, June, and Raymond reached the porch steps.

"Leave your dirty shoes outside," she said through the screen door. "And brush off as much dust as you can before coming in. Supper'll be ready by the time you're cleaned up."

Glen was the last to the table. He folded his hands, glanced at Laura, then said a short grace before reaching for a big serving bowl with steam rising from the surface.

"Beans again? I'm sick of beans." June glared at Laura, then turned to Glen. "Why can't we have something else besides chicken or beans?"

"Eat what's on the table." Glen's voice was firm as he filled each child's plate with beans and boiled greens. "You should be grateful. Lots of people are going hungry these days."

Laura passed out slices of bread and filled everyone's glasses with water. She noticed how haggard Glen looked, but didn't say anything. He chatted with the kids while they ate, then went out to the porch swing, where he stayed while Laura cleaned the kitchen and put the children to bed.

"They're out already." Laura stepped outside and joined Glen on the swing. She sighed, as she rested her head against the slats and glanced sideways.

Glen leaned forward, resting his forearms on his thighs. Hands clasped together, shoulders slumped, he didn't say a word.

They sat together in the thick silence.

Was she wrong to insist that they leave? An unbidden response to the pain that radiated from her husband, popped into Laura's mind. The answer came just as fast. No, no way were her children going to grow up like she did. She chewed her lip, wishing she could find words to help Glen understand.

The quiet stretched on, but there was no peace in it. Then Glen, his eyes cast down, said, "I told Dennis and Gladys we're leaving." His voice was low-pitched and a little hoarse.

"What did Dennis say?" Laura found she was having trouble speaking around the lump in her throat.

"Just that he understood. He begged me to let him know when we got settled, because he hates to lose touch." Glen glanced sideways at Laura, then focused back on his hands. "He'll help me get the truck ready, and with supplies and such."

"Dennis is a good man." Laura crossed her arms and stared up at the sky, but found no answers in the blanket of stars.

Glen sighed and sat back. "Gladys said I can return with the children anytime. We'll always have a home here."

Laura's sharp retort died in her throat. There was no point in making him feel worse. They rocked in silence, staring into the night.

"I'm going to bed. Tomorrow will be a long day." Glen stood, stretched, then stepped around Laura to head back inside the house.

Laura followed him inside, and watched him undress and get into bed. He laid on his back, eyes closed. She could see his hands were clenched and the muscles in his arms were tight. She changed into her nightgown, slipped under the covers, and turned toward him.

"Good night, honey," she said.

Glen turned on his side away from her and punched the pillow under his head.

Glen stayed facing the wall, but soon began thrashing and whipping his head back and forth. His nightmare visions assaulted Laura, first with familiar scenes of his brother's death, then of his mother's sad eyes accusing him of failing to save Bobby. At that point, new scenes appeared, the first one of a landscape covered with swirling colors. She heard June, Raymond, and Jimmy screaming in pain, lost in the colored mists. The children weren't visible, but the screams were blood-curdling. Glen, frantic as he attempted to find and help them, was lost in the fog, unable to reach them. Then the vision changed and Laura saw herself and the children sinking into a lake of fire. She had a smile on her face, even as she held tight to her shrieking children. Glen, panicked, reached out for his babies. They were trying to escape and come to him, but he couldn't reach them.

"I'm so sorry," Laura whispered, trying to soothe Glen out of the horrific nightmare before he woke the children.

Glen jerked awake, his face contorted with the look of horror and panic she'd seen in the dream. Without a word, he pulled away from her outstretched hand, grabbed his pillow, and left the room.

Laura stayed in bed, tears soaking her pillow. Three times she fell asleep only to wake up immersed in his nightmares once again. Each time she ached for his pain, but feared making things worse if she went to him. It had been a long time since she'd prayed, but she prayed with all her heart for Glen to find peace.

CHAPTER TWENTY-SIX
That's Not Fair

When Glen stirred on the sofa the next morning, Laura was busy firing up the stove. Without a word, he went into the bedroom and changed clothes. She poured batter on the griddle just before he pulled his chair out and sat down at the table.

"Kids waking up, yet?" Laura flipped the first cake over.

"Not yet."

Laura slid a plate on the table, then poured two cups of coffee. She curled her fingers around the steaming mug. "Guess I'd better start making plans about what to take with us."

"You do that." Glen focused his attention on his plate. When he finished, he put his dishes in the sink and started for the door. "I'll be late."

Laura nodded, then followed him, placing her hand on his arm. "Should I pack you a dinner pail?"

"Don't bother. I'll eat with Dennis."

Glen pushed through the door and walked across the porch. Laura watched him until he was halfway to his uncle's house, hurt that he never glanced back.

"Mama, is Papa already gone?" June stood just inside the screen door, rubbing her eyes.

"Yes, he has a long day ahead," Laura said. She joined June and gave her a quick hug. "Are your brothers awake?"

"Yes, and they're jumping on the bed. Raymond's teaching Jimmy how to reach for the sky when he jumps."

"I'd better bring them both down to earth before somebody gets hurt. Set the table and I'll get your brothers."

Breakfast was a lively affair, since Jimmy kept throwing his arms in the air and squealing as Raymond egged him on. Laura and June giggled right along with the boys.

After the children were fed and dressed, Laura put a fresh coating of Cloverine Salve on June's and Raymond's welts before sending them outside to play.

"Don't know what we'd do without this stuff," Laura said to no one in particular. She pulled out the drawer. "Cuts, dry skin, bug bites, it takes care of everything." She counted three full tins of the salve besides the open one she slipped in with the others.

Laura remembered the day, back in Tulsa, when she'd purchased a big supply of the salve. A boy, maybe eleven, holding his cap in his hands, had told her a sad story about why he needed to sell all his stock that day. He said his mother was a widow, confined at home with his baby sister. Since his father had passed, he had to be the man of the house and needed a wagon so he could do errands for his poor mama. There were only ten tins left, just $.25 each, and that was the exact amount he had to sell to earn the wagon.

Glen had joined her at the door during the boy's story, but hadn't said a word when she agreed to buy the last of the boy's inventory.

After the boy left, Laura had been surprised when Glen grinned and called her a softie. When she protested, he said he'd used the same kind of story when he'd sold Cloverine door to door, and he bet the boy would use the same story with all their neighbors. The next day, Laura had checked and discovered three other women on the street had also bought the story and ten tins of the salve.

"I guess I better get started on the moving list," she said out loud. "At least we'll have enough Cloverine."

Laura checked on the children, playing in the front yard, then cleaned the kitchen. Once finished, she pulled a notebook and pencil out of a drawer. "Sure can tell I don't write much." She picked up a knife and began whittling wood away from the lead until the pencil had a nice sharp point.

Laura cleaned up the shavings, dropped the knife back into the drawer, and then settled down to started her list.

Food

Pots, pans, dishes

Clothing

"This will never do." Laura put the pencil down in disgust. "Two adults and three kids living in a truck for who knows how long? I've got to rethink this."

She stood, stretched her arms, and watched the children play for a few minutes. "Enough of that, I'm wasting time."

Back in the chair, Laura started again.

<u>Food</u> - bags of wheat, corn flour, and sugar. As much canned food as we can get. Oil, molasses, jerky, anything dried.

They'd have to stick to staples, canned goods, and things that didn't need to stay cool. She tapped the pencil against the table. With space so limited, they wouldn't be able to store enough food for more than a few days at a time. Thank goodness they still had the little paraffin stove Glen purchased before they left Seminole.

Laura skipped to the bottom of her list and added the paraffin stove, a can opener, and fuel.

<u>Pots, pans, and dishes</u> — Stewpot, skillet, saucepan, pan lids, 5 plates, 5 bowls, 5 glasses, 2 mugs

We'll have to clean up every time we cook because there won't be room for storing dirty dishes. Once again, she moved the pencil to the bottom of the list and added the big metal basin for cleaning clothes and dishes. Water would be a big item, too.

Laura dropped the notebook and pencil when June burst through the door, yelling at the top of her lungs. "Mama, Mama, come see what Raymond and James are doing."

Laura jumped up and followed her outside.

"Look, Mama, they peed on the side of the house." June pointed at the evidence. Two bright smiles, Jimmy with his pants all bunched up around his ankles, and two wet circles that dribbled down to the dirt next to the house.

Laura hid a smile and reached down to fix Jimmy's clothes. "Okay, boys, you know you should use the toilet inside."

"Papa goes out here," Raymond said.

"I go pee, Mama," Jimmy said, reaching to claim his wet spot.

"You certainly did." Laura grabbed Jimmy's hand. "Don't touch. That's dirty."

"Aren't they in trouble?" June asked.

"Nobody else was around, so no. Sometimes boys just can't wait."

"What about girls?"

"Sorry, honey," Laura said.

"That's not fair." June fisted her hands and put them on her hips. "If they can go outside, why can't I?"

"Life's not always fair. And that's just the way it is."

Laura led the children inside, both boys laughing and June still fuming. Oh boy, that's one travel problem she hadn't thought of.

CHAPTER TWENTY-SEVEN
Long, Empty Miles
June 1933

They left on June's fifth birthday. Preparations took twelve days, and they updated their lists almost daily. The truck was the center of their plans, so Laura always deferred to Glen on how much they could take and how to pack everything. When they left, the back was full except for a small area around stacked mattresses. The roof was covered by boxes and bags roped together, with additional bags tied to the fenders and the sides of the truck box.

Dennis had been as good as his word and helped Glen find a full set of extra wheels and tires, and helped secure two large metal cans for storing extra gas in a custom rack on the outside of the truck above the rear wheel well. They fastened two matching metal cans for water on the other side. Dennis even gave Glen a bicycle for transportation in case he didn't want to use the truck.

The children were jumping with excitement the day they left. Glen and Laura knew having everyone in the truck cab would be cramped, but decided to start the trip that way as a treat. Glen sat behind the wheel, his right arm against his side as June pressed against him. Jimmy sat on Laura's right thigh, banging his fists against the outside of the locked door. Raymond perched on top of June and Laura, his body tilted toward the middle since June's lap was so much lower.

The children cheered as Glen started the truck. "We're stopping to see Dennis first." He glanced at Laura. "He's done a lot for us and I promised."

"That would be nice," Laura said. "Dennis is a good man."

Dennis leaned against the porch post, waiting as they drove up. Glen put the truck into neutral and waited inside, not wanting the children to leave their places.

"My goodness, you've got this cab packed tight as sardines in a can." Dennis shook his head as he leaned in and rested his hands on the window frame.

"Yes, sir. The kids all wanted to see out the windows, but it won't be long before they're ready to take turns with Laura in the back."

"That's good thinking," Dennis said. "We're sure going to miss you. Gladys, too. She'd be out to say goodbye, but she's feeling poorly this morning."

Sure, she wanted to say goodbye. Just to me. Gladys would love to keep Glen and the children here to herself. Laura kept her thoughts inside, not wanting to hurt Dennis.

"That's okay. You can tell her goodbye for us." Glen patted Dennis' hand.

"Miss Laura, I know Gladys can be a hard woman, and I'm sorry." Dennis sighed. "Mostly I'm sorry you didn't get to know her the way she was before. You would have liked her."

"I'm sorry too, Dennis. Take good care of her." Laura had a quick vision of a laughing, much younger Gladys chasing after two beautiful little boys. She kept her face impassive.

"Thank you for your kindness and your understanding."

Dennis nodded and stepped back. "Well, I don't want to keep you." He pulled a small box out of his overall pocket and thrust it at Glen. "Here, just some cookies for later. Don't open it now. You all better get going."

Glen and Laura both thanked him as they drove away.

Geddes was eight empty miles from Dennis's house. The town was tiny, and showed the ravages of weather and economy. All the buildings were in dire need of paint after years of sandstorms, and three out of the eight stores had been closed. Glen drove straight through, hoping to get as close to Delmont as he could before stopping for the night.

"Jimmy, be still." Laura held tight as he threw his body back and forth, banging hard onto her chest with his head. Instead of stopping, Jimmy changed directions and flopped first against the door then sideways hard against Raymond.

295

"Ow, that hurt," Raymond said. He rubbed his head and leaned away before Jimmy could get him again, but he bumped against June's chin instead.

Before June could complain, Raymond hit her. Jimmy twisted around to look at Laura and announced, "Go pee, Mama."

Glen pulled off the road onto the shoulder so Laura could open the door and put Jimmy down. Within minutes, both June and Raymond decided they had to go, too. Glen and the boys took the first turn, standing next to the truck out of sight of the road. Laura and June moved to the back of the truck and opened the doors. They climbed inside and sat on a stack of blankets.

"Don't either of you pee on the truck. Go in the dirt, you hear me?"

Glen and the boys traded places after they finished, giving June and Laura some privacy. When they finished, Laura joined the boys on the mattresses so June could sit in front. Glen had strung a rope through the handle of a door knocker attached to the back of the cab so Laura could let him know when to stop.

June was thrilled to have her papa all to herself in the cab. It was noisy and stuffy for Laura and the boys in the back, but the nest of mattresses and blankets was soft and they could stretch out. The only light came through the side windows, but it was enough for the boys to play with some wooden trucks and metal soldiers from the toy box next to the pallet.

Hours passed, marked only by brief stops. They ate their dinner, sandwiches packed that morning and boiled eggs, in the back like a picnic. The doors were wide open, letting in light and air. No air movement though, and the scenery stretched out flat and empty to the horizon, except for some fencing on both sides of the road. The fence posts tilted in different directions, and many of the connecting wires were missing or hanging loose. Tiny, symmetrical piles of sand sat on top of each post, souvenirs from the last wind.

"Can we have Uncle Dennis' cookies?" June said.

"Good idea." Glen retrieved the box from the dashboard. He opened it and gave everyone a cookie. "What the heck?" Glen moved the

remaining cookies aside to see the bottom of the
box, then pulled out ten one-dollar bills. "I can't
believe he did this. And telling us not to open
the box until later so we couldn't give the
money back."

Laura touched Glen's arm. "Next town,
we've got to send a note and thank them both."

CHAPTER TWENTY-EIGHT
Hoover Flags

Raymond clambered up in the truck's front seat next to Glen after they finished eating dinner. June settled on the mattresses in back with Jimmy. Laura climbed in with them, then pulled the doors closed and locked them. The small side windows provided the only light and air, leaving the interior of the truck dim and stuffy.

"Not sleepy," Jimmy said, with a pout.

"I know, but if you lie down, I'll tell a story." Laura patted the blankets next to her. "You don't have to close your eyes if you don't want to."

Jimmy stretched out and rested his head on one arm, focused and ready.

June cuddled against Laura's right side. "Tell the one about the seven good witches and the one bad witch."

"Sure," Laura smiled. They never could remember the title of Sleeping Beauty.

"Once upon a time..."

June stayed awake longer than Jimmy, but both were asleep long before the end of the story.

The motion of the truck was soothing, however, Laura's thoughts raced too fast for her to drop off. At least, that's what she assumed. She woke up with a start when the truck tilted to the side and stopped. June and Jimmy popped up when the doors opened.

"Raymond needs to go." Glen said. "Climb down and stretch your legs."

Two cars passed while Glen and the boys relieved themselves by the side of the road. Laura and June took turns using the chamber pot inside the truck since there were no trees or bushes to screen them from sight.

Laura held June's hands above the chamber pot and poured water over them to wash them, then repeated the process with the boys. She swirled the water around in the pot, dumped it out, and put it back in the truck.

"I'm hungry," Raymond said. June and Jimmy nodded in agreement.

"Peanut butter sandwiches sound like a good idea." Glen stretched and rolled his shoulders. "We should make Delmont in an hour or so, but no telling where we'll settle down." He scratched his chin, then squinted at Laura through tired eyes. "Doubt if there'll be a place in town, but we won't know until we get there."

Bread folded over a thin layer of peanut butter, washed down with water, filled everyone up. The family piled in the truck cab together, eager to get a good look at the new city.

Delmont was a little bigger than Geddes, but still gray and brown. Tired buildings, several boarded up with faded paper signs peeling from inside the windows, lined the main street. Just a few cars and a slow-moving horse-drawn wagon moved on the road.

"Can we get out and walk around?" June said, wide-eyed.

Glen pulled over and parked. "Stay inside while I check things out. When I'm done, we'll see."

He got out and walked to Laura's side. "I want to check out the grange and see what I can learn. I'll try to be as quick as I can."

June and Raymond took turns behind the steering wheel, pretending to drive, while Jimmy jumped up and down in the middle of the seat. Three men standing outside of a pool hall about five car-lengths down the sidewalk caught Laura's attention. They were all dressed in suits and passed a silver flask as they talked. A young woman, wearing a yellow dress, came out of the pool hall and joined them.

The yellow dress didn't fit well, was too short and too tight, but there was no question about the woman's appeal or her confidence in her appearance. She flipped her long, curly hair back over her shoulder, then put one hand on her hip. Shoulders back, chest forward, smiling face tilted just a little, she reminded Laura of the fashion models in color magazines.

Stop being nosy, Laura reminded herself,
but kept watching. She couldn't help wishing
the children were quieter so she could hear.

The woman leaned forward and stroked
the lapel of the man on her right. To Laura's
surprise, he stepped back, pulled his front
trouser pockets inside out, then shrugged and
turned both hands palms up. The other two
followed suit, pockets out like puppy ears. The
woman turned away from the men and stomped
into the bar.

Laura jumped, startled when Glen
opened the driver's door.

"Scoot over." He pushed his way into the
driver's seat while the children clambered
toward Laura. Glen looked at the men on the
sidewalks, pockets still flying. "Hoover flags," he
said.

"What?" Laura was a bit disoriented as
she turned her attention back to her family.

"Hoover flags. Pockets turned inside out
to show they don't have any money are called
Hoover flags."

Laura looked back at the men, who were
tucking their pockets back inside and sharing

the flask once again. "Never heard that one. I've heard of shantytowns called Hoovervilles and newspapers called Hoover blankets, but this is a new one on me."

"I'll bet we'll hear lots more. Most folks blame President Hoover for the depression, and name lots of things for him."

Glen started the truck and pulled out into the street. "The town square's a few blocks away. Most likely no green grass, but the kids could at least run around some before we get back on the road."

Laura raised her eyebrows at Glen as the children cheered. "Great idea." She glanced back at the grange. "Did you learn anything?"

"We can talk while they run around."

Just as Glen predicted, there wasn't any grass, but there was a statue of a soldier on a rearing horse and an old Civil War cannon secured in place on its caisson. There were also several stone benches scattered around, some in pairs facing each other with flat stones between them, perfect for checkers or chess.

Glen parked and turned the engine off, then got out and helped June and Raymond down. Laura put Jimmy on the ground and sent him after the others.

"They've been cooped up too long. Look at them go." Glen led the way to a stone bench.

"You're right. Stopping here was a great idea."

Jimmy caught up with Raymond, who was climbing up on the cannon barrel. June raced past the cannon and climbed on the base of the horse statue instead. There wasn't enough room for her to stand, so she sat on the base and leaned against one of the horse's legs.

Laura glanced sideways at Glen, not wanting to push for details.

"Nothing for us here," Glen said. "A few guys were playing pool and there was a poker game going for matches. Nobody even looked my way. After a while, I joined an old guy who sat alone in a corner. I bought him a Budweiser beer, ... thank you President Roosevelt for the repeal ... and we talked."

"Raymond, help your brother off that wagon wheel before you run off." Glen watched his oldest son turn back for Jimmy, then take his hand and head for the statue where June sat.

"The old guy, Charlie was his name, told me that anybody in the area who needs help shows up at the grange at the crack of dawn. There's always a line of guys waiting for work, and the first one in line gets the first job." Glen stood up, arched his back, and folded his arms. "He told me not to bother coming because only locals ever get a chance. I told him I've got a wife and kids to feed, but he laughed and said all the other men did, too."

Laura put her hand on Glen's arm. "Did he have any suggestions?"

"Only about a place we might want to stay tonight. I think maybe we'll have more luck stopping at individual farms where I can offer a hand with whatever they might need."

Packed back in the truck, the children were too worn out to fuss. Not far outside of town, Glen turned onto a dirt road that led to a weather-beaten church with a steeple that listed to one side. A small house with a wide covered porch sat behind the church. A flagstone walkway connected the two buildings.

"Why are we at a church?" June stared wide-eyed as Glen parked between the two buildings.

"This is where we're spending the night, Junebug," Glen said. He opened his door and climbed out, blocking the way when June tried to follow him. "Hold your horses. You guys can explore the grounds, but nobody goes inside the church or the house until your mom and I check things out."

Laura carried Jimmy, who had fallen asleep, to the front door of the house. "I'll bet this was the parsonage."

Glen opened the front door and led the way inside. The dim light that filtered through the dirty windows revealed a space filled with dust and discards. The wood stove appeared undamaged, and cold water flowed through the faucets.

"If there's wood for the stove, I can make a hot meal for us tonight." Laura leaned down and opened the firebox. "Not a lot of wood, but enough for supper."

They ate sitting on the porch. Hot pan bread and scrambled eggs tasted like a feast.

"Hand me your dishes so I can clean up." Laura collected plates and utensils from Glen and the children. "Then it's time to get ready for bed."

"Where?" Raymond piped up. "Where are we going to sleep?"

"Right here on the porch," Glen said. "And you can help me spread out the beds. First a canvas, then a mattress, then blankets. Sky's clear, so it'll be like camping out."

Within an hour, everyone had washed and curled up on the beds. Laura, June, and Jimmy on one, with Glen and Raymond on the other. Minutes later, all three children were asleep, snuggled against Glen and Laura.

CHAPTER TWENTY-NINE
No Other Choice

Tripp, Kaylor, Olivet, Hurley —- their old truck stuttered past those little towns.

Only once did Glen find work in a town, and that was for a farmer who'd flipped his tractor. Mr. Warner had let his hired hands go weeks before and tried to do some plowing by himself. He had miscalculated and tried to turn on too sharp a slope.

Glen parked the truck in front of the Kaylor General Store minutes before Mr. Warner arrived, disheveled and limping from the accident. Four hours later, Glen had helped right the tractor and complete the plowing. Laura and the children helped Mrs. Warner scrape down the chicken coop while the men worked in the field. The Warner's had no money, but fed Glen and Laura's family supper and sent them on their way with two jars of saltpork, a good supply of beef jerky, and a small sack of shelled corn.

The towns were a good source of water and gasoline since Glen took every opportunity to top off their supplies. He also looked for old newspapers and magazines, because gossip from the townspeople was often unreliable.

Each time they stopped in a town, Glen and Laura searched for a place for the children to play. The opportunity to run and explore made a huge difference since they spent most of their time confined in the truck.

The family followed highway 18 East, but detoured on any small roads that looked like they led to a farmhouse. Folks outside of the towns were hurting too, but they often welcomed Glen's help in trade for food or supplies.

The small detours were also good ways to find places to camp each night. Halfway between Kaylor and Olivet, Glen turned toward what looked like a good-sized farmhouse set back among several cottonwood trees.

"Let's see if we can camp in their yard. Might even be a small creek from the look of those trees," Glen said.

"Sounds good." Laura adjusted Jimmy on her lap, his feet on the seat between her legs. June was in the middle, with Raymond standing on the floor between Laura's knees.

They hadn't gone far, when a car approached from the farmhouse. Glen stopped the truck and got out to meet the driver, but was shocked to see a shotgun cradled in his arms.

"Stop right there." The man lifted the barrel. "Now, get back in your truck and drive back where you came from."

"Sir, we mean no harm. My family and I were just hoping to spend the night in your yard ... or even out here on your road... just to get off the main highway. We won't bother you at all."

"Heard that before. Last folks started out in the yard, then stayed on and worked for me and the missus for two days. They were supposed to work one more day, then we'd pay them for what they did." The man shook his head, spit tobacco juice out the side of his mouth into the dirt, then continued. "When we woke up they'd taken off in the night. Cleaned out half the produce in the truck garden, took all the eggs from the chicken coop, and stole two of my best hens."

"That's not right, sir, not right at all," Glen said. "I don't blame you for being mad, but my wife and children just need a quiet, safe place to spend the night."

"My wife and I need to eat, too, and I can't take chances again." The man raised his head and squared his shoulders. "Just go back to the main road and take the next left turn about two miles down the way. Those folks left for California weeks ago. Place is pretty well picked over, but you can park for the night."

Glen started to say more but got back in the truck when the man cocked his shotgun. He backed all the way out to the road, never saying a word.

"Was that man going to shoot you?" June asked.

"Hush," Laura said. "He just didn't want us to stay. No more talk about him, you'll scare your brothers."

Raymond thumped his chest. "I ain't scared."

"You should be," Glen said. "Foolish to face off with a man holding a gun. Enough about him. Here's the turnoff."

No one ever pulled a gun on them again, but four nights later brought another experience they'd never forget. Glen worked all day helping a farmer and his son move bales of hay. Exhausted and wanting to settle in the first decent spot for the night, he took the first turn after the intersection with highway 81.

"Good sized house and barn, nobody outside." Glen peered through the windshield as they approached. "Lots of clear space in front where we can park if they're willing."

Goosebumps coated Laura's arms. "No, something's wrong with this place."

"This place looks better than most we've seen. I'll talk to the folks first to get their permission. They might even have work for us tomorrow." Glen's exhaustion and irritability

314

was obvious in his voice. "Don't know what you
can have against a place just by looking at it."

Laura started to argue but knew he
wouldn't listen. Instead, she tried to make out
the soft, whispery words that teased from a dark
mist in her mind. She was glad June and
Raymond were in the back, afraid they would
sense what she felt.

Glen drove all the way up into the yard,
half-way between the two-story house and the
barn. Nothing stirred except for a few chickens
pecking the ground.

"Hello. Anybody home?" Glen called out,
then tried again. "Hello. Is anyone here?"

The thick silence felt ominous to Laura,
suffocating. "I told you something's wrong here.
This place looks too well kept for folks to have
taken off."

"There's a car parked next to the house.
A garden over on the left in back, but it looks
like nobody's watered it in a while." Glen, hands
on his hips, walked to the steps leading up to the
front porch.

Laura followed, Jimmy in her arms. He
squirmed to get down, but she held tight.

"Hey, you forgot about us," June said, as she and Raymond climbed out of the back of the truck and yelled at their parents. "We want to come, too."

"No! Stay back by the truck until we call you." Laura's voice left no room for argument.

"Glen, they're in the barn, but you mustn't let the children see." Laura's voice quivered. She closed her eyes, trying to block out the pictures that filled her mind of the people who had lived in the house.

"What? Who's in the barn?"

"They're both dead, Glen. He killed her and then himself. We can't help them, but we'll have to tell the police in the next town."

"You're talking crazy. The barn door's closed. You can't know what's inside." The pulse point on Glen's throat jumped, and his face flushed with fury. "You expect me to tell the police this story?" He reached for her arm. "Come on. We're both going to check that barn so you can see you're wrong."

"Wait. I'll go with you, but first I need to take Jimmy to the others and make sure they don't follow us."

Glen shook his head, lips pursed. He folded his arms and tapped his fingers, marking time until Laura came back alone.

Neither said a word until they reached the barn. Glen opened the door, then doubled over from the nauseating stench that spilled out of the hot, dark space.

"Oh, my god, those poor people." Laura rubbed Glen's back, then helped him open both barn doors as wide as they'd go to let in air and sunlight. The light from the doors and a big window in the loft revealed the silhouette of a man hanging from one of the rafters. A woman's body was draped across two bales of hay in the middle of the barn. The buzzing sound of flies filled the space, and the movement of thousands of insects created an illusion of motion on both bodies.

"Why?" Glen's voice was a tortured whisper. "Why would anyone do this?"

"The reason is on the bale next to his wife." Laura inched forward, hands clasped together over her nose and mouth until she reached the woman's body. She pointed to an eviction notice pinned to the bale with a knife.

"The farm had been in her family for three generations. Losing it meant complete failure to him as a man and as a husband. Letting her down was worse than losing life itself. He felt there was no other choice."

"Maybe we should bury them," Glen said, still back by the barn door, unable to compel himself any closer.

"That's a kind thought, but the police will want to see the scene first." Laura backed away from the bale, then hurried to join Glen outside the door. "Besides, no way we could make the kids stay back while we did that. This would give them nightmares forever."

Glen nodded his agreement, then secured the doors shut. He led the way back to the truck, his stride jerky and uneven. Without a word he got into the driver's seat and rested his head on the steering wheel.

"What's wrong?" June said when Laura reached the children. June and Raymond were standing at the back of the truck, each holding one of Jimmy's hands. They had stayed there but could see the barn door from their position. "You and papa both look like you saw a ghost."

"Yeah, what's in the barn?" Raymond's eyes were huge as he stared at his mom. "Must be something awful. Papa looked sick, like he was ready to fall over."

"All you need to know is that the people who live here passed away in the barn." Laura knelt down and wrapped her arms around all three children. "They're okay now, since they're with God. You don't need to worry. We'll find another place for the night, though, so you need to climb in the back." She turned her attention to Jimmy. "Would you like to be in the back like a big kid?"

Jimmy was thrilled to get to ride with June and Raymond, so Laura was alone in the cab with Glen. He didn't want to talk and flinched when Laura reached out to touch him.

The ride was long to their stop for the night, a wide spot in the road next to a small creek. Once the children had eaten and settled for the night, Laura watched Glen walk away and sit at the base of a small tree near the water. She found him still there in the wee hours of the morning, thrashing against his nightmares and covered him with a blanket.

CHAPTER THIRTY
Hooverwagon

Glen drove straight to the next town, Hurley, as soon as they finished eating in the morning. He didn't make a single stop, intent on putting the nightmare behind him. He dropped Laura and the children off at the elementary school playground, promising to be back as soon as he made a report about the bodies they'd found in the barn. Laura watched the truck pull away, wishing she didn't feel so alone.

"Look," June said. She grabbed Laura's hand to get her attention, pointing at the playground equipment. "Can we go play on those things?"

"Sure you can." Pasting a smile on her face, Laura followed the three as they ran toward two teeter-totters, three swings, two slides, a merry-go-round, and a sand pile. There were even three tetherballs, and a section of asphalt with two hopscotch games. June and Raymond, enthralled with the choices, ran from one piece of equipment to another. Laura stayed with Jimmy, pushing him on a swing and helping him climb the lowest slide.

When Glen arrived an hour later, Laura settled Jimmy in the sand pile to dig. She walked to a bench near the truck.

Laura sat and patted the bench seat, "How did it go?"

"Ended up in city hall. Nearest police are in Viborg, but the city clerk will forward a report." Glen sat at the end of the bench, bent forward with his elbows resting on his thighs. He smiled and waved at June and Raymond, but Laura could feel tension rolling off his body. "They didn't seem surprised. I mean, they were sad to hear what happened, but didn't look like it was the first time they'd heard a story like that."

Laura nodded but didn't try to reach out and touch him.

"Now, I want you to tell me how you knew so much about those folks," Glen said. "Did your ma give you the whole story?"

"My ma had nothing to do with this. I don't know how it happens." Laura chose her words with care. "Pictures just burst into my mind. And I knew what the man was thinking and why he did what he did." She turned and faced Glen, staring into his eyes. "I have no control of when these types of visions come, and they have nothing to do with Ma."

"Tell me the truth. What kind of bargain did you make to get those powers? You know the Bible says that soothsayers are supposed to be put to death because they're abominations." Glen's voice was tight, raw with emotion. "Is that why you wouldn't go into that church when we spent our first night at the parsonage?"

Laura fisted her hands until her knuckles were white, nails pressed into her palms. "You sound ridiculous. Quoting old testament ugliness is not like you. The new testament says a seer is just another word for a prophet, and they were consulted and revered." She took a deep breath, trying to stay calm. "And you know we didn't go into the church because the spire tilted to one side. We worried about safety, and because the church was boarded up. We told the kids they couldn't go inside out of respect, because a church is not a place to play."

"Would you go to church if I asked you?"

"Yes, providing the minister wasn't a narrow-minded bully like Rev. Lowell, scaring people with hellfire threats instead of talking about a God of love."

"It's not up to you to decide who God is. When we married you promised to love and obey me." Glen tapped Laura's wedding ring. "I want you to stop all this stuff with visions because it isn't righteous and it isn't healthy around the kids."

"We also promised to love and cherish each other. If you love me, I want you to stop using your right ear." Laura demanded, flipping his ear with her finger.

"What?" Glen jerked away, pulling his hands back into his lap. "That's a dumb thing to say. Both ears are a part of me. I have no control over using a part of my body."

"That's right," Laura said. "Just like I have no control over using something that's a part of me."

"What's wrong? Why are you two fighting?" June stood a few feet in front of the bench with Raymond beside her.

"We're not fighting," Laura said, with a quick side glance at Glen. "Just talking." Shocked that the children had approached without being noticed, she worried about how much they'd heard.

"That's right, pumpkin." Glen gestured toward the play equipment. "Show me what you've been doing."

Both children took Glen's hands and pulled him away, leaving Laura alone on the bench. She sighed, then stood and walked to the sand pile to get Jimmy.

"Oh, my word, look at you," she said, reaching out to touch his gritty body. "Your hair is full of sand."

Jimmy grinned, his lips outlined in dirt. "Watch me." He leaned forward, digging both filthy hands deep into a hill.

"Oh, no, you don't, buster." Laura grabbed his little arms before he could throw the sand into the air. "No wonder you're covered." She pulled him to his feet and tried to brush him off. "Come on, let's strip you down and shake the sand off these clothes before you get in the truck."

It was more than an hour before they were on the road headed north. Jimmy, minus pounds of sand brushed from his hair and washed off his body, fell asleep in the back curled up against Laura's legs. Raymond was drawing on a slate with chalk. June had fussed to be in front, and Glen had agreed.

Laura kept replaying the conversation with Glen, wondering what she might have said to ease his mind. He hadn't spoken a single word to her since he'd walked away with the children in the playground and it hurt. They'd had arguments before, but this felt different.

Glen pulled the truck over and stopped much sooner than she expected. She opened the doors and walked to the front, surprised by the sight of a horse harnessed to a car on the road shoulder, facing the opposite direction.

"We're supposed to stay here while Papa finds out what's wrong," June said.

"That's a good idea. Go to the back of the truck so you can watch your brothers. Make sure they stay with you." Laura's curt tone cut off June's reply. She stared at the Hooverwagon a moment, taking in the folded down windshield, the backseat half-full of piled boxes, and the storage compartment behind the middle seats packed full. The rack above the back bumper was down, providing a platform for additional storage. The patient, blonde, draft horse stood in front hanging his head. His harness was secured to the front bumper, while the reins extended through the windshield opening and hung over the dashboard. Tied to the roof was a bale of hay and a two-foot-tall canvas-covered bundle wrapped with ropes. The ropes ran from the back bumper up over the items on the roof, looped through the front window opening, threaded back through the narrow opening at the top of the back-seat windows, then down to where they were tied to the back bumper. Additional ropes secured the hay and canvas bundle crosswise, tied through the back-seat windows on each side. The rear doors were tied shut, which meant anyone riding in back would have to crawl into the front seats and exit the front doors.

Laura crossed the road, right past where Glen stood talking with a tall, thin man in a scruffy suit and a boy almost as tall as the men. All three focused their attention on the flat tire at the left front of the car. She went straight to the passenger side where a tired looking woman sat, head bowed.

"Hi, I'm Laura. Where are you folks from?"

The woman looked pale and plain until she smiled, and then, pure sunshine. "Nice to meet you, Laura. I'm Willa, Willa York." She reached for the door handle.

Laura opened it for her and stepped back. "Hi, Willa. This is quite a rig. I'd heard of Hooverwagons, but never saw one."

"Sure wasn't planned." Willa pulled herself out of the door, then stood next to Laura, resting her hands on her distended belly.

"We made it just over ten miles outside of Sioux Falls when the radiator blew and the engine seized up. Isaac had to walk about three miles to the nearest farmhouse for help."

"Did they sell you the horse?"

"No, but they drove Isaac to another place where the folks were happy to sell the horse and all the other wagon stuff. Took a big bite out of our cash, but they weren't interested in anything we had to trade." Willa shook her head and sighed. "It'll take us a lot longer to get to California now, but we didn't have a choice."

The two women walked around the back of the car to join the men. Laura could see the left front tire wasn't just flat, it was shredded. The rim was resting on the ground, and there were pieces of rubber behind it.

"Ruben, get the jack out of the box of car parts in back while we pull the spare tire." Isaac's voice was deep and rich.

Laura and Willa stepped away from the car so the men could remove the spare tire cradled in a hole on the left front fender, just in front of the running board.

"I sure appreciate your help," Isaac said.

"No problem." Glen pumped the long handle as soon as the jack was in position. "Folks should help each other, especially in these times."

"No truer words, that's for sure."

"No, no, I want Mama." Jimmy wailed from across the road.

"Uh oh, I'd better go back." Laura looked at Willa. "Would you like to come with me and sit in the truck? You could stretch out in back with your feet up."

"That sounds like heaven. My feet are awful swollen."

Laura and Willa soon had the children laughing and clapping at silly made-up songs. The two women sat on opposite sides of the bed, leaning on the truck walls with their feet pointed at each other. Willa had taken her shoes off and flexed her ankles and toes to relieve the pain in her feet and calves.

"Willa, honey, are you okay?" Isaac, Ruben, and Glen came around the back of the truck.

"I'm fine. In fact, having my feet up instead of hanging down is helping a lot." Willa pulled her legs toward the open door. "Thanks, Laura, but I guess I'd better get back. We've lost a lot of time with the tire, but it's been a pleasure spending time with you and your family."

Glen leaned against the side of the open door. "Where are you folks planning to stop for the night?"

"Our plan was to stop in Viborg, but not sure if we'll make it now," Isaac said. "And you?"

"We'd hoped to make Lennox, then on to Sioux Falls."

"Sioux Falls? That's where we come from. Take my word for it, you don't want to go there." Isaac and Willa both shook their heads. "There's a huge Hooverville outside of town that just gets bigger and rougher every day. No jobs to speak of, but bread lines around the block."

Glen looked at Laura, "I'm a good mechanic and heavy machine operator. Course, I'll do anything I can find."

"I'm sure you would, but every single man in the bread lines wants to work, and lots of them have degrees. I was a bank manager, but since the bank went under, I wasn't able to get anything at all. That's why we lost most of our money and our home. You'd do better heading south to Missouri where the Public Works Administration is planning to do a lot of infrastructure projects."

"I've heard of that," Glen said. "One of Roosevelt's New Deal ideas. If there's work in Missouri, why are you folks going to California?"

"For me." Willa's voice was soft. She reached out for Isaac's hand. "I've had two miscarriages. We only have money for this trip because we sold everything we had except what's in the car. We have a doctor friend in California who said he'd help us."

Laura took Willa into her arms. "I'm so sorry. Just wish there was something we could do to help."

"The best thing for us would be for Willa to rest. She can't get real comfortable in the car with her legs hanging down." Isaac touched his wife's cheek. "Too bad we couldn't camp here for the night together. She's plumb wore out and we don't want to lose this baby, too."

"There's just the place about two miles back. Looked like a little creek with some clear land under a few shade trees. Didn't see a road leading to it, but the ground looked level enough for the tires. Should be room for all of us." Glen glanced at Laura, who smiled back. "We didn't stop because we wanted to get closer to Sioux Falls, but now I think we need to change course to Missouri."

They left in high spirits. Willa reclined in the back of the truck with Laura and Jimmy. June rode in front with Glen. And Raymond was thrilled to ride in the backseat of the Hooverwagon while Ruben moved to the front with Isaac. The spot was just as Glen had described, and the evening was a welcome rest for all. Even the draft horse, Blondie, had plenty of grass to graze and all the creek water he wanted when they tied him to a tree.

CHAPTER THIRTY-ONE
Aurora, Missouri
One month later, July 1933

Spending the evening with the Yorks turned into an impromptu party. They made up the beds early so Willa could rest. The three other adults forbid her to take part in food preparations or cleanup, since her exhaustion was obvious. After supper, the four children played in the creek with Ruben looking after the younger ones. Laura and Willa watched from a grassy patch a few yards from the water's edge.

"Ruben sure is good with little ones," Laura said. "My three can try the patience of a saint, but they're having fun with him.

"I know. That boy has always had a soft spot for kids and animals." Willa's back was against a tree for support. Her hands rested on her belly, sometimes stroking slow circles. "It about broke his heart when we had to give his dog away before we left, but Isaac didn't think we could handle a pet on the trip. Ruben needs something to love and care for."

The two women let the children play until dusk settled around them. They filled the time talking about everything from their families to current events.

"Sure wish we could stop time right now. It's going to be hard saying goodbye in the morning." Laura kept her eyes on the children. She hadn't felt so close to any woman other than her sisters and realized how much she would miss Willa.

"Me, too. I love Isaac and Ruben, but talking with you is different. You understand what I'm feeling, so I don't have to explain myself or make excuses for my thoughts." Willa's voice had a slight tremor.

"I know what you mean. We've got to find a way to stay in touch."

"How can we? We're headed to California and you're going to Missouri. No addresses, not even sure what cities we'll end up in," Willa said.

Laura nodded. "I've got an idea. My sister, Ruth and her husband's family, have a store in Ardmore, Oklahoma. If I give you her address, you could send me a letter through her when you get settled. She can hold on to it until she hears from us, then forward it. It'll take time, but we won't lose track of each other."

"Perfect. We'd better get back while we can still see."

Breakfast the next morning was a shared affair between the two families. The children gobbled their food then raced around the clearing playing tag, with Raymond keeping the other three giggling the whole time.

Isaac and Glen worked together harnessing Blondie to the car, then checked the loads on both the car and truck to make sure each item was secure and ready for the road. Willa and Laura cleaned up after the meal and packed everything back into their vehicles.

When they finished the chores, the mood turned somber.

Isaac put his hand out to Glen. "Don't know what we'd have done if you hadn't stopped."

"You would've been fine, just maybe a little slower." Glen shook Isaac's hand, then reached out and squeezed his shoulder. "We're the ones that owe you. No telling how much time we would've wasted in Sioux Falls trying to figure out the information you shared last night. Can't thank you enough."

Glen's attention shifted to Raymond, who was tapping on his leg. "Please, Papa, can't I ride with Ruben? Or he could ride in back with us." Raymond's eyes glistened as he grabbed Ruben's hand and held tight. "You said we're going the same way."

Glen stroked the top of his son's head. "I'm sorry, but a truck and a horse don't move at the same speed. You need to say goodbye to Ruben, now."

June and Jimmy joined Raymond in a circle around Ruben, holding on to him with tears running down their faces, not wanting to let go of their new friend.

Laura leaned down and took her children in her arms. "It's okay. You'll see Ruben again, I promise. Willa and I will make sure of that." She glanced at Willa, who had wrapped her arms around Ruben's waist.

Tears streaked four faces, but soon the children were tucked in their places. Isaac and Glen shook one final time while Laura and Willa shared a long, last embrace before getting into their vehicles. Glen started the truck, then led the way back to the highway with Blondie pulling the car behind them.

Glen drove to Viborg without stopping. He parked in front of city hall. When he got out of the truck, he glanced back, but there was no sign of the Yorks.

"See the school across the street at the end of the block? Why don't you take the kids down there? I want to find out about any Public Works jobs that might be available and I don't know how long I'll be." Glen opened the back of the truck and helped June and Raymond jump down.

"Sounds like a good idea. Come get us when you're done." Laura pointed down the sidewalk. "Don't cross the street without me." The children took off, eager to run after being confined.

Almost two hours later, Glen startled Laura by plopping down next to her on a bench in the schoolyard. "Looks like they're having a good time."

"Oh," Laura yelped. "I didn't hear you coming." She nodded at the children chasing one another around in circles on the grass. "They've never even slowed down. What did you learn?"

"Isaac was right. The Public Works Administration is a new thing President Roosevelt just signed to get people back to work. He's trying a lot of ideas, calling them his New Deal. It will fund all kinds of infrastructure projects like roads and bridges, as well as things like schools, libraries, and government buildings. States have to apply for the funds, then hire companies to do the work. The PWA funds go to the states, who pay the companies. The companies hire and pay the workers.

Information about PWA projects are posted throughout the states.

"How do you apply for the jobs?"

"That's the tricky part," Glen said. "I have to apply through the companies doing the work. I learned that Missouri has a lot of projects planned. Until we get there, I'll just have to check out all the decent sized towns to see if they're doing any hiring."

With this new information, the daily patterns changed. They still tried to get permission to spend the nights on private land for safety, but Glen checked for work in every town they passed. They traveled through Centerville, Vermillion, Elk Point, and Jefferson, South Dakota, on the way to Missouri.

The best job he found was a five-day stint in Kansas City working on a road crew for Connor Construction. The crew manager was impressed with Glen's work and his abilities with large machinery. So much so that on the last day, the manager called his company's main office and recommended Glen for an upcoming bridge project in Aurora. The job was due to

start in two to three weeks, but would last for
several months.

Glen was elated with the
recommendation. Wages in hand, he jumped
on his bicycle and headed back to where he'd
parked the truck. "Laura," he said when he
jumped off the bike. "Good news. We're going
to Aurora."

It was almost noon on Monday, July 3rd
when they crossed a bridge over Badger Creek
near the outskirts of Aurora, Missouri. Glen
pulled off the road and parked. Laura and the
kids got out to stretch their legs and relieve their
bladders. "Stay by the truck until I get back."

The kids were whining and antsy by the
time he returned. "I found the perfect place for
us to settle for a little while. Back in the truck
everybody."

The truck cab was crowded, but Glen's
excitement was contagious. He drove slow and
careful, off the road, around and under the
bridge they'd just crossed. The ground was hard
and flat for about two car widths next to the

water as they drove under the bridge then continued next to a stand of trees that shaded and concealed the grassy beach from the road. Glen parked under the sheltering branches. "Everybody out. You can explore, but stay out of the water for now."

"It's so pretty here," Laura said. A breeze caressed her face, the air much cooler than it was on the road. "We could use a break to air our clothes and bedding, and to reorganize everything in the back of the truck."

"That's what I thought. Besides, it's only a couple of miles to Aurora from here, and I need to check in at Connor. I'll bicycle into town and see about the bridge project."

"That's a great idea. You won't have to worry about the time and I can get started on the truck while the kids play."

Glen lifted the bicycle off its hook on the side of the truck, hopped on the pedals and headed up to the road. As soon as he was out of sight, Laura pulled the mattresses out of the back of the truck and leaned them against tree trunks. She shook the blankets and canvasses and then draped them over branches and bushes.

"Can we play in the water now?" All three children stood at the edge of the slow moving creek.

"Let me check it out first." Laura kicked off her shoes and stepped into the water. "Oh, that feels good." She moved farther out, making sure the bottom was smooth for tender feet and the slope was gradual with no holes or dropoffs. "Okay, you can come in. But stay near the shore. I don't want you in water past your waist."

Squeals of delight filled the air as all three splashed their way as far as they dared to go.

"June and Raymond, you two make sure Jimmy doesn't go too far."

"Anybody home?" Glen sang out as he rode into sight, a paper bag in the bike basket. "We're celebrating, and I've got a surprise."

Three wet, grinning kids surrounded him before Laura could reach them. "You got it, didn't you?"

"I sure did. Heavy machine operator for a job that will run for months, maybe even a year." Glen balanced the bike on its kickstand and grabbed the bag. "I bought ice cream to celebrate. Who wants some?"

Six hands, pruney from the water, reached out accompanied by cries of, "Me, Me, Me." Glen passed out individual cups and flat wooden spoons. "Go eat it at the edge of the water, so you can rinse off when you're finished. Then bring the cups and spoons back to the truck."

Ice cream was the most exciting thing in the bag, but Glen had also purchased a gallon of milk, peanut butter, two loaves of bread and a bag of apples. He put the milk and peanut butter into a shallow spot in the creek water and braced them with rocks to keep them upright. The running water kept them cool, while their placement away from where the children played kept them safe.

"I'm so proud of you." Laura sat next to him while they ate their ice cream and watched the children. "I guess Aurora will be home, now."

"Yes, but I think we should stay right here. It's free, private, and should be safe. Until we know more about Aurora and what's available, this will be a good place for us. I'll ride to work, so the truck can stay parked and serve as our storage place and bedroom — although it might be nice to sleep out in the open."

"That makes sense. The kids will love it. You'll have to teach them to swim, though." Laura set the empty cup down by her side and looked around. The slow-moving water flowed just a few feet away, edged by sand and grass. A cluster of tall trees swayed behind them on the left, sheltering the truck, their top branches a few feet above the roadbed that sloped up to the bridge. Nothing grew under the bridge, and the area beneath it was shady, with a floor of smooth, packed dirt. "It'd be nice to set up a cooking and eating area. We'll need to figure out a bathroom plan, too. Can't have the kids just going anywhere around us."

"You're right. I can fix both those problems right now." Glen set up a firepit surrounded by creek rocks under the bridge away from all the vegetation. He explained that putting it there would make the smoke hard to see because it would dissipate instead of going straight up in an obvious plume. He helped Laura tuck their kitchen supplies and food right up against the base of the bridge, out of the way and out of sight, but convenient for meal preparations.

Next on his list was digging a narrow latrine trench away from the truck on the opposite side from the bridge, out of sight for privacy, but not too far away so the kids wouldn't get lost. He placed a little wooden box containing a roll of toilet paper and a small shovel next to the pile of dirt he'd removed from the trench.

Kitchen and bathroom arrangements complete, they told the curious children that the creek would be their home for a few weeks.

CHAPTER THIRTY-TWO
Our Country's Birthday
July 4th, 1933

The first night under the bridge was peaceful, with no pressure to get out of bed and back on the road. Glen didn't have to work since it was July 4th, so Laura was careful not to wake him when she crawled out of bed.

It felt good to be alone, listening to the music of the water slipping over the rocks and the whisper of tree branches moving in the gentle breeze, accented by morning birdsong. After stopping at the trench to relieve herself, she knelt at the edge of the creek to rinse her face and hands in the clear, cold water.

"Brrr, I'm wide awake now," she said under her breath. "Let's see if I can fix pancakes over an open fire." She lit a match and touched the flame to kindling that rested beneath a loose cone of small branches in the firepit. When the wood was fully engaged, she added three medium-sized branches and watched the fire lick around the bark. "Now to my pantry for supplies." By the time she gathered a mixing bowl, skillet, and all the ingredients for breakfast, the fire burned hot and steady.

This would take some getting used to. She placed everything on a towel near the pit, then returned to the storage area at the base of the bridge for dishes, and a clean jug of water.

June woke up first. "Morning Mama, smells good."

"It does, doesn't it." Laura flipped a pancake that filled half the cast-iron skillet balanced on the ring of rocks around the fire. "Go do your business, then wash up. There's a clean towel draped on the hood of the truck. When you're through, your breakfast will be ready."

The boys and Glen joined June minutes after she started eating. Laura cooked pancakes, poured syrup, and refilled glasses of water until everyone was full before fixing her own breakfast.

"Oh, no, you don't," Laura said when the children plopped their dishes on the ground and headed for the creek. She pointed to an empty metal dishpan next to her side. "Put your dirty dishes in the pan, then go fold the blankets before you even think of playing."

"But you said it's a holiday. Papa doesn't have to work today, so we shouldn't have to, either." June crossed her arms, not moving.

"Mind your mama, young lady," Glen said. "Lots of time to play after the chores are done."

Laura nodded her thanks to Glen but wished his intervention wasn't necessary. June was quick to follow Glen's guidance, but she seemed to defy her mother at every turn.

Glen helped the children fold the blankets and canvasses and put them back in the truck with the rolled-up mattresses. Laura heated water in a Dutch oven over the fire for washing and rinsing the dishes. When she finished, the soapy, dirty water drifted downstream from the play area.

Since the water was too cold to swim in yet, Glen started the kids digging for worms under the trees. "Take it easy now. We don't want to hurt them. Drop the worms in this can of dirt. I'll fix some lines so we can try fishing."

Laura watched Glen and the children, relieved to relinquish their care for awhile. "Some holiday," she mumbled after putting the clean dishes back in the boxes tucked under the bridge. "He can play with them while I wash our dirty clothes."

The entire process of fishing fascinated the children. The hardest part was staying out of the water while Glen waited for a bite and pulled in his catch. He threaded each fish on a stringer anchored in the shallow water.

"Okay kids, we've caught enough. Your mama can fry them up for supper tonight. It'll be a real treat." Glen reeled in his line and secured the hook. "Leave the fish alone and go play while I put the fishing gear away."

A couple of hours later June and Raymond begged to go in the water, insisting it was warm enough. "Not yet," Glen said after wading in a few feet." Your mama has bread and butter sandwiches and jerky about ready for dinner. By the time we finish eating, it'll be about time for you to learn how to swim."

When dinner was over, Glen and the children headed to the creek for the promised swimming lessons.

While Glen worked with the kids, Laura did the washing in a metal tub at the water's edge under the bridge, using a washboard and soap flakes. "Sure wish I had a washer with a wringer," she said to herself. "But I'll manage."

When she finished, the kids called for her to join them in the water. Instead, she stretched out on the grass near where the wet clothes hung from a rope tied between two trees and closed her eyes, luxuriating in the rare opportunity to rest

Crispy, golden fried fish for supper was a huge hit. Even before they tasted it, the kids declared it their new favorite food, since they had helped their papa catch and clean it. Every

single bite of fish disappeared, along with sweet slices of canned peaches.

"I like holidays," June said. "But what's July 4th for?"

"It's our country's birthday, and one of my favorites when I was little." Glen ruffled June's hair. "We always celebrated with a big church picnic, and a parade, and lots of music." He glanced at Laura, tilting his head with wide eyes.

"Parade?" Raymond asked. "What's a parade?"

"Well, folks gather all along both sides of the road to watch. First comes the Grand Marshal on a big fancy horse, waving his hat at everybody. Most years, there are two men on horses next to him carrying big flags waving in the breeze. One is always the state flag, and the other is old glory, the red, white, and blue flag for the U.S. of A. All the folks stand up and salute just like this as the flags go by." Glen stood and raised his hand in a smart military salute.

"Wow," Raymond said. "Like this, Papa?" His salute wasn't perfect, but Glen and June clapped for him anyway.

"But that's not all." Glen sat down and pulled Jimmy on his lap. "Lots more fine things follow the Grand Marshal and the flags. Prancing horses with ribbons in their manes and tails, cars all polished with bright colored signs on the sides, marching bands with folks beating on drums and blowing on shiny horns, and people in crazy costumes. Why, I once saw a truck carrying a man playing a piano the whole way."

"I like music," June said. "What kind would they play?"

"We'll show you." Laura, who had slipped away to the truck while Raymond was practicing his salute, handed Glen his guitar. She sat across from him and strummed her banjo.

The children clapped and cheered, singing "Oh Susanna," "America the Beautiful," and "Yankee Doodle." They giggled with the counting song, "Knick Knack Paddywhack, Give The Dog A Bone."

Then BOOM, what sounded to Laura like an M80 firecracker, just like men used to set off when she was growing up, reverberated from above the bridge. Glen dove to the ground, guitar forgotten. A string of loud pops followed, keeping him pinned to the dirt.

The kids jumped, more startled by their papa's strange behavior than by the sounds. "It's okay. July 4th also means loud noises, but they don't hurt anything," Laura said. "Sounds like somebody is setting off firecrackers on the bridge, so stay here underneath to stay safe." She put the banjo down and gathered the kids close. "No more singing though. We don't want them to know we're here."

The explosions and pops continued, accompanied by the faint sounds of revelry from above. Glen sat up, brushing the dirt off his clothes. He kept his eyes averted from everyone, but Laura could see he was trembling. He remained silent long after the noise stopped. Only after they heard a car driving off the bridge and down the road did he stand and make his way to the truck.

"Best get ready for bed." Glen's voice sounded raw and tight. He pulled out the canvasses and tossed them to Laura. "Holiday's over. Got to work tomorrow and I need my sleep."

The children didn't fuss much since they were worn out. Laura and Glen lay side by side on their mattress, but neither could fall asleep. Laura couldn't escape Glen's nightmares and was unable to help him. She watched as he thought and ran and tried to escape the bullets and explosions all around him, over and over, until he woke in the morning covered in sweat.

Laura poured two cups of coffee when she heard Glen stirring. He joined her at the firepit and reached for the steaming cup. When their fingers touched, Laura looked into his eyes and saw exhaustion, pain, and embarrassment. He stared back, his eyes narrowed. The emotions Laura saw changed from pain and embarrassment to suspicion and distrust.

"Yesterday was wonderful for the kids. Thank you," Laura said.

"No need to thank me. Just trying to be a good father." Glen's voice was curt. He took his cup with him to get ready and collect the bicycle, then returned to pick up his lunchbox and put it in the basket. "Don't know how long I'll be," he said as he mounted the bike and then rode up the hill.

CHAPTER THIRTY-THREE
Emergency Fund

The children missed Glen, and were disappointed when Laura wouldn't play with them. "Papa's more fun than you. I wish you could go to work and leave him with us." June pouted, hands on her hips. Raymond stood next to her, mimicking her stance and nodding his head.

"You and me both," Laura said. "Now go clean up and fold the blankets while I roll the mattresses and put them away. When you're done, I'll have breakfast ready. And I don't want to hear another word of back talk."

June, with exaggerated sighs, stalked off with Raymond. Jimmy followed, glancing back and forth between the two children and Laura.

When Laura finished the morning chores, she decided to try fishing. The children's attitude changed as they cheered her on for each catch, until the stringer was full.

Jimmy knelt by the captive fish. "Pretty,' he said, then reached out to pet them.

"No, little man, you can't play with them." Laura picked him up and carried him away from the water. "Let's find something else for you to do."

Even with an afternoon of playing in the water, the kids were fussy and bored. When Glen pedaled in, they mobbed him, begging to play.

"Sure. Let me clean up and then we can play until supper."

Glen put the bike away, then wrestled and tickled until all three children screamed in delight. By the time Laura called them to eat, they were worn out, but grinning and happy.

"How was work? Did you like the people?" Laura asked after the exhausted children had fallen asleep. She and Glen sat near the shore of the creek, away from their bed.

"The guys on the crew are a good bunch. They've got me working a dozer." He stared at the water, just visible in the moonlight, hands clasped between his knees.

"I'm glad." Laura waited for words to fill the empty space between them. "I know you're tired, but the kids love playing with you."

Glen nodded, still looking down.

"Do you think we can unpack more of the stuff from the truck? If we could get more toys down, especially the wagon and some books, the kids would have more to do. Since we'll be here awhile, I can work with them on their letters and numbers, too." Laura kept her voice soft, trying not to pressure him.

"Guess I can. I'll get some things down in the morning before work."

"Thanks." Laura was only inches from Glen, but the distance between them felt vast. "Well, guess I'll call it a night." She faced the water but glanced sideways for any reaction. "Will you be long?"

"Don't know. It's quiet and peaceful sitting here." Glen's voice was soft in the dark. "You go on ahead."

Laura hadn't planned on falling asleep before Glen joined her, but woke with a start when his body jerked next to her. She reached for him, both with her hand and her mind.

"Stop! Don't touch him right now." The voice commanded in Laura's head, loud and insistent.

Laura responded in kind inside her head, not a sound out loud. "Ma? He's having his nightmares again. They're awful. Sometimes I can soothe him so he can sleep."

"He knows you touch his mind and see his dreams. That makes it worse."

"I only want to help him stop hurting." Laura watched Glen thrash next to her, whipping his head side to side. Her hand reached for him but stopped short.

"When he wakes, he'll look into your eyes and see pity. Pity and your knowledge of his innermost fears." The voice paused so Laura could absorb the words. "Don't take his manhood away by intruding into his soul."

"But the nightmares are worse than before. How can I help him?"

"Just love him and be ready to listen if he chooses to share."

The voice had never led Laura astray, so she turned away from Glen and curled up on her side. It hurt to listen to him struggle, but she kept her arms folded and did her best to ignore the visions of his nightmares that drifted across her mind.

Laura didn't think she'd ever fall asleep, and she was shocked to wake at dawn and see Glen, fully dressed, standing next to her. "Would you get the coffee started while I unpack more of the kids stuff from the truck?"

"Of course," she said, scrambling off the mattress. "Sorry I slept in. I'll pack your lunchbox, too."

Glen pulled out all the toys they'd packed away, then resecured the bundle on top of the truck under the canvas tarps. "We've been lucky so far, but we'd better be careful about leaving too much stuff out in the open." Glen joined Laura at the firepit. "Lots of summer storms in this area and anything left out in the open will get drenched. Wind will push rain under the bridge too, so we need to be better organized."

"You're right. And I worry about strangers finding us down here. It'd be best if we kept things we're not using closed up in the truck." Laura glanced at the sleeping children. "Bound to be folks noticing us some day and coming to check."

"I know. The truck's pulled as close to the edge of the bridge as possible and it's shaded by trees. As long as the kids play under the bridge or on the shore under the trees, they're out of sight." Glen finished his coffee, grabbed his lunchbox, and hurried to his bicycle. "Got to run, but I'll think about what we can do to make this place safer."

Laura was surprised when he gave her a quick hug before leaving. She waved and watched him disappear up the hill, glad she'd heeded her ma's advice.

Each day's routine was the same. Glen left before the children woke up, the kids spent most of the day playing, while Laura divided her time between fishing for their supper, washing, mending, cleaning, and reading to the children. She kept her eyes on them every minute because of the water. The first Sunday in camp was a treat for everyone. Glen played all day with the kids, while Laura, able to relax, left the constant vigilance to Glen.

The second weekend was different. As soon as Glen got off his bicycle Saturday evening, Laura saw he'd torn his left pant-leg. "What happened to your leg? Are you okay?"

"Sprained the darn thing." Glen parked the bike against the truck, then limped to the firepit. "One young kid got a dump truck stuck, then almost flipped the darn thing trying to get it out." He sat down, pulled his shoe and sock off, then peered at the bruised and swollen flesh. "Took six of us to get the darn thing righted. I turned my ankle in the process."

"Soon as supper's done, I'll heat some water and make a poultice. You'd better stay off your feet tomorrow, and keep the ankle wrapped to give it a chance to heal," Laura said.

Glen nodded, just as the children reached him.

"Papa." June dropped to her knees and grabbed one of his hands. "Come see the fort we built by the creek." Raymond jumped up and down with excitement.

"Hurry, Papa, hurry." Jimmy grabbed Glen's other hand and pulled with all his might.

"I'll look, but no playing tonight." Glen stood, then glanced at Laura and shrugged his shoulders. "I hurt my ankle today and have to stay off it."

"Everybody needs to wash up for supper," Laura said. "I'll be dishing up the plates in just a few minutes."

Sunday morning was steamy and wet. Everyone had slept in the truck to stay dry, since Laura and Glen thought it might rain during the night. The creek level was several inches higher, increasing the speed of the water flow.

Laura and the children sat on a folded canvas near the firepit. "All of you stay out of the water today. It's much too fast." Laura held out three large serving spoons. "You can use these to dig tunnels and roads in the wet dirt by the bank, maybe even make dams like your papa does."

Their sleepy expressions transformed into excitement as they grabbed their spoons and plopped down in the dirt near the creek bank. "When I call you to eat, bring your spoon with you. I'll tan the hide off anyone who loses one."

Glen laughed. Still sitting near the firepit on another canvas, stretched out his leg straight. "Never seen them so thrilled over spoons."

"Had to think of something. With everything so wet, they'd be whining all day about having nothing to do."

Breakfast consisted of pan biscuits cut in half with a thin smear of jelly on each cut surface, and a glass of water. Laura corralled the children, and washed the dirt off their hands and faces.

"Look, Mama, my spoon." Jimmy waved his digging spoon, salting his plate with dirt particles.

"That's great, pumpkin, but let's keep the dirt off your food." Laura laughed and swept the particles of dirt off his plate. "Just leave your spoon on the ground for now."

"Here's mine." June held out her spoon. "But look at Raymond's." She pointed at her brother.

"What happened?" Laura asked, staring at Raymond's poor mangled spoon.

"I was trying to dig out a rock."

"Looks like it was a pretty big rock." Laura took the mangled thing into her hand and looked at it. "Did you get it out?"

"Not yet."

"Well, even your papa sometimes comes across big boulders that his huge machines can't move. Why don't you tell him what happened and I'll bet he suggests you change your plans and dig around it." Laura bent the spoon back as close to normal as it would go and gave it back to Raymond.

"You're not mad?" Raymond's eyes darted to his sister. "June said you'd be real mad at me."

"No, things can happen when you're digging. Just leave that rock alone." Laura sat down in front of her plate and took a drink of water.

"Can I have more jelly?" June poked at her biscuits with her finger.

"Me, too," Raymond said, holding out his plate.

Jimmy just nodded.

"Sorry, kids, but that's it for the jelly." Laura looked at Glen, who also appeared to want more. "Our supplies are running low."

"But I don't like them all dry," June said, pushing the plate away.

"Junebug, you'll eat what your mama puts in front of you or not eat at all." Glen stared his daughter down, then looked at the others. "Be patient until we can get more supplies."

When the children were back to playing and out of earshot, Glen turned to Laura. "How short are we?"

"Pretty short, out of almost everything. You're working six days a week and can't get to a store during business hours, and I can't leave the kids alone." Laura sat next to Glen, twisting her hands together. "I thought of driving them into town, but we'd have to pack everything back in the truck first, and I'm not sure I could drive it anyway. And we sure don't want to lose this space."

"We'll have to send June to the store."

"What did you say?" Laura wasn't sure she'd heard him right. "June's just five, how can she go to the store for us?"

"She can take the wagon tomorrow morning after breakfast. We'll give her a list and enough money for the items. The store is only about a mile and a half straight down the road." Glen ignored Laura's shaking head. "The houses on the way are big, real nice places where people with money live. They won't bother her."

"She won't know what to do." Laura put her hand on Glen's arm. "This is asking a lot of a five-year-old."

"I know, but with the list and the money both tucked in her pocket and the wagon to put stuff in, she'll be fine." Glen put his hand over Laura's and squeezed. "Besides, I can't take time off work to shop. There are lines of men just waiting for a job to open up, and you can't leave here. She's the only answer."

Laura hated the idea, but couldn't fault Glen's logic. "Okay, but let's only put a few basics on the list for tomorrow to see how it goes."

They worked on the list together and settled on just five things. Glen printed them on a piece of paper.

>Bread, one loaf, sliced
>Cheese, one pound
>Butter, one pound
>Eggs, one dozen
>Milk, one quart

He calculated the cost at 91 cents, but just to be careful, they'd send her with a dollar and instructions to bring the change home.

They decided not to talk to June about the plan until morning to avoid hours of complaints from the boys.

"I mended your work pants and cleaned them up," Laura said. "They're folded in the back of the truck for you." She joined Glen on their bed after checking on the children asleep in the truck. "Funny, they didn't run around much at all today, but fell asleep when their heads hit the pillows."

Glen smiled in the dim moonlight that filtered under the bridge. "They're good kids." He paused, took a couple of breaths. "You can't leave the boys, and I don't dare risk my job."

"She'll be fine. In fact, she'll be so puffed up with pride we'll hear the story dozens of times before you get home."

"Sometimes I'm so scared for them." Glen's voice was almost a whisper, tremulous and soft. "I want them to be happy and safe. I'll do anything for them, but what if that's not enough?" He cleared his throat and sat up cross-legged, hands on his thighs. "My pa loved us and worked hard as can be, never took a sick day in his life. Then one day he died, hit by a car while he was crossing the street. Just like that everything changed."

"I know how much it hurts to lose a parent you loved," Laura said, sitting up next to him.

"I did love him. Heck, he was my hero, but I also hated him for leaving us like that." Glen fisted his hands. "He loved us but left us with nothing. No insurance, not a dime of savings. Our friends and neighbors had to pass the hat to collect enough money to bury him in the poorest section of the cemetery. Ma had to go to work at a crummy laundry working a heavy, hot, machine ... I think she called it a mangle ... ironing sheets all day just to pay for a tiny place for us to live."

Laura placed her left hand over his right fist, pleased when he opened his hand and interlaced their fingers. He pulled her hand against his chest and wrapped his other hand around it.

"I quit school and did any and every odd job I could find to help. Had to lie about my age since I was just thirteen, but nobody cared. Poor Barbara had to take care of cooking and cleaning the house, and we both did our best to care for Bobbie. He was only six. I've promised myself, every single day since, that I'd never let that happen to my kids."

"Honey," Laura interrupted.

"Let me finish," Glen said. "That's why I insisted we start saving from the day we got married. I know we always said it was to buy a house someday, but the truth is, it's an emergency fund for you and the kids in case something happens. That's why I've been so adamant about putting something away every payday."

"You're a good man, honey, and a great father. Nothing's going to happen to you."

"Just in case, you need to know I buried the jar under the truck just behind the left front tire. You'll have to use the latrine shovel and dig down about three inches until you hit a rock." Glen lifted his left hand and placed his fingers against Laura's lips to silence her. "It's a good sized flat rock, so clear the dirt off and you'll find the jar below it. The rock protects the jar from being broken by the shovel. It's there for you and the kids, just in case." Glen wrapped his arm around Laura and pulled her close.

They held each other a long time before going to sleep, their slumber uninterrupted by nightmares.

CHAPTER THIRTY-FOUR
We Don't Take Charity

Laura opened their last can of applesauce and split the contents between the children's plates for breakfast. Her stomach growled at the smell of the fruit, so she drank two glasses of water to fill herself up. "Come on, sleepyheads, looks like a beautiful day."

"Can we play with the digging spoons today?" Raymond said. "That was fun."

"No, I think we'll save that for the next rainy day. Today will be extra special, but I'm not telling you why until you finish your breakfast, and get washed up."

The kids polished off their plates, got ready in record time, then gathered around Laura. "June is going on an adventure trip for us, and while she's gone Raymond and Jimmy and I will spend our time playing together."

Next came a careful balancing act, with
Laura explaining what June would do, while
making sure the boys didn't feel left out. She
told them they needed to help June memorize
what she was supposed to do. Laura showed the
children the list folded together with a dollar
bill, and explained that she would tuck them
deep in June's pocket. She told the boys their
job was to clean up the wagon, then sent them
off to complete their task.

"Now June, we have to get you ready."

"I am ready," June said.

"No, you need to look proper for town.
That means we need to brush your hair and get
you into a clean dress."

June grumbled the whole time while
being inspected. She had short bangs and long,
straight hair that reached her shoulders. She
wore a dress that reached an inch below her
knees, a sash tied into a bow, and puffy cap
sleeves, with pockets on each side of her skirt.
The right pocket held the list and money. The
dress looked white from a distance, but a closer
examination of the stitching around the pockets
and seams showed that it had once been light

green before most of the color had washed out. June's feet were bare, as usual, but her sun-browned legs and feet were clean.

"The wagon's ready." Raymond pulled the wagon, with Jimmy sitting in it, to June's side.

"Great job." The wagon's red paint had some scratches but was dry and free of dirt. The wooden slat walls reached a foot above the metal bed.

Laura and the boys walked with June up the hill to the road beyond the bridge. She ran through her directions to June once again and made her repeat them back. "All right, Junebug, straight down that road to the store. No turning on side roads. No need to run, but please don't dawdle since we'll be waiting for you."

"I know, Mama, you told me and told me."

One final hug and Laura waved her on. June marched down the middle of the road, back straight, wagon trailing behind her.

The hours crawled by. Part of Laura's mind stayed on the memory of June striding away, but the rest remained focused on entertaining her sons. They loved having her complete attention, playing, singing, and laughing from one game to another.

Long past the time she'd been expected, June called from the road. "Mama, come help me."

"I'm coming," Laura yelled and started up the hill, then whirled to face the boys. "You two stay here. I'll be right back with your sister."

The boys grumbled but stayed at the base of the hill, watching their mama race to the top, then drop to her knees and grab June into a hug.

"What took you so long? I was worried to death." Laura released June and looked her up and down. "Are you okay?"

"I'm fine. Wait until I tell you what happened." June pointed behind her at the wagon. "Look!"

Laura stared past June at a wagon packed full of groceries clear up to the top of the sidewalls. She could see canned goods stacked at the front, bags at the back, and two loaves of bread and what had to be at least two dozen eggs balanced on the top.

"What in the world?" Laura couldn't take in what she was seeing. "I know the store didn't give you all this for one dollar." She turned back to June. "You'd better explain right now."

"Can we please go down first? I'm tired from walking and some of that stuff needs to go in the creek cold spot," June said. "Besides, it's kind of a long story."

Laura took a deep breath and squared her shoulders. She reached for the wagon handle and motioned for June to walk in front of her. When they reached the boys, Laura pulled the wagon under the bridge near the firepit and began unloading the contents. "June, start talking. I want to know exactly what happened from the time you left us. And don't you dare leave anything out."

"It was easy finding the store. I passed lots of big houses on the way, maybe four or five on each side, and two cars. The drivers waved, and I waved back, but they didn't stop. I pulled the wagon inside the store and gave the list to a man at the counter."

"My word," Laura said. She lifted a metal bowl of eggs from the top of the wagon load, set them down beside her next to two loaves of bread, and shook her head. "Look at all this food. What did the man at the store say when you gave him the list?"

"He kinda grinned and then got everything for me. The total was 94 cents, so I handed him the dollar and he gave me six cents change. He helped me turn the wagon around and get it back outside on the street, then waved goodbye."

"Mama, I think there's a chicken in the wagon, all cut up and ready for cooking." Raymond pointed to a taped-up, butcher paper-wrapped package that was shaped like a bird. "Papa loves fried chicken."

"It is a chicken, Raymond, and there's saltpork and ham, too," June said. "Miss Cecilia and Miss Inez told me we should have some meat to go with the staples." June turned from Raymond to Laura. "What's a staple?"

Laura crossed her arms and stared at June. "A food staple is something that most people keep on hand. Who are Miss Cecilia and

Miss Inez and what do they have to do with the food in this wagon?"

"They're twin sisters, Mama, and they're nice ladies. They told me to call them Miss Cecilia and Miss Inez since they both have the same last name, Witherspoon."

"Enough," Laura said. "Take a deep breath and go back to when you left the store. What did you do next, and how did you meet the two sisters."

June sighed and stared at the ground. "I walked real careful so the eggs and milk would be okay. When I started past a pretty yellow house, two ladies sitting on the porch called out to me." June raised her eyes to Laura's and shrugged. "You always tell us to be polite to grownups, and they seemed nice."

Laura's expression didn't change, so June looked back down before going on with her story. "The ladies motioned me up to the porch and asked if I'd like a glass of lemonade. It was awful warm outside, and they had a pitcher on a little table between them, so I said yes. Then they asked my name and told me their names."

June stopped speaking and tilted her head to the side, eyes focused upwards.

"I'll bet you sat on the porch to drink your lemonade and visit with the ladies. And what happened next?" Laura prodded.

"They said they knew just about everybody that lived at this end of town, but hadn't seen me before. Then they asked where I lived." June stopped and stared at Laura. "We're not supposed to lie, so I told her we lived under the bridge. They said that sounded interesting, so I told her all about how we had things fixed up real nice. And with Papa working, that's why I had to go to the store because you couldn't leave the boys or our stuff."

Laura sat down, lowered her head into her hands, and closed her eyes. When she opened them, three pairs of eyes on three worried faces stared at her. "Sorry kids, I'm getting a headache, nothing to worry about." She took a deep breath to steady herself and asked June to go on with the story.

"They asked if it wouldn't be a great surprise for you if I came home with a whole wagon full of supplies since it was so hard for

you to get away. They laughed and clapped like
little kids sharing a great game, and told me to
stay still on the porch while they went inside for
some things. Then they brought out all kinds of
stuff and packed it in the wagon." June sat next
to Laura and reached out to touch her leg."
"Then I pulled the wagon home, Mama, and
that's all. Did I do something wrong?"

"No, Junebug, you did nothing wrong."
Laura patted June's hand, then pulled herself up
and stood next to the wagon. "Let's unpack all
this stuff and put it away. Dry things and the
eggs will go in the back of the truck, and cool
things in the river cold area."

As Laura put the food away, she was in
awe at the Witherspoon ladies' generosity.
There were bags of sugar, flour, beans, and oats.
A big can of Crisco, plus two pounds of butter
and two pounds of cheese were tucked in next
to more than a dozen cans of various vegetables
and fruits and a big bag of potatoes. The
chicken Raymond had spotted was near a jar
stuffed with pieces of ham and another jar filled
with saltpork. Three quarts of milk and small
jars of molasses and honey, plus little boxes of

salt and pepper. Wonder of wonders, Laura
even found a box of Kellogg's Corn Flakes and a
small bag of oranges.

June, thrilled to be the center of
attention, spent much of the afternoon
answering questions from her brothers and
repeating her story for them.

"We don't take charity." The words ran
through Laura's mind over and over. She kept
seeing her sister Ruth's face as she'd said them,
dashing Laura's opportunity to have a free piece
of hard candy offered to her by Paul. It had been
her first trip to town with Ruth, and the thought
of what that candy's sweetness would be like
still made her mouth water. But Ruth was
adamant, insisting that their pa would punish
them both if they took something free from
anyone.

The words rang in her ears still, "We
don't take charity." But she refused to crush the
innocent look on June's face. We'll find a way to
pay those ladies back. Glen's earning good
money. Besides, these kids are hungry. How was
she supposed to take the food away for the sake
of a phrase they'd never heard before?

CHAPTER THIRTY-FIVE
Just Too Hungry

Glen was welcomed home by the scent of chicken frying in the skillet and all three children running towards him. They surrounded the bicycle, almost knocking him over in their excitement.

"Papa, Papa, come see all the food."

They jumped up and down as he popped out the kickstand, then dragged him to the firepit. "Look, Mama's cooking chicken and fried potatoes. And there's canned green beans, fresh bread with butter, and milk to drink," June said, as they stood staring at the platter of chicken. Sizzling potato slices had replaced the meat in the pan, and an open can of green beans with the paper peeled off was heating on the side of the firepit.

"Don't fight it, Glen," Laura said. "I'll explain everything after we eat." She pointed at the children who still hung from their papa's hands. "Go wash up while I fix your plates."

"June didn't get all this for a dollar."

"No, she didn't. Go wash up. If we can keep them focused on eating and playing afterward, I'll fill you in on what happened."

Glen followed Laura when she carried the dirty dishes to the creek to wash them. He lugged a bucket of hot water, heated on the fire, and dumped half into the tin basin she used for a sink. Then he added some Saponini dish soap powder to the water and sat down next to her.

"Well, I gather that June met two ladies who filled up the wagon with food for her family." Glen's voice was soft, but his knuckles were white where they clasped his bent knees.

"That's about it. We've never made a big issue out of what charity is, and since they gave her lemonade and talked first, she didn't think of them as strangers."

"I know, and I didn't want to make her feel bad either." Glen strummed his fingers and watched Laura scrub the plates and utensils, then put them into the bucket holding the remaining hot water. "It just sticks in my craw, since we didn't need their charity. I'm making decent money and can afford to pay for my family's food."

"Maybe we could pay them back. Not make them think we're ungrateful, but give the sisters a thank you note with the money inside." Laura stopped scrubbing and tilted her head to the side. "How much do you think that wagon load would have cost?"

"I'd guess about five dollars. That was a lot of stuff."

"Should we send her tomorrow, or wait for another trip to the store?" Laura wiped down the cast iron skillet, then dumped the soapy water into the creek just beyond the edge of the bridge. She watched the suds float away from their camp area, then trudged back to where Glen sat. "If we send her tomorrow, they'll most likely either refuse it or follow her back here."

"I think you're right. We'll send her to the store again in a few days and have her leave the envelope with the note and money on their porch if they're not home. If they're there, she can just tell them to read it later."

"Good plan." Laura rinsed the dishes, then put everything back into the first basin, now clean and dry. "I'll put these things away and get the kids headed for bed. You coming up, too?"

"In a little while." Glen threw a stone out into the creek, watching it skip three times before it sank. "To be honest, I'm still bothered about eating somebody else's food. That brings back an awful lot of memories, bad ones, of my family after Pa died."

Laura put the dishes away, then placed the covered dutch oven over the embers. All the leftover chicken and the cut-up giblets were inside the pot ready for cooking into soup the next day. After checking the sleeping children, she fixed the bed for herself and Glen, and changed into her nightgown.

Laura was almost asleep when Glen slipped under the blanket next to her. He kissed her forehead and stroked her cheek, then turned his back to her. Laura's visions started minutes after Glen dozed off. They weren't bloody or scary like his war dreams, but vivid, sad, and painful.

Laura saw a small, dark living room with sagging curtains pulled across a front window with a taped crack reaching out from one bottom corner. Glen's mother sat in an overstuffed chair with yellowed doilies on each arm. She was resting her neck on the back of the chair, and her swollen bare feet on an ottoman covered in torn, stained leather. Three children, two Laura recognized as Glen and his sister Barbara, sat in the middle of the floor around a checkers board.

The doorbell rang, but no one stood. The children looked at their mother, who put her fingers to her lips and tipped her head toward the window curtains. When the doorbell rang again, Glen crawled to the window and nudged the curtain aside to see who was at the door.

"Ma, it's two people from the church. Looks like they've got a box of stuff with them. The guy is wearing a Christmas hat."

"Tell them I'm sleeping." Glen's mother bolted from the room.

Glen opened the door a crack. He didn't say anything, just waited for the people to talk.

"Is your mother home?" The man asked, trying to peer into the room.

"She's sleeping. What do you want?"

"We're from the Nazarene Baptist Church, and we have a holiday basket for your family."

"Thank you. I can take it for her." Glen was polite, but his stance remained stiff and defensive.

The woman bent down, hands on her knees, putting her face close to Glen's. "We'd like to invite your family to church. And we'd like to know if there are any other ways we can help you."

"I'll let her know when she wakes up. Can't think of anything you can do for us." Glen stepped back and started to close the door.

"Wait." The man put his foot inside the door and picked up the box. "Please take this. It has a lot of food for your family." He pushed the box into Glen's arms.

"Okay," Glen said. He took the box, said thanks, then pushed the door closed with his foot. He carried the box to a tiny kitchen table and began pulling things out.

Barbara and Bobbie watched his every move, stepping back only when their mother joined them.

"Look, Ma, there's turkey, mashed potatoes, and lots more." Barbara's voice rose with each new dish she pulled out. "Wow, even an apple pie." She turned to her ma, pleading. "Please Ma, I know you don't like people poking into our business, but can we have some? Please?"

Laura could see the pain on their mother's face, the tears pooled in her eyes.

"Of course you can, honey, get the plates down and you can have all you want."

The plates were soon filled and each child dove in. Their mother didn't fill one for herself, but nibbled on a small slice of turkey. Glen's expression, as he watched his mother's, was painful. He didn't want to disappoint her, but couldn't ignore the food. Glen was just too hungry.

CHAPTER THIRTY-SIX
We Move Next Sunday
Saturday, August 21st., 1933

Laura sat in the shade by the truck, chin resting on her knees, arms wrapped around her lower legs and holding her skirt in place. She nodded and smiled at the children's antics in the water, while her thoughts raced far afield.

It didn't seem possible that it'd had been over seven weeks since they first pitched camp under the bridge? Seven weeks since she'd talked to a single person other than Glen and her children? Seven weeks of living in conditions even more primitive than the sod house where she'd been born?

"Mama, watch me," Jimmy squealed. He stood in water halfway up his chubby thighs, then leaped as high as he could and plopped down on his bottom. Water sprayed around him, splattering both June and Raymond.

Laura clapped and cheered, while June yelled. "My turn now."

June leaped into the air and slapped the surface of the water with her palms as she landed. Water fountained up in a circle, covering both her and her brothers.

"Now me." Raymond launched himself up and forward, arms outstretched at his sides, landing in a belly flop. The massive spray of water engulfed all three children.

Laughing, Laura waved her arms and encouraged the kids to keep playing. A huge lump formed in her throat. She loved her children so much it hurt, and would do anything to keep them safe and happy. Seven weeks of isolation under a bridge was a small price to pay.

The splashing game continued until Laura called the kids out of the water. "All three of you look like wrinkly prunes. Time to change into dry clothes for supper." A chorus of groans followed, but when she crossed her arms and stared into each child's face, they trudged out of the creek and grabbed towels to dry off.

The sun was sinking when Glen pedaled under the bridge, long past his usual arrival time. He found his family seated around the firepit with bowls of beans and ham in their hands.

"Sit still and wait for your papa." Laura's voice froze three children in place. "He'll be here as soon as he washes up."

Laura had a hard time being patient too, since the look on Glen's face told her he was dying to share some news. She filled his bowl with steaming chunks of ham bobbing in fragrant, juicy white beans, then poured him a tall glass of water.

"Hi, kids," Glen said. "Were you good for your mama today?" He reached for his food, flashing a huge grin and a wink at Laura.

Chatter and giggles flavored each bite as the children regaled Glen with stories about their day.

After the children told their last stories and got their final hugs, they snuggled down on their bed. Glen and Laura cleaned up the supper dishes, then strolled hand-in-hand to the edge of the creek where they settled down on a grassy portion near the shore.

Laura squeezed Glen's hand and leaned against his shoulder. "Spill it. I know you've got something to tell me. It's been written on your face, plain as day, from the moment you got home."

"I've found us a place to live, and I know you'll love it." Glen's smile transformed his whole face, and his wide-open eyes almost glowed. "It's a farm across town. The house is real nice. We'll have inside plumbing and electricity again, and it's close enough to town for you to shop and for June to go to school."

Laura inhaled a noisy gulp of air. "Oh, my goodness. It sounds perfect. Can we afford it? When can we move?" She had lots more questions.

"We can move next weekend on Sunday and get settled on Monday since it's Labor Day. The best part is there's no rent to pay. All we have to do is take care of the animals and truck garden and split half the produce and animal products with Mr. Wolz, our new landlord. He lives on the other side of the property in a small house of his own. Real friendly old guy. I think you'll like him."

Laura tilted her head to the side and scrunched up her eyes. "That's kind of a crazy arrangement. Why would he do that?"

"Mr. Wolz ... he asked me to just call him Rudolf ... was getting too old to work the place himself, so he fixed the house up while his son, Gunther, was attending Tulane University down in Louisiana. The idea was for Gunther to take over after he graduated. But that plan changed when Gunther got married in New Orleans." Glen stretched out his legs and crossed his arms behind his neck for a pillow.

Laura stared down into Glen's face. "I don't understand. Is he renting it out because his son stayed in New Orleans?"

"No, there's more to the story. When Gunther sent word about his engagement, Mr. Wolz figured the newlyweds wouldn't want to room with him, so he built a little place for himself." Glen rolled over on his side to face Laura, his head held up by one elbow while his free hand played with her fingers. "Mr. Wolz finished building his cottage and remodeling the main house just before Gunther and his new bride, Giselle, arrived."

Glen patted the ground next to his side, inviting Laura to lie down with him. "The newlyweds loved the house and made lots of friends in town. They were happy as can be for almost a year, until Giselle got pregnant."

Laura stretched out on the grass and gave a low whistle. "Uh, oh, I'll bet she wanted her family around for the baby's birth."

"You got it right." Glen reached out and stroked Laura's cheek, then her lips when she turned and kissed his fingers. "Her father has been one of the main engineers on something called the Lakefront Project in New Orleans since it started in 1926. After the big Mississippi River flood in 1927, work for the city flood control increased on a massive scale, so he's become one of the rich elites on the planning board. Giselle is an only child and her parents wouldn't hear of her living and giving birth on a little farm in Missouri. They sent first class train tickets for Gunther and Giselle, who left everything behind and headed to New Orleans a month ago."

"Wow," Laura said. "That's quite a story. I'm surprised Mr. Wolz told you so much private information about his family."

Glen chuckled. "He didn't. Most of the story came from one of my bosses who shared the local gossip. Mr. Wolz just showed me the place and told me the terms." Glen's smile disappeared as he gazed into Laura's eyes. "What do you think?"

"I think we should move next Sunday."

CHAPTER THIRTY-SEVEN
Favorite Rocks
Labor Day Week-end, 1933

"Can you believe this will be the last dinner you have to cook over an open firepit?" Glen said. "We can pack the truck early tomorrow morning."

"I'll help." June's enthusiasm was infectious. Both boys joined in with their own offers of assistance.

Laura grinned at the pained expression on Glen's face. "But remember, kids, your papa will decide what goes where in the truck, so you have to follow his directions."

Raymond jumped to his feet. "I get to dump sand on the firepit and kick it apart all by myself." He placed one foot behind the other and leaned forward, ready to start.

"Good idea, son. But don't you think we should wait until after breakfast tomorrow?" Glen said. "It'd be a long day on empty stomachs."

Raymond's shoulders drooped and June giggled. "Yeah, silly, you can't break it apart until Mama finishes using it."

Glen glanced at June, standing tall with her hands on her hips. "That's true, Junebug." Then he patted Raymond on the back. "But knocking it apart will be your brother's job when the time comes."

Anticipation and excitement made it hard for the children to relax, so Glen fished his guitar out of the truck and played while June cleaned up and prepared the bedding. Lively, silly songs soon gave way to softer melodies. Bright eyes began to droop until the children wound down and settled themselves on their mattress. Not one admitted to being sleepy, but all agreed it would be easier to listen stretched out on the bed. Glen strummed until accompanied only by soft snores and rhythmic breathing.

Laura joined Glen next to the sleeping children. "They're such good kids. You'll need the patience of a saint with all their eager help tomorrow."

"I know." Glen shook his head and laughed. "Raymond was ready to kick the firepit rocks like footballs through the goalposts."

"I think the rocks would have won, and he'd be nursing bruised toes." Laura smoothed a stray lock of hair back from Raymond's forehead. "But if Jimmy helps by kicking sand, we're all in trouble."

Glen chuckled and turned to face Laura, his expression serious. "I hope you like the new place. The house is real nice, but managing a farm while I'm off working most days puts a lot of pressure on you."

"I'll be fine. I grew up on a farm, remember, and then worked on Miss Emma's place for five years." She reached out and caressed Glen's cheek. "Truth is, I'd rather work outside any day." Laura grinned. She leaned in for a kiss, enjoying the familiar taste. "Miss Emma used to tell me I'd better find a man who'd eat anything or a rich one who could hire a cook since I'd never be great in the kitchen. I'd rather work outside with stock or in a garden anytime rather than be stuck doing housework."

"I think you cook just fine." Glen stood and pulled Laura to her feet. He wrapped his arms around her for another, deeper kiss. "We need to get to bed, too. Tomorrow will be a long day, especially with all the help from these three."

The children woke up before their parents for the first time. Their giggles and conversation woke Glen and Laura, who pretended to sleep while watching them. With June on one side and Raymond and Jimmy on the other, they folded their blanket and laid it down on the sandy dirt with their pillows next to it. Next they tried to roll the mattress. When it refused to cooperate, they pulled the canvas, with the mattress on top, over to the side of the truck. The somewhat lumpy blanket and the three pillows, coated with sand, were placed on top. Triumphant, the three ran to their silently giggling parents.

"Wake up, wake up." Jimmy sang out, bouncing on Glen and Laura's legs.

"Hurry, it's moving day. We need breakfast fast, then I'll take the firepit apart for you." Raymond's focus hadn't changed.

June stood next to the mattress and pointed at the truck. "Look, we took care of our bed. It's ready to go in the truck. Now it's your turn."

"Amazing job." Glen looked first at the canvas and the pile of sand and dirt that had been dragged with it. Parts of the mattress rested on the ground, and a coating of sand lay on the blanket and pillows spread over the top of the bedding material. "I guess we'd better get moving."

Laura had the fire going in minutes. Bacon sizzled in the cast iron skillet in the center of the pit while coffee heated next to the frying pan. She had eggs in a bowl at her side, ready to fry in the bacon grease as soon as the meat was crispy.

Raymond circled the pit, waiting to pounce as soon as he got the word.

"Listen, kids," Glen said, as everyone sat with plates on their laps. "I know you're eager to help, but I've got to pack the truck just right. I don't want you putting anything inside it. That's my job. Just find all your things under the bridge and by the creek and bring them up near the truck so I can load them."

Three faces with big grins. Three mouths that chewed breakfast as fast as they could. Three heads that bobbed to Glen's words. Laura could tell the children were eager to help, but somehow didn't think Glen's plans would work quite as he'd imagined.

Sure enough, when Laura brought the clean dishes up from the creek she found Glen standing near the back of the truck with his hands on his hips, shaking his head and rolling his eyes.

"June, what is this? Why is there a stack of wood and leaves here at the back of the truck?"

"That's our woodpile. Mama will need it at the new place, and you said to bring all our stuff to the truck."

"Honey, we don't need to take the wood. I promise there's lots of wood at the new place. Please take it all back under the bridge where it was."

June kicked at a good-sized piece. "I worked hard bringing it here. I don't want to move it again."

"Sorry, but you have to." Glen raised his voice so everyone could hear. "Please, I said carry things over by the truck, but don't stack it right behind or next to it or I won't have room to move around and arrange things."

Raymond nodded, but remained intent on obliterating any traces of the firepit. Jimmy and June looked at each other and ran off to find more stuff.

"What the heck?" Glen stared inside the back of the truck. His attention focused on a large pile of rocks resting on the rolled mattresses he'd tied and placed next to the sidewall.

Laura chuckled and said, "Those are Jimmy's favorite rocks. You know he likes to build things on the damp dirt at the edge of the creek."

"Favorite rocks? We're taking rocks to the new place?"

"You told them to get their stuff, and he considers those his best toys."

"Lord have mercy." Glen picked up a handful of the rocks and held them out to Laura. "Do you think he'd notice if these disappeared?"

"He might. Can't you tuck them in a corner someplace?"

Jimmy's treasured rocks remained in the truck, and with that, Glen gave up on his careful packing plan and ended up just sticking everything in the truck willy-nilly. The whole family crowded in the cab for the drive to their new home.

"We need to make one stop on the way to the house." Glen pulled an envelope out of the glove box. "June, I need you to show me the house where the Witherspoon sisters live."

"It's the yellow one, Papa. Are we going to stop and visit them?"

"No, but your mama is going to give them a nice thank-you card."

When the truck stopped in front of the Witherspoon house, Laura eased herself out from under the children and ran to the front door. She rapped the wooden doorknocker three times. No one answered, so she slipped the card partway under the door and ran back to the truck.

"Oh shoot," June said. "I wish you could meet them. They're such nice ladies."

"Maybe another day." Glen pulled back out into the road.

Laura smiled at June. "We'll try again, honey. But at least we got to thank them for their kindness." She was relieved the sisters had not answered the door, glad she'd avoided a potential uncomfortable scene when they found money inside the card.

Glen circled around town on back roads. "Here's our driveway," he said, turning off the pavement onto a narrow gravel lane.

The road curved to the right, ending in an open area in front of a single-story, brown house. A deep porch spanned the length of the front, with posts holding up the roof. A neat picket fence, with a wide rail on top, edged all three sides of the porch. Four wide steps in the center led up to the porch and straight to the front door with a large window on either side. The minute Glen stopped the truck, everyone poured out of the cab and rushed up the steps.

"Hang on, I've got to unlock the door." Glen tugged a keyring out of his shirt pocket, pulled the screen door open, then unlocked the front door and waved everyone inside.

"Oh, Glen, it's beautiful," Laura whispered, grabbing his hand. "Look how clean the windows are, and the paint looks brand new. I love it already."

Glen hugged her hard and grinned. "Told you."

They leaned together for a kiss, then giggled when June's strident voice rang out.

"I told you we should have brought our woodpile. Look at the fireplace." June stood in the middle of the long living room, pointing to the fireplace on the end wall to the right of the front door. Dull red bricks surrounded the edges of the opening, topped by a wide wooden mantel. The bricks were free of soot, and the grate for burning wood was empty. There were no ashes mounded on the clean firebox floor. A wrought iron rack of fire tools stood to the side of the hearth, next to a wide box big enough to hold a supply of wood and kindling. "Now we have to find wood before we can have a fire," June said.

Glen couldn't help but laugh at the earnest look on his daughter's face. "There's a whole pile of firewood stacked on the back porch. It'll be a long time before you have to hunt for wood."

"Where's the back porch?" Raymond said, looking around the room.

"Straight through this door, down the hall, and out the back door." Glen crossed the living room and opened a door across from the front entrance. "Go ahead and explore. The truck can wait while we check out the house."

June and Raymond, with Jimmy close behind, whooped with excitement and raced down the hall and out the back door.

Laura stood transfixed, staring at an upright piano that stood against the wall to the right of the hallway. It wasn't grand and gleaming like Miss Emma's, and the bench was solid wood without any padding on top. The cover was raised, exposing keys which were somewhat yellowed with age. "A piano," she whispered, turning her head toward Glen while the fingers of her right hand stroked the cool keys. Her voice trembled and her eyes glistened. "You found us a house with a piano."

"Now you can make music every single day." Glen wrapped his arms around Laura and kissed her forehead. "That's one reason I knew this house was meant for us."

"Thank you," Laura whispered into the curve of his neck. "Guess you'd better show me the rest before the kids come flying back inside."

Glen gave Laura a squeeze, then led her down the hall. Fresh-looking eggshell-colored paint covered the walls and ceiling, and the wide-plank wooden floor gleamed. They stopped at the first of two doors on the right. "This is the first bedroom, and the second is next to it. Both are the same size, but I kind of thought you and I should use the second one since it's closer to the bathroom and the back door."

Laura inspected both square bedrooms, furnished with double beds, dressers, and armoires for clothing. Each had one curtained window. The beds were made with thick, multicolored quilts on top. The curtains, sky blue in one room and soft green in the other, had ruffled valances at the top.

"Here's the bathroom." Glen opened the door on the left of the hall, across from the second bedroom. "Bathtub, sink, toilet, mirrored medicine cabinet above the sink, and a wooden storage cabinet underneath. The white enamel surfaces are in great shape and should be easy to keep clean." He looked back at Laura, tilting his head. "With the way our kids sling water, I'm glad they put linoleum in here instead of wood, even if it is just black and white squares. What do you think?"

"I think it sure beats a trench and shovel and a running creek." Laura laughed, then patted Glen's chest. "I love it. This is the nicest place we've ever had since we got married."

Glen's body relaxed, and his smile widened. "Come on, you still need to see the kitchen and washroom."

He led her back down the hall, through the living room to the dining area at the end opposite the fireplace. A table with six chairs was centered in the space, separated from the kitchen by a double-wide doorway.

Laura's sharp intake of breath said more than any words. She stepped onto the green and yellow patterned linoleum floor, then reached to her left to stroke the long white porcelain counter with a big sink in the middle and long drainboards on either side. The countertop rested on multiple cabinets and drawers, painted a soft yellow that gleamed around the metal hardware. "It's so pretty. And I can look out the window when I'm doing dishes."

Glen followed her into the room and leaned against a plain wooden table pushed against the wall across from the sink. "I mean, it's not quite what you're used to, but I'm hoping it'll do." A big grin split his face as he watched Laura move into the room, touching and exploring the upper cabinets mounted on either side of the window and the tall pantry doors at the end of the countertop.

"It's amazing, fancy enough for one of those flashy magazines. Never imagined I'd have a kitchen like this." Laura turned away from the pantry storage. "Oh, my goodness, an electric stove. I've never worked one of those."

"Only the best for Giselle. The house was small by her family standards, but Mr. Woltz told me Gunther made sure she had the latest and greatest of everything." Glen pointed to the tall white cabinet with a circular turret on top to the left of the stove. "Did you check this out?"

"The icebox? No, but that is a nice big one."

"Honey, this isn't an icebox. It's a refrigerator. That thing on top is the compressor." He opened the door and pointed to the small metal box in the top right-hand corner. "And look here, it makes ice-cubes."

"Wow. I can't believe we live here now."

"You haven't seen everything yet." Glen pointed to a glass-paned door at the end of the room. He took her hand and led her out the door. "Look at your washroom."

Laura couldn't believe her eyes. The small, square room had a countertop that drained into a big soaking sink. A shiny, new electric washing machine sat in the corner. A length of hose was connected to the faucet in the sink, ready to fill the tub.

"It's beautiful. Look how big the wash tub is. That'll do a lot of laundry." Laura lifted the lid to peer inside at the metal agitator vanes. "Can it wash with hot water? Where does the water go when the washing cycle is finished?"

"The electric heating unit heats the water for you. And when the washing cycle is over, you flip the valve on this drain under the tub so water can flow through the hose. The drain hose goes out the back door and over the side of the back porch." Glen grabbed the wringer rollers and unlocked a lever at the side. "The wringer stays out of the way while you're washing, then swings over the top of the tub so the water wrung out of the clothes goes back into the washer." He opened the door to the back porch, pointing at the hose that, tucked tight against the wall of the house, ran all the way off the edge of the porch. "The dirty water runs down that gravel-lined trough straight to the garden."

"Well, I never thought things could get this fancy." Laura shook her head in disbelief. "I'm sure getting spoiled."

"You deserve it," Glen said. "Not many women could manage seven weeks under a bridge, isolated from the whole world, without throwing a fit."

Laura's response was cut off by three voices begging to get their things out of the truck.

CHAPTER THIRTY-EIGHT
I Love It Here

The whole family pitched in to help unload the truck. Glen insisted on putting all their possessions on the front porch first, so they could be sorted and put away in proper order.

When the truck was empty, Laura stood staring at everything they owned. "I'd forgotten what all we packed. It looks like a lot more spread out here instead of stuffed into the truck."

"Everything will look a lot better inside the house. Good thing this place is full of furniture so we have places to put things." Glen looked at the children who had each created a little section of their favorite things, then he glanced at Laura. "Shall we let them take their things into their bedroom? Then they can go play while we do the rest?"

"Not everything. Jimmy, your rocks go on the back porch. Raymond, same thing for the wagon. All outside toys go to the porch instead of inside the bedroom. "Three heads bobbed in agreement, ready to start. "Go on, get busy."

Each child grabbed something and shot inside the front door. Glen and Laura put all the kitchen things away first, then tackled the other items.

In just a few hours, all their possessions had been put away. The children were running in and out through the back door as they explored each new discovery with their parents.

"Wish I had their energy," Laura said, watching the children disappear down the hallway and out the back door. She sat on one of the dining room chairs and stretched her back and arms. "Are you hungry?"

"I could eat." Glen sat in the chair next to her with his legs extended straight out, then slapped his palms on his thighs. "But we have a bunch of animals to tend to first. We can take the kids to show them, then figure out what chores they can do later. Caring for cows, mules, pigs, and chickens will be new for them, especially learning that the animals have to be taken care of every single day whether they want to or not. I think we can wait to check out the garden until tomorrow."

"You're right. I'd forgotten." Laura rolled her shoulders one last time, then stood and motioned to Glen. "Come on, Mr. Farmer, we'd better get started."

They found the children sitting and staring through the pasture fence at five cows and two mules, all grazing on ankle-high grass, switching their tails at pesky flies.

"Guess we can wait until later to bring them into the barn and do the milking." Glen and Laura leaned on fence posts and watched with the children for a few minutes. "Let's go check on the pigs and chickens," Glen said.

"The pigs are on the other side of the barn." June popped up and led the way. "Come on, I'll show you."

After studying the pigs, three sows and a pen full of half-grown piglets, the children led the way to a chicken coop with a large fenced-in enclosure where the birds were pecking at the ground or settled in the sun.

"Chickens, I know. We have to collect eggs every day and keep them fed, but they shouldn't be too much work for you guys while I'm away."

Laura smiled at Glen and nodded because she didn't want him to feel bad, but a good look at the white and green piles all over the chicken ladders, nesting boxes and coop ground told her a different story. The pen needed a thorough cleaning, and that would be a big, dirty job. The manure could go straight into the garden to help prepare it for next year, but getting it scrubbed off all the surfaces and into the garden would take hours of hard labor. And that job would fall on Laura's shoulders.

"Mama, can we pet the chickens?" June said. She and her brothers stood at the cage door, ready to join the birds inside.

"Not now. Why don't we go inside and have a bite to eat. You kids can wash up, then set the table while I fix something."

The rest of the day, Laura stayed inside organizing and planning. The children ran in and out, exhausting themselves exploring. Glen told her he wanted to get familiar with the things stored in the barn, garage, and storage shed, and ended up outside most of the afternoon.

By evening, the house felt like home. The truck, empty and clean, was in the garage, while Glen's tools were arrayed on shelves and hooks along one side of the garage above a long workbench.

After finishing the household chores, Laura accompanied Glen to the barn. He got all the cows and the mules into their stalls, fed them, and milked the cows. The warm, frothy liquid was then poured into tall milk cans and stored in a room in the barn.

One cow had put her foot in the bucket, so they carried that milk out to the pigpen. The fresh milk poured into a trough with the rest of the pig's food caused a mini-stampede with each pig pushing and shoving for his share.

"I'm glad you collect eggs in the morning," Glen said, shaking his head as he led the way to the coop. "I'm bushed."

"Still work to do with the birds. We have to make sure there's enough straw in all the nesting boxes, then secure the door and side panels so predators can't get in after dark."

Laura grinned at Glen's puzzled expression. "Chickens aren't the smartest creatures around and often kick straw out of their boxes, or mess in it. You want the nests soft for the eggs." She opened the lid on a large wooden box inside the coop and showed him the straw packed inside. "Just grab some here and put it where it's needed. Then check all the chicken wire on the pen walls to make sure there aren't any holes or sections pulled out. We don't need foxes or skunks getting in." She pointed to a hammer, a pair of pliers, and some wire hanging next to the wooden door. "Always smart to make sure everything's secure before locking the pen door for the night."

Glen watched her every move. "Good thing you know what to do." He patted her shoulder as they made their way to the back porch of the house. "I didn't mean to create so much work for you, I was just excited about this place."

"I love it here. We'll manage."

The next day, they took a tour around Aurora so Laura would know where everything was. Glen assured her she'd be able to walk to the places she'd need, but wanted to be sure she could find them. The kids were just excited to be in town.

"Look, June, there's the school." Glen pointed to a two-story building in the middle of the block. "That's where your mama will take you tomorrow morning." The building was close to the sidewalk but had a wide grassy area on the side. Several children were playing tetherball and hopscotch, while others played on slides and climbed on a circular metal thing with bars going different directions.

"Tomorrow?" June squeaked.

Laura patted her leg. "You'll be fine."

Glen drove at a crawl, pointing out a grocery store, a service station with a huge red winged-horse and the word Texaco on the sign, a post office, a feed store, and even a barbershop and a beauty parlor. Laura took note of the places she'd need to visit, hoping she'd remember.

"Papa, where do you work?" Raymond looked from side to side.

"I'll show you the office, but I don't go there each day." Glen turned down a side street that had more office buildings than stores. "I go straight to where we're working on a bridge."

They drove past a bank, an insurance office, and a doctor's office. "There's Connor Construction," Glen said, pointing at a large square building with double glass doors that had the company name painted on the glass. "That's the company I work for."

Glen turned again onto a street that paralleled the one they'd come in on. "And now for a surprise." He drove down a block and parked. "Everybody out."

"Where are we going?" Laura asked once they gathered on the sidewalk.

Glen didn't say a word, just led the way past two store fronts and opened the door to the third. "This is Annie's Ice Cream Parlor, and you can each choose whatever flavor you want."

Glen drove the truck to work the next morning, not having allowed enough time for animal care and not wanting to be late. Laura decided the chickens could wait until she returned from walking June to school. She didn't wake the children until Glen left, knowing their help would just slow him down.

"Come on, sleepyheads, get yourselves washed up for breakfast. You can get dressed after you eat." She poured glasses of fresh milk to go with plates of eggs, bacon, and toast. "Hurry, we're walking June to school this morning."

The pace picked up, as all three children chattered with excitement about the hike into town. Laura stopped them at the front door for a final inspection, then escorted them out the door and down the stairs.

It didn't take long. June led the way with Raymond next to her for most of the distance. Jimmy started out walking, but soon tired and raised his arms to be carried. "You're getting heavy," Laura said, groaning as she picked him up. He grinned and wrapped his arms around her neck. June's pace didn't slow down until they were right in front of the school, when she stopped and grabbed Laura's arm.

"Do I have to go in?" Her voice sounded shaky and thin.

"Yes, and I promise you'll love school, just like I did." Laura put Jimmy down and gave June a hug. "We have to go to the office first, then we'll take you to your class. And remember, we'll be right here waiting for you when school is over today."

They left June with a happy smile on her face, talking to a little girl with curly red hair. The teacher, Mrs. Maxwell, waved them out the door after promising everything would be fine.

CHAPTER THIRTY-NINE
Scary Bunch of Little Monsters
The Next Three Years, 1933 through 1936

Mrs. Maxwell was right. June did just fine in school, and so did Raymond when he began two years later. By the time he started, Laura no longer needed to walk the children each way.

Glen continued working full time for Connor, but had been cut back to five days per week instead of six to save on overtime. He worried about the income loss, but found it much easier to keep up with the animal and garden chores.

Once the weekends were free, Laura and Glen hosted impromptu dances every Saturday night for a large circle of friends. They'd push the dining and living room furniture against the walls and roll up the living room rug. Everybody who came brought something to snack on or to drink, piling their offerings on the dining table. People even brought their own cups, plates and utensils to make it easy on Laura.

No alcohol was allowed, since the dances were family affairs. All the guest's kids were put down on blanket pallets in the children's bedroom by 8:30. The parents didn't care if they slept, as long as they stayed in the room. The adults couldn't hear them once the music started, so the children could talk and laugh to their hearts' content. Once in a while, a grownup would notice the door to the hall ajar with wide eyes peeking around the edge, but the door always shut as soon as an adult discovered the child.

Laura and Glen didn't dance much, even though they both loved dancing, because they spent most of their time playing various instruments. June almost always sat at the piano, while Glen switched between guitar, or

banjo, or harmonica. Some folks brought
instruments and would play a few songs to give
Laura and Glen a break. Most of their breaks
were spent dancing, since neither could resist
the music.

Laura enjoyed the people in Aurora,
most of all the shopkeepers who were quick to
smile when she came in. One of her favorites
was Mr. Niederman, the postmaster. Short and
round, with a white wreath of hair that circled
his crown, he always wore bright green
suspenders. He also kept a pipe in his mouth
that was almost never lit, no matter how often
he stopped work to relight it. Mr. Niederman
had been a widower for many years and never
seemed to pry, but somehow asked just the right
questions to start a conversation.

"Come on in, Mrs. Webber. I've got
something for you today," he'd sing out,
grinning around his pipe, whenever she got a
letter from her sisters or from Willa. "This one's
from Ruth," he'd say. He'd learned about each
member of her family and loved to hear all the
news. Laura felt safe sharing, since nothing
she'd ever told him came back as gossip.

"That's wonderful. Congratulations," he said. He'd clap and cheer when she told him about the birth of Becca's twins, a boy and a girl, born just before she'd moved to Aurora. News about Ruth's boys' fascination with bicycle racing elicited a grin, especially when he heard about little sister Maggie wanting to follow them on her trike.

Mr. Niederman worried about how Ruth and Paul were doing during the depression and wasn't surprised to hear they'd tabled plans to build a house for themselves.

"Just hope they can hold on to both of their stores. Not easy in these times." He'd shake his head and pat Laura's shoulder when she'd told him their news. "Lots of stores have to close because folks just can't buy like they used to."

"You're so right. They've laid off most of the help. Jake, Martha and Paul have to do almost all the work. Ruth even helps some with the bookkeeping and store paperwork at home. They might still have to close one, but are trying hard to hang on."

Laura didn't go to the post office every day, once June walked Raymond to and from school, but always stopped at least a couple times each week when she needed to go into town.

On Friday, October 30th, Laura surprised June and Raymond by meeting them outside of school. Jimmy held the wagon handle, proud to help.

"Hi, Mama," June said. "Guess what, Raymond and I both won prizes for our costumes. I was the best witch in second grade and Raymond was the best scarecrow in kindergarten."

"That's wonderful."

"Next year, I'll have the neatest costume in the whole school." Jimmy chimed in, not to be outdone. "Look how scary I am." He held up his arms, trailing gauze strips. "I'm a mummy."

"Since you're all dressed up, I thought it would be fun to spend time visiting downtown before we go home. I have a few errands and you can look at all the store decorations."

The three children skipped and waved at people on the sidewalks, with Laura pulling the wagon behind them. They stopped at the bakery, the grocery store, and the dress shop.

"One last stop at the post office, then we'll head home." Laura gestured at the wagon that held her parcels and handbag. "I think Mr. Niederman will love seeing you, but mind your manners and don't interrupt if he's helping someone."

Three people were in line at the post office when they arrived. Mr. Niederman helped two of them in a few minutes, but an older man with a cane examined several new stamps before he made his selection and left. The children pranced from one foot to another waiting for what must have felt like a lifetime before they had Mr. Niederman's attention.

"Oh, my goodness, Mrs. Webber. Did you know a witch, a scarecrow, and a mummy were following you around?" The postmaster put his hand on his chest and bent down to get a closer look. "What a scary bunch of little monsters."

"You've got that right," Laura said. "I have two letters to mail, one to Ruth and one for Willa." She handed the stamped envelopes to him and received one in return from Willa. "Thank you so much."

Laura made the children take off their costumes when they got home and shooed them outside to play. When Glen arrived right at dusk, he brought the kids inside with him. They all washed up in the washroom before trooping through the kitchen to the table.

"My favorite meal, fried chicken, mashed potatoes and gravy, and creamed corn," he said, then gave Laura a hug and a peck and sat down. "Thank you, this is the perfect end to a rough week."

"You're welcome. And we have chocolate cake, too." Laura passed him the platter of chicken, then filled the children's glasses with milk. "Jimmy, stop fidgeting or you'll spill your milk."

"Uh, oh, makes me wonder if you're working up to something," Glen said. He glanced at Laura and smiled.

Laura finished the dishes and put the children to bed before joining Glen in the living room. He sat on the sofa, leaned his head back, and closed his eyes. He looked like he was napping instead of listening to the radio. Laura knelt facing him on the couch, both her legs tucked under.

"Sleepy?" she said.

"A little. Just peaceful sitting here listening to the news." He chuckled and turned his head toward her. "Those kids of ours are like wind-up toys, but they never seem to run down. Sure wish I had their energy."

Laura nodded and raised her head, rubbing her hands together in her lap. "They are good kids though, all three healthy and smart, never been any trouble."

Glen's tipped his head to the side. "That's true." He stared at Laura. "What's going on? You sound kind of funny. Is something wrong?"

"No, not wrong." She took a deep breath, then blew it out. "At least I hope you won't think so." She paused once again, glancing around the room then back at his face. "We're going to have another baby."

CHAPTER FORTY
Hindenburg Disaster
April 1937

Laura moved around the dining table, leaning sideways to position plates, utensils, and napkins in front of the chairs. When they were in place, she pressed both hands into the small of her back and stretched, shrugging her shoulders and rolling her neck to loosen the muscles.

The sound of thundering feet racing down the hallway toward the living room interrupted her brief respite. "Slow down. No running in the house." The thunder changed to a soft, slow patter of footsteps just before the children reached her and settled into their chairs.

Glen followed the children into the room. "Not sure how good a job they did washing up." He stopped behind Laura and massaged her shoulders and neck. "You look beat, honey. Sit down and I'll finish setting the table."

"Thanks. If you'd bring in the pitcher of milk and fill their glasses, I'll get the food." Laura sat down with a groan after they finished.

Raymond, seated next to Laura, giggled. "Mama, you can set your plate on your tummy."

"You've got a point." Laura rubbed her belly and grinned. "But then one good baby kick and my food will be on the floor."

Glen filled the children's plates, then Laura's. "Okay you guys, no more jokes about your mama's belly. Won't be long before she'll be able to chase you down again when you tease her."

"How soon will the baby be here?" June cocked her head to the side and studied Laura's abdomen. "Remember you're supposed to have a girl for me, so the girls will match the boys."

"Junebug, you know your mama won't know what the baby is until it's here. We've explained that to you before. Be patient for a few more weeks."

Laura smiled, grateful for the way Glen handled June. She was sure it was a boy, but wouldn't say a word ahead of time.

June shrugged and sighed through pursed lips, looking down at her plate. Then her head popped back up. "Where's the baby going to sleep? Our bed is already crowded with the boys and me, no room for another kid."

"Don't worry about that. The baby will sleep in the crib in our room for a long time." Glen reached out and ruffled June's hair, then looked across the table at Laura. "We need to get set up pretty quick though, not much more time left."

"My old crib?" Jimmy asked.

"The same one you all slept in. Your mama made sure we brought it with us." Glen looked across the table. "Your mama's one sharp lady."

Baby conversation continued throughout supper, but petered out long before Laura followed the children to their bedroom and tucked them in. Once kisses, hugs, and prayers were over, she gave each child a final pat, then headed for the door. "Good night, sleep tight."

Three little voices joined her for the last line of the familiar refrain. "Don't let the bedbugs bite."

Laura switched off the light and pulled the door closed behind her. Just before it clicked shut, she heard, "Remember, we need a girl this time."

Rolling her eyes, Laura joined Glen in the living room. He sprawled on the sofa, work boots kicked off under the coffee table, stockinged feet resting on top. His once white socks had yellowish brown sweat-stains from the leather boots. Just as she reached the center of the room, the drum solo at the beginning of Benny Goodman's, Sing, Sing, Sing, started blasting on the radio.

"I love that song," Glen said, patting the couch cushion next to his side. "Come, sit by me. I'd grab your hands and start dancing right now, if we weren't both exhausted."

"We're getting old. Never thought I'd pass up a chance to dance to Goodman's band." Laura lowered herself onto the couch, kicked off her shoes, and put her feet up on the table next to Glen's.

"Feels so good to sit down." She groaned, then rolled her feet and ankles around in circles in time to the music.

The two sat with their eyes closed, toes and shoulders moving along with the rhythm. Seconds after the last notes, the sound of Hawaiian music ushered in Bing Crosby's mellow voice, singing Sweet Leilani. "Man, talk about a change of pace," Laura said. "But if they'd played Bing first, I might have fallen asleep."

"...You are my dreeee-aaamm come true." Glen sang the last words along with Bing, then stood up just as the Sunbrite Cleanser commercial started. "I'm going to the bathroom," he said. "Should be back before FDR's chat starts. If I miss something, let me know."

After President Roosevelt signed off, Laura sighed, shrugged her shoulders, and rubbed her hand on Glen's thigh. "That Hitler is sure stirring things up. Sounds like he's taking over Germany, even though they're supposed to be a democracy like us." She turned sideways, pulling one leg up on the couch next to Glen.

"When the last war ended, everybody said it was the war to end all wars, but this sounds scary."

"Things will settle down, you'll see." Glen's skin was pale, his facial muscles tense. "No need to worry."

"I hope you're right. In her last letter, Willa said Isaac was getting nervous. If things in Europe keep getting worse and worse, the U.S. might get drawn in. No telling what could happen then. She's frightened for Ruben." Laura clasped her hands together, fingers white at the knuckles. "He's not old enough to enlist, but if things go bad like before, who knows how long it might last."

Glen stretched sideways, reached for the radio sitting on the end table, and flipped the switch off. "No more talk about Europe or war. Too many folks died last time. Nobody'd be stupid enough to want that again. Besides, everyone keeps saying whatever's happening in Europe is their problem, not ours. I just can't see the President sending our army off to fight again."

They went to bed soon after, but sleep didn't come easy. Laura was still wide awake when Glen dozed off. He was quiet at first, then started thrashing. She saw his brother Bobby die over and over as the nightmare repeated itself in Glen's mind, fresh torture each time. She knew better than to touch or wake him, but lay with her hands clasped, praying he'd slip into a peaceful sleep.

Glen looked tired and drawn the next morning, but Laura didn't say a word. His sleep was uneventful with no more nightmares until May 7, the day after the horrible Hindenburg disaster.

"What's wrong," Laura said when he entered the house, his face a mask of pain and disbelief. "What in the world happened?"

A quick head shake was the only response, then he opened his arms and hugged the children that mobbed him. "Hey kids, I've missed you, too." His voice sounded tight and strained. "How about you guys go get cleaned up while I talk to your mama, then you can tell me about your day during supper?"

The children galloped down the hallway. Glen wrapped his arms around Laura. "On the radio, the announcer said the German airship

Hindenburg was landing in New Jersey." Glen held Laura tight and pressed his face into her hair. "It caught fire while trying to land. The whole thing turned into a fireball. Thirty-eight people died."

"Oh, no," Laura whispered into his chest. "How did it happen?"

"No one knows yet. But the news report, with the screams and cries of the people waiting for their friends to land, played over and over on the radio. That announcer, Herb Morrison, was doing a live broadcast and broke down. Couldn't hardly talk, he was so choked up."

Laura squeezed her eyes shut, unable to get the awful images out of her head. She and Glen clung to each other, sharing strength and solace.

"Papa, we're ready," June said, patting Glen's back.

"Good job." Glen gave Laura a final squeeze, then released her. "Let's set the table while your mama finishes the food." The smile he'd pasted on for the children slipped when they headed for the kitchen.

They didn't say a word about the disaster until after the kids went to bed and Laura joined Glen in the living room. Once settled on the sofa, Glen reached for the radio out of habit, then pulled his hand back. "I'd like to listen to the news, maybe some answers about the crash, but don't want to hear the details again."

"I know what you mean," Laura said. "We could listen to music or Fibber McGee and Molly, but it doesn't feel right to be enjoying ourselves after such an awful thing."

The evening was long and quiet, and they went to bed early. Glen never woke during the night, but his old nightmares haunted both him and Laura, augmented by the screams on the newsreel.

CHAPTER FORTY-ONE
David Edwin Webber
May 1937

David Edwin Webber was born on May 24, a little earlier than expected. An exhausted Laura cuddled the sleeping newborn in the crook of her arm when Glen burst into the room.

"Honey, are you alright?" He stroked her cheek, then kissed her forehead. "I should have been here. I'd have left work early if I'd thought it was time."

"Mr. Webber. "Dr. Farnsworth, a gray-haired man with a small goatee and mustache, reached out his hand. "Your wife and new son are both doing fine. I'm all done here for now." After shaking Glen's hand, he turned his attention to Laura. "I'll see you and the baby in six weeks. If you have any problems before then, just let me know."

"Thank you, Doctor Farnsworth." Laura's voice was soft. As soon as he left, she turned to Glen who was sitting on the side of the bed. "Better let the children in before I fall asleep. Besides, might as well face the music with June when we tell her she has another brother."

Glen kissed her fingers, then cupped his hand around the baby's tiny head. "They were on the front porch when I got here, running races and playing tag. To be honest, I didn't even stop to talk to them." He stroked his son's tiny palm, which closed around his finger. "Welcome, David, your sister and brothers will love you, although June will have to get used to another boy." He looked at Laura. "By the way, how did Dr. Farnsworth know you were in labor?"

"I realized the baby was coming just before the kids were supposed to leave for school, so I sent June. His office is just a little ways past the post office, so she had no problem finding him. I think she ran the whole way."

"I'll have to let her know she did a great job." He kissed the baby's head, then rubbed his cheek against the downy hair. "I'll be right back with the kids."

Raymond and June burst through the door with Jimmy right behind, with Glen taking up the rear. Laura sat up in bed and placed the baby on her legs. She unwrapped his blanket so they could see and touch him. No more complaints from June, who was won over when little David's tiny hand clasped her finger.

The new baby changed the household routine for everyone. June and Raymond took over morning chicken duty, feeding them and bringing in the eggs, which meant the two of them had to get up extra early to get the chores done. At first, Laura wanted them to go to bed earlier to make sure they got enough sleep, but since school was almost over, she didn't enforce the new bedtime. Jimmy's job in the morning was to keep an eye on David while Laura prepared breakfast. The baby was almost always asleep, but it kept Jimmy out of mischief and happy to have a job of his own.

Laura insisted Glen buy a playpen for David, so she could keep him in sight while she worked during the day. The first time she set it up by herself after Glen left for work, she almost shoved it back in the box. "That darn thing looks more like a cage than a playpen." She folded a big, soft blanket to cover the wooden bottom. "I hate the thought of putting David in there, but at least I'll know he's safe." She sat back on her heels and looked at the wooden contraption. "I guess it's not so different from his crib. I'll keep him outside with me and give him toys to play with so I can get my work done."

David spent most days of the summer in the playpen, first near the chicken coop where Laura double-checked the nesting boxes for eggs the children might have missed. She also made sure the brooding hens' eggs hadn't been bothered and that the spring chicks and poults were okay. The adult chickens liked to spend time loose in the yard for a few hours each day, so she let them out of their pen and checked on them each time she passed through the yard. Once, about every two weeks, on a day when she didn't have much to do in the garden, she'd select either a young rooster or a hen that had stopped laying eggs and wring its neck. Removing the feathers and cleaning the bird was a tedious process, but all the work was worth it when the golden-brown, crispy pieces graced the supper table.

After caring for the chickens each morning, Laura moved the playpen to the garden. She spent hours hoeing weeds, thinning and pruning plants, and picking ripe produce. In addition, she also had to water, which meant moving the heavy rubber garden hose from row to row, and soaking the plants from the bottom. Bug control meant picking the pests off by hand, since chemicals were just too expensive. Laura remembered how much she'd hated being put on bug duty, and wasn't surprised that her children hated it, too.

As the season drew to a close, many afternoons and evenings included canning, with David's playpen inside the house parked between the kitchen and dining room.

* * *

One Sunday, David giggled and drooled from where he lay stretched out on his papa's lap. The older children were outside playing, so Laura and Glen enjoyed a rare bit of quiet time together with the baby. "He's such a calm little guy," Glen said, making faces and playing with David's hands and feet.

"Thank goodness. Poor little squirt spends a lot of time in the playpen outside with me, but doesn't seem to mind." Laura stretched her legs out so her feet could rest on the coffee table. "I can't believe summer's nearly over and it's almost time for school to start. The kids have helped a lot, but they'll have to focus on their schoolwork soon." Her thoughts turned to her pa, and how he hadn't supported his children's education at all. "I want our kids to get as much schooling as they can."

"I do, too, but I wish you didn't have to work so hard." Glen pulled David up and turned him around into a sitting position. The baby's back rested against Glen's stomach so he could hold the little hands, clapping and playing with them. "I love this place, but sometimes I wish I'd found something that didn't involve as much work for you."

A loud wail sounded and the back screen door slammed, interrupting Glen's comments. "Raymond pushed me down," Jimmy said, running into the room just ahead of his brother.

"Did not. He fell down all by himself," Raymond shouted in self-defense.

"Hush, both of you." Glen's voice stopped both boys. "Jimmy, looks like nothing's broken since you can run down the hall and shout. Are you bleeding?" Jimmy shook his head. "Then I think you'll live."

June started to speak, but stopped when Glen raised his hand. "You guys have been playing just fine, so either go back outside and be more careful, or I can come up with a list of chores to keep you out of trouble.

The same horrified expression graced all three faces. The children turned and ran back out.

CHAPTER FORTY-TWO
Shell Shock
Summer 1938

The days shortened, school started, and the household routines changed again. By Thanksgiving, David was crawling and rebelling against confinement in the playpen. The older children did homework after supper, their books spread out on the kitchen table, within view and easy reach of their parents when they needed help.

The radio was a big part of each evening, with the family listening to music and their favorite family programs, Sergeant Preston of the Yukon and The Mercury Theatre. Laura and Glen kept up on the news too, but waited until after the children had gone to their room for the night to turn on the CBS World News Roundup with Edward R. Murrow.

"Those three can come up with more excuses for not staying in bed," Laura said, closing the hall door behind her then returning to the living room. Her smile disappeared when she saw the look on Glen's face. "What's happened?"

He held his hand up for silence and leaned closer to the radio. "Dear God, it's starting all over again."

"What?" Laura crossed to the sofa. "What's happened?" She sat down and put her hand on Glen's shoulder, staring at his stricken expression. "Please, tell me what's going on."

"Hitler's troops have not only invaded Austria, they've annexed it and installed a new government. Hitler kicked out the Austrian Chancellor who tried to stop the invasion and put his own people in charge." Glen's voice was thick and shaky, his hands clasped so hard his knuckles were white.

"That's awful, but it's still in Europe, not here."

"But that's two places now. Japan has already invaded China and killed thousands. With war on two different fronts, I don't see how we'll be able to stay out of the mess for long."

"I can't see America getting involved unless somebody attacks us, and they'd be crazy to do that." Laura put her hands over Glen's and held them.

"Hitler won't stop, you'll see. And Japan is bent on spreading their empire. One of them will come after us, or there will be some kind of aggression against one of our allies that forces us to take action. Mark my words, we'll be at war just like before and it won't be long. And then the dying starts again." Glen stood and headed for the front door. "I've got to get some air."

Laura was asleep on the couch when Glen came back inside. He shook her awake and said, "I'm sorry, but I can't understand how we can face war again. I hurt so much when I think about another war."

Laura didn't attempt an answer, just stood and wrapped her arms around him. When they got into bed, she could feel the tension in Glen's body and feared he wouldn't be able to sleep for hours. Sure enough, she fell asleep first, then woke to a muffled scream. This time she couldn't bear the thought of him suffering all alone and stroked his face and arms, hoping to soothe him out of the familiar nightmares.

The news didn't get better, nor did Glen's sleep. As spring approached, he smiled less and less. He was obsessed with making sure everything on the farm was perfect, pushing himself as long and hard as he could, as if the family's survival depended on his never shirking, never resting. The Saturday dances stopped because he didn't feel right taking the time to relax and have fun. He no longer played guitar for the children either, saying he didn't have time. He made sure he got to work early every single day and was the last person on the work crews to leave, terrified of losing his job.

"I hate peeling carrots." A reluctant June was helping Laura prepare for supper. They sat in rocking chairs on the front porch, watching David walk behind Jimmy and Raymond on shaky legs as the older boys tried to catch butterflies.

Laura started to respond, then noticed their truck, followed by two cars, coming up the driveway. She put the bowl of potatoes on the porch floor next to her chair and marched down the steps to meet the procession.

"Mama, why is Papa home so early? Who's with him?" June followed Laura out to the yard.

When the three vehicles pulled up in front, a stranger climbed out of their truck and brought the keys to Laura. "I'm awful sorry Mrs. Webber," he said. "There was an accident at work, so I had to drive your truck home."

"An accident? Oh, dear God, no. Where's Glen?" Laura whispered, her heart pounding so loud she thought the driver must be able to hear it.

Another man approached from the second car. "Mrs. Webber, My name is Mr. Zimmerman. Glen wasn't in the accident. Please, let me explain." He reached for Laura's hands, wrapping his own around them. "A young man, his name was Ralph, died in an accident at the job site today. A cave-in, that no one could have anticipated. Glen joined the other men and dug him out, but they were too late to save his life."

A third man joined Laura and Mr. Zimmerman, while the driver backed off the porch and walked back to the second car. "Ma'am, I'm Dr. Bailey. I had to pull your husband away from Ralph in order to treat the poor fellow. When I had no choice but to pronounce the death, your husband collapsed, moaning and screaming. He kept saying he was sorry to somebody named Bobby, over and over, even though he knew the man's name was Ralph."

All the color leached from Laura's face. "Bobby was his brother," she whispered. "He died in the war and Glen never forgave himself."

"I'm so sorry to hear that," Dr. Bailey said. "But it explains a lot. I had to give Glen a strong sedative to calm him down. I think he'll sleep for a couple of hours, so we need to put him to bed."

Tears poured down Laura's face. She felt June's hands tugging at her skirt, horrified that the child had heard what happened. She leaned down and held June tight. "Honey, I'll explain all this later. Would you please take your brothers to the back porch and keep them there until I come get you?" June shook her head no, holding even tighter. "Sweetheart, I need you to be strong now for me and for Papa. Please do as I say, and I'll be with you as soon as I can. Please, baby, I need you to do this for me."

The men waited with Laura until the children went into the house. As soon as the back door closed behind them, Laura said, "Bring him in now and I'll show you the way to our bedroom."

The men left, after putting Glen to bed, and giving her their condolences. Without the strength to stand a minute longer, Laura sat down on the bedspread and watched Glen sleep. There was no peace in him, just a drugged out blankness. She heard a soft knock, then whispers from the other side of the door. She took a deep breath, rearranged her face, and opened the door. "I'm sorry kids, come on in and I'll explain what's happening."

They clustered around her, tears streaking each face. Laura knelt and wrapped her arms around them. "I know you're scared ... me too ... but we'll be okay. I promise." She looked into their frightened eyes. "I have a story to tell you about your papa." Laura took a deep breath and searched for the words that would convey truth without making things worse. "Your papa had a sister named Barbara and a baby brother named Bobby. When their father died, Papa had to be the man of the house and help take care of his mama, Barbara, and little Bobby."

"You mean we have an Uncle Bobby and an Aunt Barbara?" June said.

"You have an Aunt Barbara, but Bobby died in the war." Laura paused, not wanting to continue, but knowing she must. "Bobby insisted on joining the Army to fight for our country, so your papa joined with him and promised their mama he'd look after Bobby. He tried his best, but Bobby was shot and killed during a battle. Papa blamed himself, even though there was nothing he could have done." She could see the three oldest children's faces absorb what they'd heard, while David just watched them and reflected the emotions he saw. "For all these years, Papa has missed his brother and felt awful about his death."

Laura stopped again, knowing the rest of the story would be hard for them to understand. "Today there was a terrible accident where Papa works, and a young man died. Your papa tried his hardest to save him but wasn't able to. The man reminded Papa of his brother, and it was just like he had to watch Bobby die all over again."

The children's eyes filled with tears, and the three oldest looked at Glen as he lay unresponsive on the bed. David began to cry because he hated seeing the others sad. "Now, for some reason we don't understand, your papa can't seem to pull away from that awful memory. The doctor gave him something strong to keep him asleep for a while, and we're hoping that he'll wake up and be okay."

"Poor papa," June said. Her lips trembled as she placed her hands on Glen's blanket-covered arm. "He's got to be okay. We need him."

The boys nodded in agreement, then stepped to the bedside next to June. They reached out their hands and patted Glen's body. Laura picked David up to soothe him, but let the others take their own time to come to terms with what was happening.

"Mama, will Papa wake up?" Raymond's voice was filled with hope and innocence.

"I don't know, sweetheart. We hope so."

Glen didn't stir until hours later, not knowing where he was. "Bobby, oh my God ... Bobby, not Bobby ... Get up Bobby ..." The heart-rending pleas went on and on, interspersed with bouts of crying and shouts, then silence for a few minutes before they started again.

Laura tried to wake him, stroking him with gentle fingers, then shaking his body hard to bring him back. Nothing worked. She could see he was caught in time, unable to shake free. She knew the man's accidental death was the trigger, but didn't know how to release Glen from his living nightmare.

Laura knew the children were terrified, needed her to comfort them and to know what was happening to their papa. Frightened by what they saw and heard through the bedroom door, they stayed in the hallway. "Glen, I've got to leave you for a few minutes to talk to the children," Laura said. "I'll be back as soon as I can."

Her heart broke to see her babies shaking with fear for Glen, begging her for answers she didn't have. "I'm so sorry, but we have to get help for Papa. June, do you think you can go get Dr. Farnsworth? Tell him it's an emergency."

"I'm going, too," Raymond said. He was stiff with determination. "I can help her."

"That's a good idea. You and June need to leave right now, but be careful." She hugged both children, then watched them race out of the house.

"Jimmy," she said, "I know you wanted to go, but I need you here. Can you please help me with David? He doesn't understand and needs someone to play with him."

"I don't want to play." Jimmy cried and crossed his arms. "I'm not a baby. I want to help Papa, too."

"Honey, keeping David calm and away from your papa right now is the best thing you can do for both of them. I know it's hard, but if you could do that for me, it would be a huge help."

Jimmy sighed, then nodded. "Come on, David, let's play trucks on the porch."

Laura paced back and forth between a tormented, unresponsive Glen, and the little boys playing on the back porch. Each time she joined them, a silent Jimmy would look for some change in her face, then resume moving trucks around with his brother.

After what seemed like hours, she heard a car pull into their driveway. She was out the front door and off the porch before June and Raymond burst through the car door. Dr. Farnsworth was a little slower to reach her, medical bag in hand. "Mrs. Webber," he said. "Has there been any change?"

"No change at all. I've tried everything I can think of and can't get through to him."

Laura led the way back to the bedroom as they talked. "Kids, Dr. Farnsworth will need to examine Papa, so please wait on the back porch with Jimmy and David. I'll come after you as soon as I can. And thank you so much for fetching him."

Dr. Farnsworth repeated many of the same things Laura had tried, in an attempt to snap Glen out of his disconnected state. Nothing helped or even seemed to affect Glen at all. "Mrs. Webber, I wish I had an answer for this, but I'm afraid that your husband is suffering from a severe delayed attack of shell shock. His recent experience caused him to flash back to what happened to him during the war. There is no medical cure for the condition. It's possible he'll come around on his own, but he needs time and rest."

Laura's hands flew to her mouth to stifle the moan she couldn't control. "Isn't there anything you can do? He's in so much pain."

"We can try something to break this cycle. I'll give him an injection to make him sleep." He pulled a syringe and a bottle of medicine out of his bag, filled the syringe, then plunged the needle into Glen's hip.

"He'll be groggy when he wakes in about ten to twelve hours, but should be manageable. Give him one of these pills." He pulled another brown glass bottle out of his bag and placed it on the bedside table. "This drug is strong and will keep him in a drowsy state. He'll be able to hear you, and with your help should be able to eat and drink and go to the bathroom. Give him one pill three times a day for a week. I'm hoping that by then, the war memory will have receded enough for him to wake with all of this behind him."

"I can do that," Laura said. "But Dr. Farnsworth, what if the pills don't work?"

"Let's not think about that right now. I'll stop by each evening to check on him." He patted Laura's shoulder, then glanced back at Glen before leaving the bedroom.

CHAPTER FORTY-THREE
Come Back To Us
Summer 1938

Sleep was all but impossible, but she refused to leave Glen's side during the long night. Laura knew the injection was wearing off when his body tensed and he started muttering. The sounds weren't words, but the cadence varied like speech. Laura could tell when he began dreaming, but all she could see were disjointed flashes of color and light, shot through with buzzing, unintelligible sounds. His agitation increased as dawn light appeared through the curtains. "Glen, I'll be right back." There was no reaction. She hurried to the kitchen for a drink of water, then shook a pill from the bottle Dr. Farnsworth had left.

The house was silent as she padded back to his bedside. "Glen, I need you to take this."

She tugged him into a sitting position and pushed a pillow behind him. "Here, honey, Dr. Farnsworth prescribed medicine to make you feel better." She poked the pill into his mouth, put the cup to his lips and tilted it. "Swallow." To her surprise, he followed her directions, then laid back down and closed his eyes.

"Mama, is Papa better?" June peered around the door, then stepped toward the bed. "He looks better."

"He took something from the doctor, so we'll see." Laura stood and led June into the hallway. "Come help me start breakfast, then you can wake your brothers. I'll get your papa when everything's ready." Please God, let the medicine help.

The medication calmed Glen down, so much so he was like a shadow-man when it took effect. He followed Laura's directions and dressed himself in the clothes she handed him, then followed her to the table and ate what was placed in front of him. He showed no emotions and wasn't able to participate in conversations with the children.

"We need to take care of the animals, now," Laura said to the kids as they cleared the table. "It's already late for the poor cows. They've got to be miserable." She stared at a placid Glen, then took a deep breath. "Let's make Papa comfortable on the back porch. Jimmy, you and David can show him how you make your forts. In fact, you can take the box of Lincoln Logs outside and make the biggest buildings ever."

Jimmy looked puzzled, like he was trying to figure out if this was an adventure or a way to leave him out of something the older kids were doing. "Can you please do that for me, Jimmy? I need your help with David and with your papa while he's not feeling well."

Jimmy nodded, then ran for the Lincoln log box. Laura settled Glen in one of the rocking chairs on the back porch. Jimmy joined them there, dumped the contents in a big pile at Glen's feet, and motioned for David to help sort them.

Laura led June and Raymond toward the barn. She was so thankful she'd been raised on a farm, even if it's been a long time. "It's time you two learned how to milk the cows. Won't it be fun to surprise Papa and show him how you can help?"

Laura secured the first cow in place, settled herself on a stool with the bucket under the cow's swollen udders, then leaned her head against the heifer's warm side. June stood at her side next to the cow's back legs, while Raymond bent down behind the cow where he could see the bucket better. "Just pull and squeeze down, one teat after the other." The rich streams hit the bucket with an easy rhythm. "Watch me with this cow, and I'll let you each try with..."

"Aaahhh, no!" Raymond yelled and jumped, a look of shock and horror on his green speckled face. He reached out and stared at the warm, wet manure splashed all over the front of his body.

June brayed with laughter, then covered her mouth, choking as she tried to stop.

"Oh, no, Raymond. I'm so sorry." Laura paused a moment from the milking, but didn't dare stop. "Guess I should've warned you not to stand too close behind the cow." She tried to convey sympathy, even while giggles threatened to erupt. "Don't smear it. Go to the faucet in the corner and let June clean you up with rags."

"No," June wailed. "That's yucky, I don't want to touch him."

"I can't stop milking or I might ruin this bucketful. We can't risk wasting anything with your papa sick. I don't want to hear another word from you, so stop whining and help your brother clean up."

June glared, mutiny written all over her face, but led a now tearful Raymond away.

Laura got the big animals out of the barn into pasture, while June and Raymond worked together to feed the pigs and chickens. After they cared for the animals, Laura and the children headed back to the house. "You two were a great help. Your papa would be proud of both of you." She patted both of their backs. "Come on, let's see what I can make for dinner."

An excited Jimmy and David met them at the edge of the porch, eager to show them the log town they'd created. "Wow, that's the best fort you've ever made." Laura congratulated them, then glanced at Glen, who didn't look like he'd moved since they'd left him in the chair.

"I'll let you know when the food is ready, so you can wash up."

After the children took their places, Laura led a docile Glen to his chair at the table. He could feed himself and handle the cup, but moved in slow motion and paid no attention to the children's questions and comments.

"Mama, what's wrong with Papa? I asked him a question three times, and he never said a word." June, lips pursed tight, put her fork down with a clatter.

"We don't know." Laura chose her words with care. "We're hoping the medicine Dr. Farnsworth left will help him feel better soon."

"He doesn't look like he's sick." Raymond looked close at Glen's face, then turned back to Laura. "But he doesn't act like himself. It's like he doesn't even know we're here."

"I know," Laura said. "But not all kinds of sicknesses show on the outside. Your papa's kind of sick is inside his mind."

"But if the doctor can't see inside his mind, how can he fix it?" June leaned closer to Glen, tilting her head and squinting her eyes.

"I don't know how for sure, but Dr. Farnsworth said the medicine should help him. It may take a week or so, so we have to be patient."

Laura found understanding what Glen was suffering made no sense to her.

When Dr. Farnsworth arrived that evening, Laura led him into the living room, where he found Glen sitting on the sofa while music played on the radio. The doctor sat down, put his medical bag on the coffee table, then opened it to access his stethoscope. He checked Glen's vital signs and reflexes, but couldn't get him to answer questions. "Mrs. Webber, there's nothing physically wrong with your husband. How did he sleep last night?"

Laura knew better than to share the disjointed images she'd seen in Glen's mind. She sat on the other side of her husband with her arms wrapped around her torso. "His sleep was restless all night, but got worse toward morning. He looked like he was dreaming, but I couldn't understand anything he said."

"Did you have trouble getting him to take the medication?"

"Not at all. I didn't wait for him to wake up all the way on his own," Laura said. "I sat him up, put the pill into his mouth, and got him to swallow."

Dr. Farnsworth nodded, then leaned forward and closed the clasp on his bag. "Well, keep giving the medication three times a day. I'll stop by each evening to see if there's any change."

"You mean he might stay the same?" Laura's heart thumped so hard in her ears she was sure he could hear it. "What happens if the pills don't bring him back?"

"Mrs. Webber, I told you before, it looks like the accident triggered your husband's shell shock from the war. We don't know much about how the mind works or how to reverse something like this." Dr. Farnsworth stood, picked up his bag, and took a few steps toward the front door. "The pills put Mr. Webber into a kind of mental fog, but I'm hoping that by slowing his mind down it will return to normal when the drug wears off, rather than going back to the frightful place where he was yesterday."

Laura's hands flew to her face and her eyes opened wide. "You're just hoping the pills work? You don't know if they will or not?" She rose and followed him. "What happens if they don't work? What else can you try?"

Dr. Farnsworth shook his head and put his hand on Laura's shoulder. "My dear Mrs. Webber, I wish I had more to offer. Just pray that the pills work, because they're all I have." He squeezed her shoulder, then dropped his hand. "If this medication doesn't work, we'll have to commit him to a mental institution where they're equipped to deal with his problem."

"Oh, no, please God, no." Laura whispered. Her entire body shook. She watched Dr. Farnsworth leave and pull the door closed behind himself. She didn't feel strong enough to navigate the few feet to the door, so she dropped back on the sofa and wrapped her arms around Glen. "I know you're in there. You have to come back to us. Please honey, we love you and we need you. Your brother's gone but we're here and we need you back."

CHAPTER FORTY-FOUR
Make Him Well Again
Summer 1938

Day two, three, and four were smoother editions of day one. Glen spent each morning on the back porch with Jimmy and David after breakfast, then moved to a chair in the garden near where Laura worked. He sat at the kitchen table while she prepared meals, then in his chair at the dining room table when they ate. The only improvement were occasional nods or one-word responses to questions.

"Mama, did you hear Papa?" June ran to the kitchen where Laura was pulling a bottle of milk from the refrigerator. "I asked Papa if he'd like some milk and he said yes."

"That's wonderful," Laura said. When they reached the table, she filled the children's glasses. "Glen, would you like milk, too?" He spooned mashed potatoes into his mouth, but didn't look up. "Glen, do you want milk?" She tried again, but there was no response.

"But he said yes a minute ago." June's voice was tight and high. "Ray and Jimmy heard him, didn't you?" She looked at her brothers, who nodded their heads.

"Honey, I believe you." Laura filled Glen's glass, then sat down.

June looked like she was either going to cry or yell as she focused on him. "Papa, it's not polite to ignore someone when they ask you a question. That's what you always told us. If you can eat and dress yourself and follow mama's directions, you can hear my questions and answer me." She stomped her foot and leaned against the table.

Glen continued eating his supper at the same pace, with no outward sign he heard his daughter. June watched him, arms crossed and breathing hard, then burst into tears. "Can I be excused? I'm not hungry, anymore." When Laura nodded, June ran from the table.

Raymond and Jimmy looked at each other when they heard a door slam from the hallway, then resumed pushing food around on their plates. David's lower lip trembled as he looked from face to face, then reached his arms out to Laura.

"It's okay, David, June's okay. You stay here and eat like a big boy with your brothers and I'll go talk to her."

When Dr. Farnsworth arrived, Laura waited until after he examined Glen, then led him outside to the front porch. "Doctor, I need to ask a question." Laura's voice was soft but firm. She crossed her arms and looked into his eyes. "Do you see any changes or improvements?"

"I wish I could say I did, Mrs. Webber, but that wouldn't be the truth."

"Sometimes he nods and gives one-word answers to questions. Is it possible he's better, but the drug is making it hard for him to communicate?" Laura rubbed her hands over her upper arms, but kept her focus on the doctor's face.

"That's possible, but we don't know for sure. We won't know much at all until he stops taking the medication." Dr. Farnsworth held his medical bag in front of his body, both of his hands on the handle.

"How long will it take for the medicine to leave his system so we can see if his mind is back to normal?"

"Well, that varies with patients. It can take a long time. It might be best to taper him off rather than just stop."

"Then let's start that tomorrow. Maybe two pills tomorrow and one the next day. The first day with no medicine at all you might know something." Laura put her hand on the doctor's arm. "This is tearing my children apart."

Dr. Farnsworth sighed, glanced at the front door, then looked back at Laura. "I understand. Your plan's a good one. I only wish I knew more about these things. I'd better be going now, but I'll see you tomorrow."

Laura nodded, then watched him until he drove away. Tomorrow, She'd give Glen two pills, then only one the day after. Could the answer be that simple? She opened the front screen door and joined Glen on the sofa. He didn't react at all. He stared at something only he could see.

"Would you like some music, honey?" Laura stood and turned the radio on, then sat with her legs tucked under. She patted Glen's leg and leaned against his side. Nothing. she might as well stroke the couch. Then Bob Hope's voice singing Thanks for the Memory filled the room. Laura couldn't hold on any longer. Tears flowed throughout the song. When the last notes faded, she kissed Glen's cheek and left the room.

Acknowledgments

This book could not have been written without the help of my mother, June Azevedo. Her stories about growing up helped me create the emotional framework for the fictionalized characters and events. She told me about her mother's love of music, and how the family moved around during the depression. Mom remembers the summer they lived under a bridge as the most fun they ever had, since the children had no idea they were poor and homeless. She even remembers walking to town pulling a wagon and chatting with friendly, generous strangers.

I also have to thank many writers in the Sacramento community for their support, patience, and guidance. The superb critique group led by Gini Grossenbacher helped me every step of the way, especially Margaret Duarte, Elaine Faber, and Carolyn

Radmanovich, who toiled over my work each month. Other special people, both writers and beta readers, who kept me going with their skills, humor, and kind words were Judy Pierce, Norma Jean Thornton, Tammy Brandon, and Marlene Meineke.

Writing can play havoc on home life. I am blessed with a marvelous husband, Stan Darrow, and daughter, Sheryl Wilson. They put up with my lack of attention while I agonized over the manuscript and loved me anyway.

Thank you all.

About the Author

I've been passionate about three things my whole life: reading, flying, and animals.

I was one of those kids who walked down the halls holding an open book, glancing up to keep from running into people or walls. I no longer read walking down the street, but I do manage to read a few sentences on my Kindle at red lights. Reading is as important to me as breathing, and one of my greatest joys now as an author is getting to know other writers. What could be more awesome than reading a fantastic book and being friends with the writer?

Thanks to a marvelous husband who knows how much I love flying, I've been up in a hot air balloon, a two-man helicopter, a glider, and an open cockpit bi-plane. He even encouraged me to get my private pilot's license, and sympathized when I had to quit during the economy crash in 2008. Every minute in the air was amazing, and today I'd go up in anything, with anyone willing to take me, anytime, and anywhere. No wonder one of my writing idols is Richard Bach, pilot and author of Jonathan Livingston Seagull and my favorite book ever, Illusions, The Adventures of a Reluctant Messiah.

My love of animals made me want to be a veterinarian, but I fell in love and married during my first year of college. In spite of dropping out, I still made a contribution to animal welfare by raising 514 bottle-fed kittens, working an all-volunteer cat spay and neuter clinic every month for 20 years, and writing books about animal rescue.

I believe that a supportive family is key to a happy life and am blessed with an understanding husband who has been my best friend and life partner for 54 years thus far.

Sacramento, California has been home for most of my life. Stan and I live next door to my parents, and share our home with our cats Gracie, Portia, Bonnie, Becca, and Ash. We now also have four chickens, Bernice Williams, Goldie Girl, Anna Banana, and Miss Cluck, that fertilize and cultivate our garden while taking care of insects throughout the yard.

My philosophy of life is simple. If you find harmony within, you can make a difference to the people around you. That in turn spreads out and makes a difference in the world. Life just gets better each year as long as you keep dreaming and loving.

One of the best thing in life for a writer is hearing from readers. I'd love to hear your comments, questions, or suggestions. You can find me on my website, https://www.sharonsdarrow.com, on Facebook at https://www.facebook.com/SamatiPress, or email me at sharon@samatipress.com.

I hope you enjoyed Strive and Protect, Book Two in the Laura's Dash series. If you'd like to learn more about what happened before, here is the first chapter from Book One, She Survives. Interested in a peek ahead? I've also included the first chapter from Book Three, Desperate Choices

She Survives

CHAPTER ONE

Hardscrabble Birth

August 1903,
Five miles outside of Ardmore, Oklahoma

"Look, Jon, ain't she pretty?"

"She? She? Another damn girl? What's the matter with you, woman. Five young'uns so far, and only one boy. And him the last a'fore this'n, so he's no use to me on the farm for years." Jon turned away from the bed with a disgusted expression and headed toward the open door. "Pretty? Hellfire, just another useless mouth to feed."

Vera watched her husband shove five-year-old Becca aside as he pushed past his four older children to get through the doorway. He went straight to the wagon, jumped up on the wooden bench, and grabbed the reins.

"Miz Dobbs, aint you 'bout ready to head home?" he yelled.

The youngsters, clustered around the

open door in the sweltering August midday sun, stared at Vera and Miz Dobbs. They were careful to not look back at their father, hoping he wouldn't focus his attention on them. Ruth, the oldest, made sure Lizbeth and Becca stayed just outside the threshold where Miz Dobbs had told them to remain. She held Ben, just turned three, by the hand to keep him from rushing through the door.

Miz Dobbs patted Vera's arm and shook her head. "I got to go, Miss Vera. Mr. Cavanaugh sounds mighty impatient. You and the baby'll be just fine."

"I know. Thanks for your help. Can't imagine having to birth a baby without you." Vera squeezed the midwife's hand.

Miz Dobbs started to turn away, then looked back and whispered. "Miss Vera, you know your baby was born with a caul on her head. Ain't never seen part of the birth sack stuck to a baby's head like a hat before, but I've heard some folks believe that's a sign that the baby's born with the second sight. Least ways, that's what my gram told me. Do you want to keep the caul?" "I'd love to keep it for Laura when she's grown, but Mr. Cavanaugh wouldn't like it. Would you keep it?" "Yes, ma'am, I'll be proud to keep it for you." Miz

Dobbs smiled, packed a collection of bottles, jars, and rags back into her battered leather bag, then hurried out the door.

As soon as she settled herself on the wagon bench, Jon slapped the horse's back hard with the reins. The horse lunged forward into the harness, jerking the wagon onto the rutted road.

Vera waited until the sound of hooves faded in the distance, then pressed her lips against the baby's damp hair. "It's alright, sweet Laura, it's alright. Mama loves you."

Vera stroked the baby's forehead, remembering how she'd looked at birth with the glistening white membrane stuck tight to her tiny head, covering her eyebrows, hair and ears. Poor little one. There should be a ceremony to guide your path and protect you, with all the clan members taking part. "What will it mean for you, my sweet Laura?" Vera whispered in her ear. She knew Laura's life path would be hard, no doubt of that, but she'd also have strength, luck, and special gifts of the spirit. "No tellin' what kinds of gifts they'll be."

Unable to resist their imploring looks, Vera raised her right arm and waved the other children, still waiting in the doorway, to come over to her bed. "Come on now, time to meet your new baby sister."

They rushed forward, jostled for the best positions as they gathered around the bed, stroking the baby's face and arms, holding her tiny hands, and assuring themselves that their ma was alright.

"That's enough for now," Vera said, after each child

had a turn with the baby, "I'm awful tired. Ruth, will you fix something to eat for supper? And please close the curtain so the baby and I can sleep."

Ruth nodded, then herded the little ones away from the bed. She closed off the area by pulling together two blankets suspended from a rope stretched from wall to wall just below the muslin-covered ceiling. Something moving on top of the muslin above the bed caught her eye, a clear sign that some type of vermin had fallen through the sod and been caught by the cloth. Wooden pegs, pounded diagonally into the angle between ceiling and plaster-covered sod walls, kept the fabric taut. Ruth could see that Ma would need to replace the muslin soon since it had torn away from some of the pegs and sagged in many places from the weight of the dirt and small creatures it held.

Vera cuddled her daughter's soft, warm body against her breasts. She listened to the

faint, whispery sounds of the baby's
breathing, then drifted off to sleep, newborn
in her arms, both exhausted from the rigors
of birth.

Hours later, Vera woke to the sound of
her husband stumbling to his side of the
bed. She kept her eyes closed and her
breathing regular, hoping he'd think she was
still asleep. He stank of alcohol and sweat,
cursing in the darkness as he pulled off his
boots, overalls and shirt, then dropped on the
bed and shoved his legs under the covers, still
dressed in his dirty long-johns.

Vera heard the children stirring, disturbed
by the sounds their father made, before they
slipped back into sleep on their straw pallets just
a few feet from her bed. Jon's heavy, rhythmic
snores let her know when he was asleep, so she
could climb out of bed with baby Laura in her
arms.

Vera knew the baby needed to nurse but
didn't want Laura to wake up enough to cry.
Moving in slow motion to avoid making any
noise, Vera sat down in an old wooden rocker
near the foot of the bed and brought the baby
to her breast. Little Laura rooted around for a
moment before she latched on and suckled
with greed, working her tiny, contented fingers
against her mother's skin. As she rocked,

soothed by the quiet perfection of the moment, Vera began to sing the Cherokee Morning Song, an ancient melody passed down from one generation to another, just as she remembered hearing it when she was little. She loved the words, but the meaning—I am of the Great Spirit, Ho, It is so, It is so—was even more precious.

We N' De Ya Ho,
We N' De Ya Ho
We N' De Ya,
We N' De Ya
Ho, Ho Ho Ho
He Ya Ho, He Ya Ho
Ya Ya Yaaa

She thought only Laura could hear the words, but she was wrong. All of a sudden, her body snapped forward propelled by a hard slap to the back of her head. "I tole you about talkin' Cherokee in my house. If'n I hear it again, I'll knock you clean out'a that chair."

Jon's voice was low, more like a menacing growl than speech. The threat was real as demonstrated by the force of the blow, the promise of more violence clear.

Vera didn't make a sound, nor did she

turn to look at her husband. She could sense
his presence as he stood behind the chair,
looming over her. Squeezing her eyes closed
against the pain radiating from the back of
her head, she fought against the urge to react.
She stayed still, her head bowed forward over
her daughter's body, then resumed rocking
and nursing after she felt Jon move away
from behind her. Within minutes, Vera heard
a liquid torrent as he used the thunder-jug
from under their bed, then the noisy creaking
when he lowered his body back onto the rope
mattress. The pungent urine odor stung
Vera's nose as she sat, waiting, until his
snores once again filled the sod house. Only
then did Vera let the tears run from her eyes
while she changed Laura's diaper and rocked
her back to sleep.

Vera stayed in the chair a long time,
rocking and stroking Laura's warm little
body, because she didn't
want to climb back into bed next to her
husband. How could I have thought he was a
good man? If only I'd taken more time to get to
know him. There's worse things than being
alone.

Jon had first introduced himself at a
church picnic. As Vera helped the other women
set out bowls of food on long wooden tables,

she noticed him watching her from where he stood with two other men. She felt his eyes on her throughout the afternoon, but he didn't speak to her until people started leaving.

"Hello miss, I'm Jon Cavanaugh," he'd said. "You're the schoolteacher, ain't you?"

"Yes, I'm Vera Miller." They talked a long time, seated on wooden benches in the churchyard. She told him about her students, and he told her about purchasing a homestead.

Vera enjoyed talking to Jon and considered him a handsome man. He was tall with dark brown, wavy hair, deep blue eyes, a dark complexion, big, strong looking hands, and a muscular, powerful build. He also had a scar running from just below his right eye to the base of his ear. The scar was pale, a wide, raised welt standing out against his dark skin. Vera tried not to stare, but couldn't help wondering what had happened to him.

Jon was courteous but didn't smile as they talked.

One week after they met, Jon caught Vera at school after her students had all left. He wasted little time before getting to the point of his visit, a marriage proposal. He explained that he needed a wife to help him work his homestead, and she needed a husband.

They were both strong, young, and living
away from their families. They were also
God-fearing, so should share the same ideals
about the commandments to marry and raise
children. Vera, after a day to think about it,
accepted. It seemed like a reasonable decision
based on sound ideals, a good match for
them both.

Vera remembered her wedding day and
wished she could go back and change things.
No fancy clothes, flowers, or music, just
standing in front of a preacher early in the
morning. After saying "I do," she'd watched
Jon nod to the parson, then lead the way
outside to his wagon, piled high with their
belongings. No kiss, no hugs, not even any
soft words.

Reaching Jon's homestead had taken all
day, and the condition of the place when they
arrived was much more primitive than Vera
had expected. No house at all, just a crude,
three-sided lean-to built into the side of a
small hill. She hadn't said a word, though,
just followed her new husband's lead, helping
him transfer the wagon contents inside and
then trying to create some order. When the
wagon was empty, Jon put the horse and
wagon into the barn which was in much
better condition than the lean-to, while Vera

started a fire and began to prepare supper. Vera hadn't known what to expect when the sunlight faded, and the darkness drove them inside by the fire. She'd hung a blanket over a rope stretched across the length of the open side of the lean-to, providing them with shelter from the night. When she'd finished, Jon had reached for her without a single word, pulling her toward their bed against the wall. Vera sat down on the thin straw mattress next to him, then was shoved flat on her back and taken like an animal in the field. Vera hadn't fought or protested, understanding it was her duty as a wife to submit to her husband.

Jon wasn't a talkative man, but during long hours trapped together during their first winter, they'd talked about their family histories.

Vera's parents had died in a fire the year before she'd started teaching, only six months after her brother had gotten married and moved away to be with his wife's family. Vera couldn't rebuild the burned buildings or work her father's farm by herself. No clan members lived nearby, and the tribal reservation was miles away. Teaching in a nearby town was her only choice. The previous teacher had married and moved away, so the School Board was happy to accept her. Her education at a Christian off-reservation day school was sufficient for her to teach elementary school students.

Jon's mother had died giving birth to him, her fourth baby. His father had neither the time nor patience to deal with a baby, so he hired a newly freed slave, Millie, to take care of the home and the children, and to serve as a wet nurse. Jon's father had grown up with slaves in the family, so he treated Millie the same way. Jon had one sister, the second oldest child, whom Millie taught about women's work and about a woman's place. Jon's father was a firm believer in punishing youngsters who disobeyed him, using either a razor-strap or riding crop. The scar on Jon's face came from his father's whip, when Jon had tried to turn away once to escape punishment, a lesson he'd never forgotten. When Jon's pa died, the oldest son inherited everything, forcing Jon, his other brother, and their sister to leave and find their own way.

Vera's thoughts were interrupted when Laura started fussing against her shoulder. The motion of the rocker and comforting touch of Vera's hands on her back soothed the baby to sleep. Vera kissed the top of her head. If only they'd talked about family and raisin' young'uns earlier. Never would have married a man with no softness or love inside him. Wasting time looking back though, no way to change things now. Got to get some sleep.

Vera carried the sleeping baby back to the bed, tucked the warm little body tight against her side, and was soon dreaming, breathing in the sweet smell of her baby's breath.

Vera and baby Laura were together almost all the time for the first few weeks, a cloth sling holding the baby tight to Vera's body. Laura slept to the soothing sounds of her mother's breathing and heartbeat, comforted by the warmth of her mother's voice and body, and the familiar scent of her skin. When Vera needed a few moments without the sling, she would hand the baby to Ruth, always reminding her to hold baby Laura with care.

"I know, Ma, I know how to hold her." Ruth would roll her eyes each time and reply. "I'm nine now, you don't need to remind me every time." The baby took only seconds to settle into Ruth's thin arms, so different from Vera's rounded body. "See, she likes me holdin' her."

"She sure does, Ruth." Vera smiled as she

replied, enjoying the sweet picture of her daughters together. "She knows you and loves you already."

Of course, whenever Ruth helped Vera with baby Laura, both Lizbeth and Becca clamored for their turns.

"Ruth, you've had her long enough, it's my turn now." Lizbeth always whined. "I'm seven, nearly big as you. Let me have her."

"Me, too. If Lizbeth gets a turn, I do, too." five-year- old Becca would chime in.

Ruth knew it was up to her to handle the two girls' requests. "You can both have a turn, but you gotta sit down first," she'd say, positioning baby Laura into one small lap after another.

Vera never worried about the baby with Ruth in charge. She loved watching and listening to her daughters care for baby Laura, their love for her clear even while they squabbled with each other for their turns. Vera also loved seeing how content the baby was with her older sisters whether Laura was sleeping or watching them with wide open eyes.

"Ruth is quite a little mother," Vera said one day, as she sat rocking and sewing. It was much too hot to work inside, so she'd dragged the rocker and a basket of mending outside and placed them in the shade next to the front of the house. Ruth sat near her, caring for baby Laura. Lizbeth, Becca and Ben played hide and seek, running and giggling, in and out of the barn.

Ma and Pa would've loved them so much. Vera sighed as she watched her children. Near fourteen years and she still missed 'em every single day.

"Ma," Ruth asked, breaking into Vera's thoughts. "Laura is such a pretty baby. What was I like as a baby?"

"You were the happiest of all my babies. Didn't cry, just made little noises right after you were born. Miz Dobbs didn't even have to slap your bottom."

Happy with that answer, Ruth turned her attention back to Laura.

Vera's thoughts drifted back to the day Ruth was one week old. She'd never forget that day, never till the day she died. Vera sat in the same rocking chair where she sat now, bursting with happiness, holding her baby daughter. She'd been singing softly to the sleeping infant, the same song she liked to sing to Laura, when Jon walked over to her.

"What's that song? Didn't sound like no reg'lar words I ever heard," he'd said.

"Just a lullaby my uncle taught me when I was young. Men sing the lullabies in Cherokee culture," Vera answered.

"Cherokee? Your uncle's a Cherokee? You tellin' me you're a damned half-breed?"

Vera stood up and placed the baby into her basket.

"No, I'm not a half-breed, I'm full blood Cherokee." Jon's slap split Vera's lip and knocked her down.

His hands were fisted at his sides as he stood staring at her on the ground, his entire body stiff with rage. "You tricked me into marryin' a dirty Indian? You lyin' whore."

Vera had tried explaining that she'd never hidden anything. It wasn't her fault he'd never seen an Indian teacher before, or an Indian woman who wore her hair up. It wasn't her fault that the Christian name she'd been given by parents educated off the reservation had confused him. He'd never asked, and she'd assumed he knew and didn't care. But her words had no effect. "Iffen anybody in town ever finds out about you bein' a Indian, I'll never live it down. And now my own blood daughter isa stinkin' half-breed? So help me God if this gets out I'll beat you to death myself." Jon's words, spoken in cadence with his fists striking her face and body, left no doubt he meant what he said.

That day was the first time Vera had

been beaten. She'd never been hit before, but from then on, she had to endure both her husband's contempt and his thoughtless violence.

Shaking her head, Vera brought her attention back to the present. The past was over. She couldn't change it. Just got to protect the young'uns best as she could.

Vera kept a smile pasted on her face, not wanting her facial expression to invite questions about her thoughts. She watched Ruth handle all three of her younger sisters, moving the baby from lap to lap without ever losing her patience.

Ben, her only son, showed little interest in the baby. It made Vera sad, but she understood. He was three years old and already trying to follow his father's instructions to "be a man." Although his face and body still had the soft contours of babyhood, he almost never let her hold him anymore. And on those rare occasions when he came to her for comfort, he'd pull away if his pa came near them.

Poor Ben. He'd do anything to get attention from his pa. But if he got hurt, all he'd hear was "Stop that cryin'. Men don't cry." If he got caught havin' fun playin' with his sisters, Jon would yell at him, "What's the

matter with you, boy, playin' sissy games
with girls." And the rare times his pa'd see
him huggin' her, Jon'd tell him to "stop bein'
a baby."

Sometimes Ben would poke at baby Laura
as she rested on one of his sister's laps, but he
seldom talked to her or asked to hold her.

And Jon's relationship with the baby? He
demanded respect and obedience from his
children, not considering affection of any
value. Vera took care to keep baby Laura out of
his way, knowing it was safer for both of them.

Desperate Choices

CHAPTER ONE

Is Papa Crying

July 1938, Aurora, Missouri

Three more days. Three more to find out if Glen would be back to his old self. Laura watched her husband sleep, his sandy brown hair curled against his forehead. The drugs in his system kept him from dreaming, a blessed relief from the nightmares that had haunted him since his mental breakdown. Dr. Farnsworth had suggested weaning him off his medications, skipping one of his three doses each day.

The next evening, Glen didn't seem any different after taking two pills that day. She wondered if his behavior would change after being cut to one pill the following day.

When Laura woke in the morning, she was shocked to find Glen sitting on the edge of the bed, staring at the window.

"Good morning, honey." She padded around the bed, knelt down and looked into his blue eyes. "You're awake early. Are you hungry?" She kept her tone light, hoping he'd respond. His eyes were open and appeared focused, but he wasn't looking at her, he was looking through her.

"How about some coffee before the kids wake up?" Laura thought she saw a faint flicker of something in his eyes. She grabbed her old, green chenille robe and pulled it on. "Let's stop at the bathroom first, then you can keep me company while I put the coffee on and start breakfast."

Laura noticed that Glen held his head a little more erect at the table. There was a slight tremor in his hands. He didn't speak though, so she stopped trying to engage him in conversation.

"Here, Glen," Laura said, handing him his pill. She made sure he swallowed it, grateful that he didn't fuss about taking his medication. She'd better get the chores done fast, since there was no telling how long it would last.

Laura worked as fast as possible, caring for the animals and garden, keeping Glen close by. "Good thing we bought these folding chairs when we used to have people over," she said.

"You can keep me company while I'm working." Glen sat, feet and knees together, back straight and eyes focused straight ahead, at the edge of the garden while Laura watered and pulled weeds.

"It was a lot easier when you helped with chores around here, honey. The kids try, but they're too young to accomplish a lot." Laura glanced at Glen, but his face remained blank.

She made many trips to the house and outbuildings to check on the children as they first did their chores, then played. She carried the chair with her when she moved from place to place, while Glen followed, sitting down when she unfolded the chair. "Here you go," she'd say each time. "Are you comfortable? Would you like a glass of water?"

At dinner, June sat on Glen's right at the table. She stared at him while Laura started filling the children's plates. She observed him following Laura's motions with his eyes. "Papa, do you feel better?" Her voice was high and full of hope. No answer, but Glen seemed to twitch as if he'd been touched.

Laura willed him to respond to his daughter, but saw no indication he was aware of her at all. If he could eat and drink at a normal pace, why wouldn't he answer his daughter? Or at least look at her. "I'm sorry, Junebug, I guess he needs more time."

June nodded, her blue eyes bright with unshed tears. "But how much time, Mama? When will Papa get well?"

Laura shrugged and shook her head. "I don't know, honey."

All four children looked glum as they finished their meal.

"I have an idea. You guys have been working so hard to help me and keep an eye on your papa this last week, I think you need some extra play time and a treat. No more chores for you this afternoon, and I'll bake a cake for supper." Laura leaned forward. "How about chocolate icing, too?"

The smiles were a little slow in coming, but then all four cheered and ran out the back door with June carrying David on her hip.

Laura spent the rest of the afternoon in the kitchen baking, first the promised cake and then oatmeal raisin cookies. The kids ran in and out, checking on the progress, while Glen sat on a chair next to the small table where she worked. "Smells good, doesn't it?" She dropped spoonfuls of dough on the cookie sheet, as the sweet aroma of the cake in the oven filled the room.

"Can we have some dough?" June begged from the washroom doorway, her brothers peeking around her. "A little bite for each of us?"

Laura started to say no, then laughed and relented. "Okay, then out you go until I'm done." She handed each child a small spoonful of dough, and waved them out the door. "Our kids are pretty special," she said to Glen.

He stayed in the room with her while she worked, but grew more and more agitated. The muscles in his face and arms twitched, his hands clenched, and his legs bounced up and down. Now and then he cocked his head as if listening to someone, and more than once Laura thought she heard him mumble under his breath. As she pulled the last batch out of the oven, Glen stood and stalked through the dining room and out the front door.

Laura left the cookie sheet on the stove top and followed, afraid to let him out of her sight. He stopped on the porch, one hand on an upright post in front of the steps leading to the yard. Laura stood about two feet behind him. "It's pretty out here, isn't it, honey? Feels good to stretch your legs."

Not a word in response, but Glen's head moved toward the right as if to hear her better. If only she could think of something to say. Then Laura noticed Dr. Farnsworth's car coming toward the house. "Glen, Dr. Farnsworth is coming to visit. He'll be pleased to find you outside." Thank goodness. Maybe the doctor could do something to help him.

Glen didn't say anything, but Laura saw his hand clench tight on the post, his knuckles white, while he tucked his other hand into his front trouser pocket. Glen's breathing sped up as they waited until the doctor parked his car and approached the steps.

"Hello Dr. Farnsworth, you're early," Laura said. She stepped from behind Glen. "Look who came outside by himself today." Her voice sounded brittle and artificial.

Dr. Farnsworth looked as dapper as ever in his dark suit as he approached the steps, his gray hair, mustache, and goatee impeccable. "Good afternoon, Mr. and Mrs. Webber. I had a cancellation today and hoped you wouldn't mind my coming out early." Dr. Farnsworth's tone and facial expression were neutral, devoid of sentiment as he approached the porch, his gaze focused on Glen. "It's good to see you outside, Mr. Webber, beautiful day isn't it?"

Laura saw Glen's jaw clench and move side to side, but he didn't speak. She placed her hand on his back, surprised when his muscles tightened and he pulled away at her touch.

Dr. Farnsworth climbed the first two stairs, one slow, deliberate step at a time. "Mr. Webber, you appear much better today. Would you mind my giving you a quick checkup?"

Glen didn't look at him, but moved back two steps toward the middle of the porch. He stepped backwards again as the doctor climbed the last two stairs, keeping the same distance between them.

Laura opened her mouth to speak, but after a quick head shake by the doctor, remained quiet. Her hands were clasped so hard she could feel the nails biting into her palms.

Dr. Farnsworth paused at the top of the steps, then moved toward two chairs and a small table grouped together near the door. He placed his medical bag on the table and removed his stethoscope. "Mr. Webber, would you mind sitting down for a few minutes? I'd like to check your heart and lungs. Won't take long, I promise."

Glen turned his body and faced the doctor. Laura noticed his forearm muscles flexing and his hands tightened into fists.

"No, I'm not leaving him," Glen said, staring at the porch floor where there seemed to be something no one else could see. He focused on doctor. "I know he's gone, I know that, but I'm not leaving him." Glen's body was a study in defiance and pain. He dropped to his knees, threw his head back and began to wail. His entire body shook with the force of the ungodly cries that ripped from his throat.

"Please, please do something." It was hard for Laura to breathe, much less talk. "I can't bear to see him hurt like this. Can't you do something?" She grabbed Dr. Farnsworth's arm with both of her hands.

"Mrs. Webber, all I can do is give him something to knock him out. This breakdown is far beyond my abilities. The only help available to him is the Springfield Mental Hospital. I've spoken to them about your husband, and they have room."

"How can I do that to him?" Laura clasped her hands together, kneeling near Glen.

He continued to rock on his knees, arms tucked around his torso, screaming and moaning. "What am I supposed to do?"

The screech of the screen door opening behind her startled Laura. "Mama, what's wrong? Is Papa crying?" Laura leaped to the door, pushing hard to keep a frightened June from coming outside. "Stay inside, sweetheart, you and your brothers need to stay inside."

"Dr. Farnsworth, do what you've got to do. Please, the kids can't see this."

The doctor, his own eyes glistening, nodded, pulled a syringe from his bag and filled it. Glen didn't react to the needle plunging into his arm, just continued rocking and yelling. In minutes he stopped making the awful noises and his body relaxed. The doctor pulled him to his feet and began walking him down the steps. At the foot of the stairs, he turned to Laura. "I'm taking him straight to the hospital before the shot wears off. I'm sorry there isn't more I can do for him."

Laura's entire body shook as she watched the men make their way toward the car. She realized June had stopped screaming and banging on the door, then heard footsteps pounding away from the door toward the hallway. Within minutes June and her brothers came running around the side of the house as Dr. Farnsworth was putting Glen into his car.

Laura ran down the steps and caught June in her arms, holding her tight until the doctor's car pulled away. "Honey, your papa is sick, and the doctor is taking him to get help."

"No, no, bring him back." June's fists beat into Laura's chest as soon as her arms were free. The boys clustered together next to Laura. June, crying and calling for their papa to come back, stared at the car as it disappeared from view.

Laura didn't even try to stop June's blows, absorbing them until June wore herself out. She dropped to her knees and wrapped her arms around all four children. "I want him here, too, I didn't want him to go away. But Papa's hurting and we can't help him. You don't want your papa to be in pain, do you?"

Their cries and tears hurt Laura much more than June's punches, and the worst pain was not being able to help them. "Dr. Farnsworth is taking Papa to a special kind of hospital. They have a room all ready for him, and know how to make him well again."

The tears and cries diminished, but all four children held tight to Laura. "Mama, when will Papa come back?" June's raspy voice was hard to recognize.

"I don't know, sweetheart. I wish I knew."

"But they will fix him, won't they?" Raymond's eyes were huge, and his voice was filled with longing.

"Of course they will, honey." Laura tightened her arms around her babies. "That's what doctors and hospitals do."

Laura almost added the words "I promise" but somehow held them back. Memories of sad endings when she worked in the hospital in Tulsa flashed through her mind. More memories came of doctors ready to "let nature take its course" and nurses who let patients die who'd been deemed hopeless.

"Papa will be fine, but it may take a while for the hospital to find the right medicine to make him well," Laura said, trying to soothe the children she held in a tight huddle, rocking until the sobs subsided.

At long last, Laura stood and lifted David into her arms. The other children stayed close to her sides as they walked back into the house. Please God, if you're listening, please help him.

"God always listens, honey, but sometimes his plans aren't easy to understand."

Laura's steps faltered as the words rang inside her head. Ma? Can't you help me? I can't stand this. It's too much. Laura hadn't heard her ma's voice or felt her presence in a long time.

"Yes, you can. You're a strong woman, and can do whatever you have to. Your children need you. I know you won't let them down."

Laura started to reply, but her ma was gone. She'd left right after she'd delivered her message.